CHEAP AS BEASTS

Visit us at www.boldstrokesbooks.com

CHEAP AS BEASTS

by

Jon Wilson

2015

ISBN 13: 978-1-62639-318-9

THIS TRADE PAPERBACK ORIGINAL IS PUBLISHED BY
BOLD STROKES BOOKS, INC.
P.O. BOX 249
VALLEY FALLS, NY 12185

FIRST EDITION: FEBRUARY 2015

CREDITS
EDITOR: JERRY L. WHEELER
PRODUCTION DESIGN: SUSAN RAMUNDO
COVER DESIGN: GABRIELLE PENDERGRAST

Dedication

For Margaret

Striving to better, oft we mar what's well.
—William Shakespeare, *King Lear*, 1.4.346

CHAPTER ONE

I've always been partial to redheads, especially the fair-skinned, svelte, doe-eyed type with full, demure lips and naturally rosy cheeks. Nothing drives me more wild than smooth, creamy flesh, either naked or draped in just the right finery, sprayed with a light scattering of freckles. Naturally, none of that described Lana O'Malley, who sat cross-legged in one of the two chairs facing my desk. She was blond and tanned and about as soft as granite.

"The police are useless." She fiddled with a cigarette and a butane lighter, neither of which she appeared to remember how to operate. "And I'm beginning to believe coming here was another waste of time."

"Now, Lana." Morgan O'Malley patted her hand and held it. Unlike his sister, he fit my wish list to a tee and was the only reason I hadn't tossed the pair of them into the hall. He looked at me, plaintive. His eyes were a subtle mixture of green and brown and gold. "Can't you help us, Mr. Colette?"

I think I'm pretty good, but he had me, mostly because he didn't know he was doing it. With him, it was all innocent, lethal instinct. I had to look back at his sister just to get my lips working. "I don't know. I'm still not clear on what it is you want me to do."

Lana slid forward, perching on the edge of her chair. "That monster killed our father. We want you to prove it."

"Never mind the police, who says he died from natural causes?"

"The police!" She spat the word like it tasted as bad to her as it usually did to me. "Show him the paper, Morg."

He slipped his hand into his breast pocket. "This is an affidavit signed by father's doctor." His voice was low, calm and steady, quite the contrast to his sister's. "He had a physical last year. There was no sign of any heart disease."

I accepted the document, pretending to admire its face. "But he was, what? Sixty? Sixty-five?"

"Sixty-two," Lana snapped. "In great shape. He played tennis twice a week. He could've beaten you."

That was childish, of course, but arguing with such filial devotion seemed futile. With the old man's ashes in a jar on a mantle somewhere, it could never be settled. "I'm sure he was an animal," I told her. "Still, people that age die."

She threw down the cigarette, preparing to spring. "How dare you speak that way about my father?"

Yeah, yeah. Like he was God.

Not that he was far off. Even up in Pacific Heights, the O'Malley mansion stood out. The old man had made his money in real estate, none of it local, but had re-invested heavily in San Francisco. Then the war came, and he took his bundle and lent and leased it into lots of other, bigger bundles. I heard the mayor used to have to call O'Malley's secretary just to make an appointment to call back later and ask him to lunch. Something like that. Anyway, when he was found sprawled on his bedroom floor, the newspapers went berserk. But there hadn't been even an allusion to foul play.

"Not that I should have expected better. Not from someone who works in a hole like this." Lana O'Malley, continuing her tirade.

"Which brings me to my next question," I told them both. "Why exactly did you pick on me?"

She settled back into her chair, twisting her bright red lips sourly. "You weren't our first choice, I assure you."

"Well, that makes me feel better."

Morgan interceded again. "Really, Mr. Colette, no one even wants to listen to us."

Lana turned on him. "Oh, don't indulge him, Morgan. He's already convinced himself he's a clever little man. He needs to be put in his place."

That seemed to deserve an appropriate response. For instance, I'm six feet tall and weigh a good two hundred pounds, and, while I was not exactly flush, I had just that morning delivered some photographs of a philanderer to his wife's attorney in exchange for a sizeable stack of dough. So, I was financially predisposed to give them the boot. But there was Morgan to contend with, or, more precisely, that heroic jaw and those multicolored eyes. And, yeah, the ginger hair.

I sat back in my chair too, stretching my legs out under my desk and crossing my ankles. "What is it exactly you're saying that no one wants to hear?" I let sister know I was ignoring her statement about me being small by addressing my question to brother.

He played along. "Just what we said. We think it wasn't... *natural*. We think he was poisoned, or well, I don't know about poisoned. I mean, the police have scientists, right? They would've found poison. But we think something..."

"You think something." That was rich. I wondered if they knew the only reason they were being politely ignored by the police, as opposed to being aggressively told to go soak their heads, was because of their last name. Lana started up again, something about how Morg was telling it all wrong, but he placed his hand on her shoulder and looked me straight in the eye.

"We suspect Miranda had something to do with it."

I reiterate that he was good. The way he was looking at me, like something about my eyes mesmerized *him*, tipped me that he suspected I was close to being hooked. And also that he knew *why* I was close to being hooked.

I looked over at Lana. Her expression said there was absolutely nothing mesmerizing about me at all. As the feeling was exceedingly mutual, I told her to tell me more about this Miranda.

Miranda O'Malley, born Miranda March, and, for a few years, called Miranda Reed, had wed Lawrence O'Malley during the war. She was apparently a succubus. That was Lana's word and, I admit, I wanted to look it up to be certain it meant what I thought it did. She used a few other choice descriptors such as viper, temptress, witch, and a certain word which rhymes with witch, but I could tell that succubus was her favorite.

Adam Reed, Miranda's first husband, had died in France. As there'd been a war on, that didn't strike me as an astounding coincidence, although from the way Lana told it, I half expected to be told the succubus had a hand in that event as well.

As to how her father and Miranda had met, Miss O'Malley was a bit vague. She appealed to brother, but he seemed either to have forgotten or never known himself. The succubus had just suddenly appeared in their lives, on their father's arm, an affront to their mother's memory, a black mark against their father's fine judgment, etcetera. Clearly a spell had been cast. Never mind that Miranda was beautiful, charming, and half Lawrence's age.

"How long had your father been a widower?"

The question brought Lana's head up sharply. "What does my mother have to do with any of this?"

Exactly, I thought.

Morgan, who still held his sister's left hand in his right, offering an occasional squeeze to help her through some of the more trying details of her story, reached over to soothe her with his other hand. He lowered his heroic chin slightly, aiming his swirling eyes at me from under a manly brow. "Our mother died right after the crash, Mr. Colette. December of twenty-nine."

I made myself meet his gaze, thinking that if I did end up working this silly case, I'd best be able to withstand the client's eyes. My chin floated up, tilting my head back slightly so that I was gazing down the side of my nose at him. "How'd that happen?"

"How is this—" Lana started up, but Morgan squeezed again.

"She had been sick for a while. She caught the flu and never fully recovered. But I don't see how this can have any bearing on anything."

"No," I said, "you're probably right. And the fact that Miss O'Malley here had ostensibly been the woman of the house for fifteen years clearly has no bearing on her opinion of the succubus who displaced her."

Morgan let me see his disappointment. The sadness in his eyes made sure I knew how profoundly he felt it. "Please, Mr. Colette, there's no need—"

But that was as far as he got, because sister was through. "Come on, Morgan." She was on her feet and fumbling with her wrap and purse. She probably could have done better, but all her attention was focused on me. "You're all in this together. Joe warned me. He told me you'd be worse than useless!"

To his credit, Morgan attempted a couple of intercessions, all of which earned him squat. Neither he nor I had risen when Lana jumped up, though she was, strictly speaking, a lady, and I understood that he harbored hopes of coaxing her back into her chair. Again, he came up with squat. Finishing with me, she screamed at him again to "Come on," then propelled herself to the door and on out.

On his feet finally, Morgan watched her go, then turned to me as I reclined in my chair with my fingers laced atop my middle. He didn't say a word but let me see his disappointment had given way to frustration. For a man I estimated to be securely in the middle of his third decade, he struck me as rather adept at corralling his expressions. It made me want to try him out at cards, say pinochle or five-card draw. But I just smiled sympathetically, then he went after her, leaving the door standing open.

CHAPTER TWO

I went for lunch to the counter at Jack's, around the corner on Pine Street. Eating a Denver omelet and home fries, I caught up on *The Chronicle* and *The Bay Clipper*, a week's worth of daily news. Neither sheet had anything at all to say about Lawrence O'Malley. I took that as confirmation that I'd done the right thing in making no move to stop his brats from storming out. His death was less than two months old, so if any whiff of a story lingered, it would have rated a mention at least. I considered calling a friend of mine, Gig Barton, a scribe for the *Clipper's* crimebeat, just to do some casual fishing but decided no head of ginger hair was worth that much effort.

I got back to the office at two. For my professional services, I rent two rooms on the third floor of the Rooker Building. You've probably seen it. At six stories, it's one of the three tallest buildings on that section of Pierce. You probably just don't remember seeing it. Despite its height, it somehow manages to be eminently unremarkable.

The first of my two rooms, entering from the hall, is the reception area, with a small but serviceable reception desk I hope to someday hire a quiet gal to sit at and, contingent upon her abilities, possibly screen my incoming calls and type occasional correspondence. Two chairs are in the opposite corner with a little table squeezed between them, which I also hope to someday find occupied—preferably with prospective clients eager to hire me. But that day, like most every other, reception showed no signs of life whatsoever.

The second room, approximately twice the size of the first and, therefore, half the size of a Pullman dining car, was my private office.

It was equally devoid of human habitation, but less distressingly so than its smaller sibling. I hung up my jacket and hat on the rack, opened the one window, stood looking out across the alley, and loosened my tie. To show you just what an optimist I am, I only smoked a single cigarette before going to the phone to check for messages.

There was one, and the girl at the service seemed every bit as surprised as me. Not that I mean to complain, about my business, that is, not the attitude of certain telephone operators. I enjoy moderately steady work. For instance, that philanderer's wife's attorney I mentioned. Also, I do some subcontracting for both Walter Cobb and the Zenith Detective Agency. I could probably go full time for Cobb. He's mentioned it once or twice, hinting that I'd almost certainly bring in more cash, but I haven't yet grown weary of seeing my own name on the door when I get off the elevator. Although it had been misspelled for nearly three months after I moved in.

The name and number the operator gave me were neither Cobb nor the Zenith. But just to show you also that I can be realistic, I got comfortable in my chair, loosening my tie a bit more, and lit up another Camel before dialing the phone.

It rang nearly half a dozen times, and I was on the verge of throwing in the towel when it sounded like the receiver at the other end was grabbed, throttled and thrown against the wall before a breathless female voice came on and told me, "Not yet!"

According to my grandmother, that is no way to answer a telephone. I glanced down at the note I'd scribbled. "Hawthorne-seven, two-six-five-eight?"

The female voice sounded as if it moved some distance from the transmitter and said, "Yes, Florence, but with the other hat. The *other* hat!"

I thought about tossing my towel again, but I'm nothing if not tenacious. "Hello?"

Of course, allowing that the female ear was located in the usual vicinity of the female mouth, there was a fair to middling chance that the female brain didn't get the message. Then, the voice came back to the mouthpiece and demanded, "Hello?"

"Hawthorne-seven, two-six-five-eight?"

"Of course it is. Isn't that what you dialed?"

I took a breath, a deep one, through my nose, hoping she heard it. Having sampled more of her, I had deduced that she was young, possibly a girl, but almost certainly not a woman. Somewhere in that excitable in-between, when bobbysocks give way to garters and hose. It's not an age I have much patience for. "I'm calling Ramona Wyman."

She took a breath too, I assume. I didn't hear anything for a moment. "And who shall I say is calling?"

"Whom. Declan Colette, returning her call."

"Whom, what?" That time there was no pause, but lots of curiosity. "*Who* is this?"

I decided my best bet was to stay professional, at least until I ever had occasion to meet this dingbat in person, which would probably result in my giving her a swift kick on the sitter. "Declan Colette. I was given a message that Ramona Wyman had telephoned while I was away. I am now endeavoring to return her call. May I speak with Mrs. Wyman please?"

"Mrs. Wyman lives in Ohio. There's two of them, I think, if you count my brother's wife, which I guess you have to, considering. I'm Ramona Wyman. Miss Ramona Wyman. But I didn't call anyone, not anyone named Dec—wait a minute! Is this the detective guy?"

"This is that guy."

"Dexter Coleman?"

"Declan Colette."

"That's right. I remember now because when George told me the name, I remember thinking it sounded French. Are you French? I have a letter from France. Troyes. Only they pronounce it *trois*, like the number three. It's in the Champagne region, only I don't know if they make champagne there. You don't sound French."

I wondered how she knew, seeing as I'd managed to say so little. I tried to even the score. "I'm not French. I've been to France, but only passing through. I don't know if I sent any letters. Does it say it's from me?"

"Huh?" She was clearly better at giving; my spiel seemed to leave her stumped. "What are you talking about?"

"The letter. The one you say you got from Troyes, pronounced *Troyes*. Didn't you call me about a letter you say you received from France?"

"I didn't call you about *that* letter!"

"Oh, my mistake. How may I help you?"

She took another moment. "You talk fast."

I nearly dropped the telephone receiver. Actually, I nearly picked up the entire set and tossed it across the room. Fortunately, my other hand was busy with a cigarette. My lips shared that burden a moment, readying myself for a final assault. I spoke slowly, with a measured tone. "Maybe we should start again. This is Declan Colette. I'm a private investigator. I'm returning the call of Miss Ramona Wyman."

Her own voice was softer, more restrained. "Well, you needn't be rude about it."

"You're right, of course. I needn't. How may I help you?"

"I actually think it's a rather nice name, actually."

"Thank you."

"There's an author called Colette. Did you know?"

"*Gigi.*"

"No, I think it's just Colette. One name. Listen, can I make an appointment to see you? It's very important."

I sighed loudly, hoping she didn't hear that time. It was just such an overwhelming relief. I almost managed to overlook the fact that it threatened me with the prospect of being stuck in the same room with her. Of course, there was always the possibility of giving her that kick.

"Certainly," I said. "When would you like to come by? I have some time tomorrow, both morning and afternoon."

"Oh, no, I couldn't possibly come there. Couldn't you come here? Or, I suppose, we could meet somewhere. Yes, actually that's best. We could meet somewhere. Say the park? No, that's too public. How about the public library?"

I appreciated her irony and considered paying a compliment, but the last thing we needed was another sidetrack for her mind to go sprinting along. "Wherever is convenient for you, Miss Wyman."

"Do you know Eisley's?"

"The deli?"

"No, Eisley's the mortician. Of course, the deli."

I bit my tongue so hard I'm surprised it didn't snap off. "Tomorrow noon?"

"Oh, I can be there in an hour. I have to pick up something for Auntie anyway. No one will suspect anything if we meet at Eisley's. Half an hour."

I looked at my wrist and then confirmed my findings with the clock on the wall. Eisley's was down on Market Street, but I could make it at a brisk pace. "Three-thirty?"

"Swell. How will I know you?"

"Grey suit, light blue shirt. Blue and black striped tie."

"Really?" She was amazed. "How old?"

"I bought the tie last month. The shirt and suit are a little older."

"No. How old are you?"

"Oh, right. Thirties. Early."

That actually earned me another of her quiet moments of reflection, or maybe she was just distracted by something shiny on her end. "What color hair?"

"Brown, but I'll have a hat."

"Beard?"

"Goodness no."

"I rather like beards. Uncle Larry had a beard, actually. Very distinguished."

Fearing how much she might decide to pontificate on facial hair, I cut her off. "How will I know *you*?"

"I'll be wearing a green dress with a blue—no, white—no, blue coat. I'll wear my lavender scarf. Auntie got it for me at Christmas. It's got little designs that look kind of like peacock feathers only they aren't. Oh, and I have blonde hair. Medium length. I'm trying to decide if I want to grow it out. I'm not sure if that will be the fashion next season."

"And, um, how old are you?"

"Twenties," she said, allowing me another relieved sigh. Then she appended, "Well, nearly. In three years."

CHAPTER THREE

B etween my legs and a convenient street car, I made good time to Market and up the few blocks to Eisley's, arriving about twenty minutes past the hour. There were no green dresses with coats of any color at the half dozen tables outside, and, at that time of day, there was no one who wasn't employed inside. Despite their full assortment of meats and the fact the big sign over the picture window reads *Eisley's Delicatessen*, the place was mostly renowned for desserts. I got a slice of pie and a glass of milk and joined the *al fresco* diners to await my *rendezvous*, as our meeting might have been called had it been mentioned in Miss Wyman's letter from *Troyes*.

By the time I finished the pie, it was a quarter to four and the glass of milk got me nearly to four o'clock. Two cigarettes saw me through the full hour I had decided to wait. On the way back to my office, I decided Miss Ramona Wyman had truly earned a swift kick on the sitter.

The note with her name and number was still on my desk, but I didn't call. I did check with my service, but that time nothing was doing, doubtlessly reassuring the operator that God was in His heaven, and the sun might safely be expected to rise again tomorrow.

At five-of-five, I broke down and called Walter Cobb to see if he had anything I might help him out with, but he'd already called it a day. I hung up, got my hat, and did the same.

With the pie still settling, I opted for a movie first and saw the new John Garfield. I've been a fan of Garfield since *Four Daughters*, and I met him once after a USO show. He's shorter in person.

On the way back up the hill to my apartment, I grabbed a sandwich at an all-night counter, washing it down with another glass of milk. I rent one room for my living space, but it's shaped like an L and is slightly larger than my office. Most importantly, it has its own attached bath. After three years fighting in Europe, I swore I'd give up eating before I'd ever hunker down in a place that didn't have a private bath.

I read some and smoked a lot, then splashed water on my face and went to bed. All these details are admittedly that, but I include them to show I was absolutely not expecting the pounding on my door three hours later.

I used to sleep quite soundly, but the Germans cured me of that. I was sitting up by the third pound and fully awake for the three that followed. "Open up!"

I switched on the lamp and growled at my watch when it told me it was two thirty-nine. I swung my feet out from beneath the covers and onto the floor. I didn't call out *Who's there?* I didn't care. I just didn't want them to pound any more.

But they did. Another half dozen that was clearly some bozo who had never learned to use his knuckles properly. It was the sound of the side of a fist landing hard against the wood. I stumbled over and turned the bolt, reaching down for the handle when the door flew open and two men charged in, nearly knocking me flat.

"Alright Colette?" That was from the second guy, a crumpled-looking older specimen I knew and loathed named Oscar Dent. Lieutenant Oscar Dent, San Francisco Police Department. He had stopped a few paces into the room, looking ready to draw his guns. The uniformed man two steps in front of him, whom I did not know, continued on around the bend in my room.

I had backed up and stayed back to avoid being trampled. While I might have had a moral case for escorting them back into the hall, and physically I had a good chance of success—especially with Dent, who, though several inches taller than me was quite a few pounds lighter and nearly twice my age—they were officers of the law, and it might prove legally problematic. Not that I wouldn't have liked to try.

The uniform had opened up the bathroom door, the closet door and even gone down on one knee to search under the bed. Dent was helping, though just with his eyes. "You alone?"

I appealed to him. "Listen. You can't do that, and you know it."

"You're a lawyer now?"

"I don't need a law degree. If you got a warrant, let's see it."

"Maybe I thought I heard a woman's voice. Maybe I thought she was calling for help."

I tsked at him. It's an admittedly bad habit I have which has gotten me into more than one scrape. But I was disgusted. I have two nice chairs in the front half of my room, one that I like to read in and the other I keep to maintain my optimistic outlook. I sat in the second, leaning back and getting comfortable. "Fine. Look away. I mean look around. Search away. Constitution be damned."

"Save it. When did you last see her?"

"Her who?" I was staring at my bare feet, wiggling my toes. August is probably the best you can expect in San Francisco, weather-wise, so I was in nothing but my shorts and a t-shirt. "Did you even say hello?"

Dent watched me watching my toes. Past experience told me he was probably scowling, as that was just about all his ugly mug did in my vicinity. The uniform continued to search, though my place is small enough I'd wager he was merely putting on a show at that point for his so-called superior officer. The lieutenant apparently wasn't impressed because he barked, "Wait in the hall, Jones."

When we were alone and Dent had closed the door, he took up a position in the center of the room with his feet planted too far apart and his fists on his hips. He scowled some more, doubtlessly thinking that he was towering over me and obviously expecting me to buckle. "Spill it. When and where did you last see her?"

I was lighting a cigarette and didn't rush to answer. Finally, I waved out the match and used it to gesture at him and the room and the whole unseemly business. "Even if I did know to whom you were referring, you think I'd talk after that performance?"

He used his mean smile. "Oh, you'll talk. Get dressed, we're going downtown."

I didn't hide my skepticism. "Nothing doing. Get your boy back in here and have him tackle and cuff me and then you can talk to my lawyer tomorrow. Today. Later today."

He chewed on that notion for a while. "Ramona Wyman. We know you met with her today. When and where and what for?"

It's harder to act nonchalant when someone delivers a sucker punch like that. It helped that I was sitting down. I mean, I knew he wouldn't have burst in, spittle flying, with good news, but why her? Did I neglect to mention that Lieutenant Dent works homicide?

I said the first thing that popped into my head. "Gigi."

"What was that?"

I decided it was my turn to scowl, and I aimed it up at him. "Ramona Wyman's dead?"

"I'll ask the questions. You get dressed." Then he decided it would probably be in the morning paper. "She was found a few hours ago. What was your business with her?"

"None of yours." I didn't get up. I didn't move. I sat there still staring at my feet but not seeing them. "We had an appointment to meet, and she stood me up."

"When and where?"

"Eisley's, downtown. She called sometime around noon, and I called her back at about two-thirty. She said she had to meet me, that it was important."

"Yeah? What was important?"

"*That* she didn't say. She wasn't alone when she called, though she wasn't exactly being sly about it. She did mention something about no one suspecting her if we met at the deli."

"Yeah, she went there a lot, nearly every day. We haven't found anyone who works there yet. The place opens early, and the bakers or whatever they have come even earlier, but nothing yet."

"We were scheduled for three-thirty, and I made it early. She hadn't shown by half past four when I left." I stubbed out my cigarette in the ashtray at my elbow and then fumbled another one out of my pack. "When did she...?"

He took a deep breath, expanding his sunken chest, then gave up trying to look imposing and paced a few steps to stretch his legs. "No one wants to commit. She was found floating under a pier by some tourists at about nine p.m." He stopped pacing and watched me strike another match. "Did I tell you you could smoke? Get dressed, we're going."

I finished with the match and deposited it in the ashtray. Reclining in the chair, I crossed my ankles and took a long drag on my smoke. A second. I didn't look up at Dent, but I wasn't exactly looking it over either. There was nothing to look over. She hadn't called me about a letter from France, nor a French author named Colette, yet that was nearly all we'd talked about. "It sure would be nice to know why she had to see me."

He made a strangled sound, and I wondered if the bile might kill him. "I'll say. Get your goddamned clothes on!"

I finally did look up at his red speckled face and his bulging rheumy eyes. The man was a walking coronary. "I never saw her. I can't help you."

He clenched his hands into fists and clamped his jaw. I expected him to lurch over and grab me or clutch his chest and drop to the floor. He did neither. "Just my goddamned luck to find you in this. Things looked bad enough with her uncle."

"What about her uncle?"

"The family's been raising a stink for a month now that he was actually murdered. Now I guess people will start listening."

I sat forward. "Hang on. Who's her uncle?"

"What did I say about asking questions? Get dressed."

On my feet, I reminded him that we weren't too far off from eye-to-eye. Also there was my weight advantage. And his age. "Who's her uncle?"

Like any bully, he sort of shrank in the face of opposition. "Lawrence O'Malley."

Pathetic. Not just Dent, but all of it. There I had sat eating pie. My cigarette was only half gone, but I stubbed it out anyway. "I'll get dressed."

CHAPTER FOUR

They cut me loose just before noon. I think the ADA who was questioning me had a lunch date. He kept checking his watch and right about eleven-thirty, got a call, his end of which included in its entirety, "Is it that time already? I'll be right down." Not that I wasn't ready to go; he was my third interrogator of the day. After Dent came Dent's boss, Inspector Ackerman, and after him, Assistant District Attorney Holloway. They asked a lot of questions, or maybe I mean they asked a few questions a lot of times.

All three started out on the girl, Ramona Wyman, aged seventeen, hailing from Williard, Ohio. But Ackerman and Holloway both segued quickly over to the O'Malley kids. Of course, not long after I got downtown, either Lana or her brother had spilled that they had visited my office that morning. They had not been hauled to headquarters—money and familial connections matter—but that didn't mean they weren't questioned and well. So I was twisted deeper into the mire.

Holloway was the smoothest. He made the transition seem almost natural. Had Ramona Wyman mentioned anyone else during our telephone conversation? Her aunt, Miranda O'Malley, for instance? How about her cousins, Morgan or Lana? Was she concerned about their visit to my office earlier that day? Did she ask what the O'Malleys spoke with me about? Did she suspect them of something? Did I tell her what the O'Malleys said? What did I tell her about the O'Malleys?

Then he was off. What had the O'Malleys said about Ramona Wyman? How did I think they felt about her? Was there animosity?

Nothing, No Comment and No Idea. Neither Lana nor her brother had mentioned they even had a cousin. Of course, I furnished very little in the way of answers anyhow. And it was only partly to do with my attitude toward cops. This was simply a case where I knew decidedly little. I hadn't actually met with Ramona Wyman, and the O'Malleys had stormed out of my office half way through our first meeting.

But it wasn't a complete waste of time, at least on my end. I may, to quote Lieutenant Dent, be nothing more than a lousy snoop, but even I manage to sniff out the occasional clue. For instance, after turning his attention to the O'Malleys, Ackerman especially, phrased some interesting questions. What proof did the O'Malleys possess that their father had been murdered? What about that proof had been insufficient to persuade me to take their case? Did I not consider their proof authentic? *Did it strike me as having been fabricated?*

He was clearly addressing something specific, some actual piece of evidence. He and Holloway thought that I had seen it or at least had it described to me. I couldn't quite decide if *they* had seen it or even knew exactly what it was. But it was something, and they were keen on it.

Also, being, to quote both myself and my license, a private investigator, I was able to piece together an assortment of other pertinent facts despite the universal attitude of everyone I spoke with not to answer any questions. For instance, Ramona's personal info. I also learned that she stood five-foot-four, weighed a hundred and ten pounds, and wore red lipstick. There hadn't been any sign of sexual assault. No purse had been discovered, but the ocean is wide and deep, and they hadn't yet found where the actual murder had taken place.

About that. She'd been strangled with her own scarf, still bound tightly in place when the body was recovered. It was apparently purple with something like peacock feathers on it. No prints. A few coins were found in a pocket, making theft seem unlikely, despite the absence of a purse. Although a thief, having lost control and killed, might be unnerved enough to forget to check all the pockets. The only article found on the body in addition to clothing was a slip of paper with my name and number, the words "Gray Suit, Blue Shirt, Striped Tie, Old" and a time, three-thirty.

Dent had some fun with that word *old*, of course. And him gazing fondly back at fifty, yet nothing but a lieutenant. He decided to take the line that I was dogging the Wyman girl and, how pathetic, she thought I was old. That attack made no sense for any number of reasons, but the mere sight of me sets the old bird's blood pumping at such a pace it's a wonder he manages to form any words whatsoever. Busting through my door like he was Elliot Ness. I should have filed a complaint, but it would have taken even more time, and I had things to do.

When I hit the street, I used the first phone booth I could find. Of course, the Hall of Justice has public telephones, but after nearly eight hours of sitting, sitting and more sitting, the muscles in my thighs were twitching, and I needed to pound some pavement. I stopped at a drug store on Kearny, south of the Square, and tried Gig Barton, my reporter friend at the *Clipper*, but he wasn't available. I trudged to California Street and tried again at a diner. Same result. I started up California, moving at a fair clip, got to Stockton and another drug store and got him.

"Why aren't you in jail?"

"I escaped," I said. "Where are we having lunch?"

"We aren't. You probably look like you've been hung out to dry and smell worse. Besides, I work."

"You do. And I occasionally help. Now I need help—info. I'll buy you clams at Sym's."

"All the way out there?"

"I recall you agreed with me about Sym's clams. I'll change my shirt."

"You do know your clams." He made some noises that might have been his brain working but were probably just his lips flapping around an annoyed sigh. "I can get away for about an hour, but it has to be now."

That suited me perfectly, and I told him so. We rang off, and I dashed outside to jump on a passing streetcar. It carried me to the top of the hill, and I started down on foot, getting about half way before lucking into an empty hack. That brought me to the Rooker building, and the elevator took me the rest of the way. Getting out on the third floor and turning right to head down the hall to my office, I saw that someone was fiddling with my doorknob, or at least he had been. He'd apparently looked up when the elevator binged. He didn't think to remove his hand from the knob until after we'd made eye contact at which point he smiled, putting both hands into his pockets.

I sort of recognized him, but not really. He looked like Tyrone Power had before the war, and that's not the sort of comparison I am apt to make lightly. Tall and slender, draped in a suit that someone had taken care fitting and finishing, he wore a hat set back to show off the black hair that swung down across his forehead. His face had all the right parts arranged in just the right way, nothing too big or too small, skinned in a light olive shade that made you notice his dark eyebrows, which in turn set off his dark eyes. His lips weren't really red, or even pink, but were perfect at showing off his white teeth. You got the impression he spent some time at the mirror working to get that smile just right. Basically, he was that sort of guy who is too pretty and knows it. The sort your knuckles just itch to plug.

"Why, it's the man himself," he told me in a firm tenor.

I eyed him skeptically as I approached. "Is it?"

"Declan Colette, yes?"

I neither confirmed nor denied it. I reached the door, and he stepped back to let me use my key. That my key fit the lock probably went some way toward answering his question.

"You don't remember me," he said, following me into the foyer, past the someday-receptionist's desk into my office. "We worked together on that bank notes caper last year. Joe. Joe Lovejoy. I'm with Cobb."

By the time he'd said all that, I was around my desk and seated in my chair. I didn't get up to take the hand he extended to me, but after a momentary hesitation, I did shake it. As soon as he'd mentioned the bank job, I remembered him fine. Half as smart as he thought and twice as smooth. But he did work full time for Walter Cobb. As I recollect, the old man once told me he kept Lovejoy around because the ladies liked him. I didn't doubt it. But my knuckles were still itching, and clasping hands with the snake didn't help.

He put his hands back in his pockets and looked around at the window and the filing cabinet, at the couch against the wall and the two client chairs facing my desk. But he didn't sit. "This is a nice office.

Cozy." He offered me another askew glance, angling his head slightly to give his eyes a coy slant. "You do remember me, don't you?"

"Sure. Sure I do, Joe. How you been?"

"Great! And you?" He was energized, which made me remember how tired I was. I watched him pace a few steps to the left and back another four steps to the right. He continued to admire the decor. "Must be swell being your own boss. Not that Cobb is a bad guy, no! He's always done all right by me. You know, he thinks well of you, too. Says you have potential."

That made my hand twitch, and I had no choice but to make a fist. I can't say he noticed. He was eyeing me but trying to be sly about it, or rather playing at being sly in such a way as to ensure that I knew exactly what he was doing. I cleared my throat and told him, "Is there something I can do for you? Did Cobb need me to call him? I'm a bit busy at the moment. In fact, I just came in to change my shirt."

"Carry on. This is just a friendly visit, professional courtesy. Walter sent me, but informally, you know? He likes you. Did I tell you he told me he thinks you have potential?"

I got back up because it would be easier to knock him down that way. Not that it would have been much of a chore lying on my back. Admittedly, he probably fought dirty and maybe even kept assorted tools tucked away, but the mood I was in, I wouldn't have felt anything less than a sap over the head. Not that I was planning on knocking him down. Professional courtesy, you know. It goes both ways. I just went over to the bottom drawer of the filing cabinet and got a new shirt.

"You mentioned it," I said in answer to his question.

He lodged his fanny on the edge of my desk, his feet set wide. His hands were still in his pockets. "Well, we all heard about the police taking you in this morning. We heard that girl who got killed, she had arranged to meet you. We also heard that Miss Lana O'Malley and her brother, Morgan O'Malley, came here to the office." He had been watching me take off my tie and shirt, but at that point decided the toe of his shoe was more interesting. "That surprised us. You see, I've been working for the O'Malleys nearly three weeks. I mean, Cobb and I have. They hired us to look into their father's death. You don't mind if I smoke?"

I didn't answer because it wasn't really a question. He had his long, brown ridiculously expensive cigarette out of its silver case and nearly to his lips. He flicked a matching silver lighter and started puffing. When he looked back up he said, "God, you're a gorilla."

I had taken off my undershirt and was using it to wipe under my arms. I don't know what exactly prompted his remark. There's some hair on my chest, I suppose, and I am not ashamed of my physique, which is broad at the shoulders and less so at the waist. But my arms aren't especially long. My knuckles rarely drag the floor. Maybe it was just an involuntary reaction to my muscles; I was downright burly compared to him. Admittedly my phiz wasn't in the same ballpark. If he was a young Tyrone Power, I'm James Cagney, say in *City for Conquest*, only *after* his ill-fated fight with the champ.

I didn't have a spare undershirt at the office, so I donned the clean shirt over my skin. He watched me because, you know, animals in their habitat can be fascinating.

"You can imagine we were surprised," he was saying. "And now, of course, we'll be taking on this new business. Well, along with the police. You do understand?"

"Professional courtesy." I moved back to the chair behind my desk, carrying my tie in my hand. I figured he was going to talk, and I couldn't do much about it short of risking a charge for assault, but I didn't have to listen. I dialed my service, then juggled the telephone receiver as I looped the tie back around my neck. "Declan Colette, messages."

The operator told me, "I hope you're sitting down, Mr. Colette." I am not fudging this. Those were her words.

Meanwhile, Lovejoy went on. "Also, you understand, we're interested in asking you a few questions. I mean, I am, here and now. Or if you're busy, we could meet for a drink after."

I had my pad and pen ready. "Shoot," I told the phone.

I had nine messages, and the operator did absolutely nothing to conceal her incredulity. Three were from Gig Barton, asking me to call, so I skipped those. Two were from Sam Weingarten, who wrote for the *Chronicle*, but we were not friendly, and I skipped those too. Two more were from Walter Cobb, the first asking me to call and the second reiterating that request and adding that it was important. Since his heartthrob was standing right there in front of my desk, I skipped again.

I finally got to use the pen for Mr. Morgan O'Malley, Finchley-five, seven-one-four-three. The call itself was not so earth-shattering a development considering, but the time at which the message had been taken was indeed noteworthy: ten o'clock p.m., the previous evening. *Indeed.*

The last message was from Mrs. Lawrence O'Malley, at a number I recognized as one I'd written down the day before.

"So, I guess things are looking up." That was the operator, sounding as if something like a smile might be playing on her lips.

I thought a crack was in order. I almost demanded her name, planning to feign some outrage and telling her to connect me to her supervisor. But she seemed quite smart enough to mistake it as a clever ploy to get her lined up, and I like to avoid misunderstandings. "I'll let you know," I told her, hanging up.

When I turned my attention back to Lovejoy, I discovered he had ended his soliloquy and was craning his neck to see what I'd scribbled on my pad. *Good luck with that*, I thought. I could barely read it myself right side up. I tore off the top sheet and crammed it in my pocket. Rising, I said, "You're Joe Lovejoy!"

It startled him. His handsome brow dipped over his flashing eyes. That was enough to tell me I was onto a tack. "You aren't the same Joe who told Miss O'Malley I'd be worse than useless? No, it couldn't be. Must have been another Joe. Professional courtesy, and all that."

"I don't know what—"

"Skip it," I said, waving my hand. "This was just a friendly visit. Informal."

He backed up a step as I came around the end of my desk, which did my heart a world of good. He may have been too arrogant to be intimidated, but that didn't mean he had to be incautious. You never know what a gorilla might do. "So, we understand each other?"

I gestured him toward the door. "Sure. But let's agree that you use the elevator, and I'll take the stairs. Professional courtesy."

He shook his head, preceding me into the hall. "Don't play it that way, Colette." He made it an appeal, addressing my back as I locked up. "I was there first. It's mine."

"Go then, my boy. Run with it. But I didn't invite the O'Malleys down here yesterday. They came on their own. Three weeks after hiring you."

He showed me his hands as he backed away down the hall. "You've always been a jackass. I was just trying to be professional."

I didn't watch him go. The stairs were in the opposite direction, I had nothing more to say, and I was in real danger of being late for my lunch date.

CHAPTER FIVE

In addition to clams, Syms has a variety of great Cajun cooking. And, growing up in my grandmother's house, I know from Cajun food. It also boasts the huge advantage of being located just a few blocks from my office and being owned by a man who will be eternally grateful for some help I provided him back when I first came to the city.

Gig, who prided himself on his palate, had never been before I took him there. That was partly because it's a Negro establishment in a predominantly Negro neighborhood, and Gig is so white, he practically glows. But it's also because the place is a secret treasure, and only the best people know about it.

I beat Gig there and managed to score my usual table at the back. Gina, the hostess, who might live in the place for all I know, since I've yet to visit and not see her, brought me a Manhattan in a highball glass. "You don't look so good."

"Is this some new scheme to score a bigger tip? I question the merits."

She has the loveliest black skin, just a few shades lighter than my grandmother, and huge almond eyes that must take ten minutes to paint each morning. Her amber irises reflect the subdued lighting of the room beautifully. "You question everything, Dec. It's the only reason I don't marry you."

"Is that the reason?"

She laughed, a deep, throaty, barely-audible baritone that she's somehow learned to make resonate in a man's lower spine. "Well, one of them. I'm not quite sure I approve of your line of work. Look at you. Did you sleep last night?"

"As a matter of fact, I did. Which just goes to show you." I took a sip of my beverage and glanced once up and down her long form. "You look well."

"That's *my* job."

"And the reason I don't marry *you*. I'd be down here every night hunched in the corner in a jealous rage."

She looked disappointed. "You wouldn't make me give up work? Now I have two reasons."

"Drats. Foiled by my own wit." I took another drink. "My only excuse is I'm bushed. I slept last night but not much. Did I remember to order clams when I asked for this drink?"

"You did. You're not completely done for." She nodded at my half-empty glass. "You may want to slow down on that until your friend gets here."

I hoisted the glass to my lips and swallowed a healthy sample. "I may need to inform Sym of the way you're trying to dissuade patrons from spending money." I could see she wasn't amused, however, so I added, "Don't bring me another until you bring his."

I didn't have to wait long. She was halfway to the front when the street doors opened, and a tall blond fellow stepped in. He stood blinking at the darkness while Gina greeted him. She pointed back at me, then went to the bar as Gig Barton made his way toward me.

He dropped a manila folder down next to my drink. "Happy Christmas."

"Merry New Year. What's this?"

"Everything I could smuggle out under my jacket." He settled into his chair. "Don't say I never gave you anything."

"I wouldn't dream of spreading such a vicious lie." I opened the folder and nearly fell out of my chair. It was packed with photos and draft prints of articles, copies of morgue biographies and even some handwritten notes. "Jesus, Gig, I'm flabbergasted."

"Yeah, well, I also brought this." He tugged a notepad out of his inside breast pocket and slapped it down on the table. "So understand I expect a fair exchange. Say everything you've got now plus first crack at anything you dig up. Regarding Ramona Wyman, of course.

What exactly is your involvement in this thing? Did you meet this girl or only converse on the telephone? Is it true you met with Lawrence O'Malley's kids yesterday?"

"How's Betsy?"

"She doesn't like you, and she wouldn't approve of our having lunch. Try to stay focused. I've only got an hour. Maybe two if you drink enough of those so that you can't control your tongue." He indicated my empty glass.

I looked up and around for Gina and saw her already on her way with a tray. Sadly, only one glass was riding it, and its contents looked too clear to be a Manhattan. Probably it was Gig's gin fizz. That's what he likes. Nobody's perfect. I told him, referring to Betsy, "I thought you said she didn't trust me. I had no idea her opinion crossed the board. Now my feelings are all hurt."

"Well, we'll just have to soldier through the pain."

"Can I at least take a look at this first?" Gina had arrived, so I said, "Maybe taste your drink. You remember Gina. Gina, Gig."

They acknowledged they knew one another as she deposited his drink, inquired after my thoughts on a second, and departed to get it. Gig tasted his gin fizz, wiped his lips, and went straight back to work.

"First thing this morning, I was told you were under arrest. What happened with that?"

"That was merely Oscar Dent trying to show he still has teeth. Nothing was filed, and by the time I got into the ADA, they'd bought me coffee and donuts and considered me a friend of the force. Who's George Kelly?" I was glancing over the bios, and I didn't recognize that name.

"Another cousin. Lawrence O'Malley's sister's kid. Well, kid no more. He's our age. The only one of the bunch not loony, I gather. War hero, North African variety. Morocco maybe? Member of the bar. Patrician's right hand. Did surprisingly well in the old man's will. In fact, if there had been any question about O'Malley's death, Kelly would have topped my list of likelies."

"If? Surely this new murder makes it better than even that O'Malley didn't go without help."

"If so, you'll need to explain the how to me. Zack Nolan had the story for three weeks and came up with nothing. I admit Nolan's not me, but he's at least half as good and would have dug up something provided there was something to dig up." A waiter deposited a steaming bowl of clams in the center of the table. Gig took up the large serving spoon and shoveled a good portion onto his plate. "No sir, O'Malley died of a heart attack, plain and simple. The cops brought in three different experts to be sure." He popped a clam into his mouth. "You aren't planning to help me with these?"

"Sure. I'm just trying to get through this." I flipped another page, scanning a short article published the day after O'Malley's death. "You said you only had an hour."

"Nuts. Have it to me by the end of business today. I mean it. Tony'd have my hide if that went missing. And, like I said, I expect some quid for the pro quo. You can start by telling me why it was you were meeting with Ramona Wyman."

"Sadly, I can't. I don't know why. It was about the only thing she refused to tell me."

"Okay, then. Why did the O'Malley kids come to see you?"

"Sad again. Nothing you'd be interested in. Unrelated."

"Ha!" It wasn't so much a laugh as a scoff. "Now you're just trying to goad me. They were peddling the notion their father had been murdered. You weren't the first to hear about it. They'd been to the police and a few lawyers. You weren't even their first private dick."

I let him see that I was hurt. "Then why ask?"

"To show how much better a friend I am than you. Did you buy into their fable?"

"I never got the chance. Miss O'Malley decided she didn't like my haircut and called the whole thing off." I helped myself to some clams, spooning them on my plate and splashing a generous portion of the sauce atop them. I'd already closed the manila folder and shoved it aside for later, when I was alone. "Tell me about those kids."

"They do add some color. You've seen her. She's not exactly hard on the eyes, but she's cold. A dutiful daughter by all accounts. Went to Mount of the Olives rather than Brown or Vassar. People tell me that speaks volumes, but maybe she just doesn't like to travel. Was engaged, but he didn't make it back, also apparently that—"

"Where was he killed?"

"One of the atolls. We were brothers at arms, but of course I never heard of him. Langston maybe? Something or other. Good family, I hear."

I put a finger on the closed folder. "He's in here?"

Gig shrugged. "Probably. Peripherally. I had no idea you were so thorough."

"Yeah? You were about to say something. Also apparently what?"

"Huh?"

"You said he was killed and that also apparently—" I left it hanging just the way he had.

He tried to remember. "I think I was going to say also apparently that didn't help Miss O'Malley's disposition. She took it hard. The whole Greek tragedy, wailing woman bit. I hear there may even have been hair-pulling and ashes. Hasn't mixed much with men since."

All that actually raised my opinion of Lana O'Malley several notches. I drank a silent toast to her. "What about her brother?"

"Even more color, only darker shades. Black, for instance. As in black sheep." He drew a deep preparatory breath. "Disowned by Father, though no one knows why exactly. Has the usual vices— cards, ponies, girls—but nothing to excess. Thirsty often and enjoys quenching it. Also prefers fast cars to walking. But never arrested, never accused of treating any particular girl in an unchivalrous fashion. Still, disowned. Ostensibly before the war, but the will made it official. I believe the line was, 'To my son, Lawrence Morgan O'Malley, I bequeath nothing.' I suppose that could also be considered a motive for murder, but everyone claims the boy is sweet and sensitive. Tried to make a go of it in Hollywood but flopped. Betz tells me he's better looking than Peter Lawford. I don't see it."

"Me neither. Tell me about the widow."

Gig sat back in his chair, taking a break from the clams to stretch. "Not until you buy me another drink." He grinned.

I flagged Gina, and she seemed to flow over to us. She was not dressed for evening, but she was nevertheless stunning. I hadn't been aware music was playing until I watched the movement of her hips as she crossed the room. The joint had live bands in at night, of course, but it was the juke box that time of day, and the music and Gina coming toward me put me in mind of Billie and *Lover Man*. Only when she reached us did I realize it was Ella crooning longingly about a *Cabin in the Sky*.

Gig must have seen the way I was watching her, because when she left us with our refill order, he asked me, "Is that why you like this place?" He turned his head to watch her go. "She *is* a Nubian goddess."

That made me chuckle and succeeded in bringing me out of a reverie that had absolutely nothing to do with Gina's charms. I said, "Let me call her back and you can tell her that. Then, when you pick yourself up off the floor, you can tell *me* about Miranda O'Malley."

The widow O'Malley turned out to be Gig's favorite topic of the day, which, in light of what I'd already surmised, surprised me not at all.

Most of what he told me was a rehash of what Lana had shared the day before, only filtered through the admiring eye of a healthy young man rather than the jaundiced eye of a bitter almost war widow. The single most startling revelation he provided was that Miranda had not 'suddenly appeared' in the O'Malley's lives; she'd been there nearly ten years before marrying the old man. Her first husband's father, Jasper Reed, had been Lawrence O'Malley's attorney for most of the century, right up until the war started. George Kelly, Miranda March, and Adam Reed had all attended Stanford together.

There were a few other random facts: she liked to dance, wasn't much on public service, threw wild but intimate parties, didn't like riding or betting on horses, but she frequented both Bay Meadows and the new Golden Gate Fields. Men liked her. I guess that was not news in and of itself, but the feeling was seldom mutual. In other words, Gig told me, grinning, she rarely danced with the same partner twice. And one time at the track club, two Romeos had skinned their knuckles over claiming the seat next to hers while she, bored, had awarded the chair to someone else.

Gig wasn't keen to move the conversation along, say to Ramona Wyman, which was poised to be *my* favorite topic. He had more praise to heap on the widow. I told him to save it for a sonnet he should forget to copy me on. He laughed, but only relented to talk about Ramona Wyman when I got Gina to bring us two more drinks, his third and my fourth.

I tried to start as close to the beginning of my interest as possible. "So, why was the kid living with her aunt rather than with her parents back in Ohio?"

"Her mother died somehow, nothing sinister as I recall. I do know how your mind works. But it was either aunt or grandma, and she was a kid and aunt married well—I mean the first time too. So there you are. This is good gin for the afternoon." He squinted around the restaurant; it was only about a quarter full, and we were the only non-Negroes. "I wish we could get in here at night sometime."

I could probably get us in at night through a side door, I know, because I've snuck myself in that way, but he didn't really mean it. He preferred the Torrent Club on Telegraph Hill, which was artsy and swank at the same time. Sym's was not artsy, just very swank, and the clientele that filled the place most nights wouldn't have welcomed two white men. "So there I am. Ramona moved in with Auntie."

He shook his head. "Pushy bastard." He was just starting to slur his words, and his cheaters were sliding down his nose. He pushed them back up. "She spent summers with Adam and Miranda Reed and moved in full time when he left for Europe. Also, it had been decided she would follow Auntie through Stanford and preparations were in the works. It was going to require preparations—monetary preparations—because Miss Wyman was not the brightest bulb."

"She was cute, though. Was there a boy?"

"None anyone could or would name."

"Too bad. Girls tell things to boys who hold their hands, don't they?"

"Nothing a boy can bank on, if memory serves. In your case, I imagine it was a lot of 'Stop, you're hurting me.'"

"A wit like that and they don't have you on the funny pages?" I tossed back some Manhattan. "So they all live together there in the big house?"

"No." He shook his head, then sat frowning at his glass, his lips puckered and on the verge of a frown. It was the sort of expression that might bespeak deep rumination at a desk somewhere. But at that table covered in the wreckage of slaughtered clams, in that dim restaurant, the ice cubes rolling lazily around in his half-empty glass, it simply said that I'd about drowned his usefulness for the time being.

"Well, all except the O'Malley kids. Go figure. Lana O'Malley has a swank apartment at Hilltop just down the street, and Black Sheep keeps a bungalow in North Beach. I hear the place is opened regularly to artists and musicians down on their luck. Apparently the boy is a patron."

"So, despite being disinherited, he's not hurting for green. He works?"

"Not at anything you or I would recognize as work. His mother's family was flush. They set him up with a trust Betz and me and you— if I could get you to cut back on the booze—could retire on and still manage to live a damned sight better than we do now."

He was sprawled in his chair, his right arm hooked up over the back of it and his long legs stretched out to the side. His left hand was on the table, meandering around in drunken circles on the tablecloth. I wouldn't quite describe the look he was giving me as a leer, but it was definitely time to send him on his way. Did I mention that he's several inches taller than me? Well, he's also nearly fifty pounds lighter.

I signaled for the check. "So, who did it? Who killed her?"

"The butler? Isn't it always? His name is Fenton, by-the-bye. A youngish fellow. Colored. Apparently they're progressive like you."

"Damned racist. Maybe I *should* get Gina over here to crown you." I made the threat in hushed tones, however, because she was already on her way.

He laughed again and I joined him, thinking it was as good a way to end things as any other. Not that I meant it—about him being a racist. I believe he's all for civil rights, at least in the abstract. Though, back when we first met, he'd done some digging for a profile piece and, discovering I'd been raised by a colored woman, killed the story because he worried it might hurt my budding business. Not that keeping it a secret appears to have helped much.

Once we were outside, me with my manila folder clutched safely in my hand, he waved his notebook in my face, showing me a blank page. "Look at that! Not a word. Damned cheating bastard."

I filled my lungs, stretching my arms out to the side and letting the sunlight tickle every corner of my face. "Think of it as an investment. Besides, your belly's full and your brain is well-lubricated. Go back to the office and enjoy your nap."

He placed his hand on my shoulder and leaned in toward me, breathing heavy gin-soaked vapors across my ear. "Let's go back to your office and play some cards. Penny poker. Or, if you're short of dough, we could play strip poker." He flicked my tie with his other hand.

I shrugged the hand off my shoulder which proved ill-advised because it nearly sent him tumbling into the street. I had to catch hold of his upper arm to keep him erect. I neither looked at his face nor addressed his ridiculous suggestion, patting him on the back and telling him, "Give Betz my love."

He offered me a parting raspberry as we went our separate ways. Mine soon delivered me back to my office where I planted myself behind my desk to give the contents of the manila folder the scrutiny it deserved. In addition to the bios and clippings, it had photographs of all the major players. Morgan's happened to be on top, and I decided that entitled it to a longer look.

He was in uniform, at ease, with his hat tucked under his arm, three-quarters profile, but his face aimed directly toward the camera. The insignias proclaimed his rank as first lieutenant, but I was left wondering whether he'd started there or if that was where he'd ended up. Nothing indicated when the photo had been taken. The phiz looked identical to the one that had confronted me across my desk the day before, brow slightly furrowed, eyes sharp and somewhat accusatory, lips straight, neither smiling nor frowning, but with just the faintest hint of a pout. He could have been sculpted by Michelangelo. He should have been. He was better looking than Joe Lovejoy and probably every bit as aware of the fact. But in his case, my first impulse was not to give him a punch in the eye.

I grudgingly moved his picture to the bottom of the stack, revealing his sister.

She looked completely different than she had when I'd met her. Shown the image out of context, I might not even have recognized her. For one thing, she was happy; it was in her eyes as well as her smile. Doubtless that had something to do with the fellow standing beside her, an honest-looking schlub I took to be the deceased fiancé. The photograph was the sort you'd see in the society pages alongside the announcement of a betrothal. They were in evening wear, the ritzy kind, with her sporting enough diamonds to pay my salary for a year.

Her face was softer, more reminiscent of her brother's. Only she had more points. It wasn't just her nose and chin, but also her eyebrows and ears. Sprightly, you might call her, or perhaps *spritely* if that's even a word. But in that picture she was a good fairy, not the evil creature that had stormed out of my office the day before.

Next in line was George Kelly, also in uniform, also at ease. He'd been a major, which sounds impressive until you recollect the state of the world five years ago. I'd known a major once, but the best I can say is he wasn't a total sap. Kelly was not as tall as his cousin Morgan, nor as handsome, but he cut a respectable figure. Maybe it was the clothes. Lots of mediocre fellows took some handsome photographs between 1941 and 1945. In fact, I have a few of myself that I've even shown people.

George Kelly looked honest and earnest and proud to be wearing the outfit. Probably he did all right by it too. Gig had mentioned something about war hero. I decided to give him the benefit of the doubt. Notwithstanding that in my estimation most of the men truly deserving of the title war hero never made it back to claim it.

Pictures four through nine were all of Miranda O'Malley. Leave it to Gig. She was also in uniform. Cocktail dresses mostly. One photo taken on a boat, showed her in a swimsuit with a flimsy gauze wrap. I'd already seen her in a couple of different papers, so the vision didn't take my breath away. Not that she wasn't worthy of all the buildup she'd been given. At five-eight, she stood tall and stately, with a tiny waist connecting her more shapely top and bottom, a dancer's gams, and arms that seemed to curve and flow without any annoying elbows.

I still hadn't looked up the word succubus, but I figured if the dictionary provided an accompanying illustration, that image looked nothing like Miranda O'Malley. Of course, neither would her likeness have been shown alongside the definition of seraphim found a few pages earlier. She had a perfect oval face with a small but pronounced chin, the sort you always imagine taking between your thumb and forefinger, with your thumb nestled gently in the faint dimple. Her eyes were enormous, but the lids were seldom at anything higher than half-mast, so she clearly disliked sharing them. Maybe that was why I preferred the swimsuit photo to the others. Most men would, of course, but for different reasons.

There on the boat, she hadn't done so much to her face. Perhaps she'd just come out of the water. And her eyes were open. She wasn't smiling. Judging just by the pictures, she never did smile. Nor frown. Such emotional displays seemed to be beneath her. On the boat, however, when whoever it had been called her name or whistled or just said hey, and she'd looked over, half-reclined on her acre of towel, arching a brow and letting on that at that precise moment, even if she didn't find it particularly funny, at least she got the joke, there was an unmistakable echo of the clever girl from Ohio. The one who had made her way West to find the kind of money and comfort that would consume and sublimate her, turning her into the woman she was meant to be. The woman captured so perfectly in all the other photographs.

My phone rang. I reached and missed, then dropped the pictures and managed to wrangle the receiver up alongside my head. "Hello?" The sound of my voice confirmed what my clumsy hands had suggested: I was drunker than I thought. Swigging Manhattans from a highball glass over lunch was bad enough, but four of them? I cleared my throat and tried again. "Hello?"

"This is the office of Declan Colette?" It was a woman's voice, a matron with a heavy accent that I tagged immediately as Kraut.

"Yes. Hold please." I put the receiver down on the desk and stood up. I stretched again, just as I had outside Sym's, loading up both lungs and rolling my fists out to my sides as far as they would go. I lit a cigarette, sat back down and hoisted my right ankle up onto my left knee. Leaning back, I loosened my tie, then reclaimed the telephone receiver. "This is Mr. Declan Colette. May I help you?"

"You are the private detective?"

"I am. But I should warn you I rarely accept German clients." That was the Manhattans talking. I wouldn't necessarily turn down an honest fee just because the client's second cousin might have taken a shot at me a few years earlier. I harbor no particular animus toward the Jerrys, at least the American ones. And I actually rather like a lot of the Italians I've met. Now, a Jap I would just as soon cross the street to trip on the sidewalk, and heaven help the one who ever pokes his ugly yellow head through my office door. But I can tolerate an occasional Kraut.

"I am Swiss," she sneered.

"Well then, *guten Tag. Wie geht's?*" Having about depleted my supply of *Deutsch*, I switched back to good old American English. "How can I help you?"

"I am calling on behalf of Mrs. Lawrence O'Malley. She would very much like to meet you."

"Yeah, how much?"

"I beg your pardon?"

"No need, I offer it freely. When would she like to come?"

Another pause. "Under the circumstances, she would rather that you might come here, to her home."

I nodded my approval. And, no, I hadn't forgotten that we were talking over a wire. "Under the circumstances, I accept. Shall I come now?"

"Madame is resting now. Please hold the line." I heard a sound as if the transmitter was covered, and I listened to nothing for nearly a minute. "She would like to invite you to come this evening at six o'clock." Then, perhaps worried I might misunderstand, she added, "After dinner."

"Really? Mrs. Lawrence O'Malley eats early." I sighed. "I suppose I can do the same. Six o'clock you say?"

"Yes, sir."

"So, not too much."

"*Wie bitte?* I—I beg your pardon?"

"You told me she very much wanted to meet me. Now she seems willing to wait several hours."

"Yes, sir. Shall I give you the address?"

I was casual. "What sort of detective would I be if I needed all that?"

"Yes, sir." Swiss or not, the old gal had all the sense of humor of a Kraut.

A moment of heavy silence followed. Finally I breathed at her. "Well, then, I guess this is where we say '*Auf Wiedersehen*'."

"Good-bye, sir." She hung up so gently, I barely heard the click.

CHAPTER SIX

I slipped Gig's folder into a heavy envelope, addressed it to his attention, Personal and Confidential, then took a cab to the *Bay Clipper's* offices. My intention was to reach the front desk without encountering anyone I knew and leave the envelope in the care of the attendant on duty. It wasn't, admittedly, the most honorable return on Gig's generosity, but I was tired and wanted to stop off at my apartment to freshen up before meeting the succubus.

The first part of my plan came off without a hitch, but after I'd stripped and showered and fallen atop my unmade bed thinking I'd rest my eyes a moment, I found myself rocking gently in the surf at some beach while a shadowy figure sat beside me trying to feed me grapes. I decided it wouldn't hurt too much to get a good look at whoever was holding the grapes, so I set the alarm for five-ten and rolled over. But I never made it back to the beach. There was only darkness until the clock started chiming, and I got up.

My phiz required a razor, as it often does in the late afternoon, but I have learned to clean up fast. I was out the door by five-forty, garbed in my best suit and tie. I only have two hats, so while the one I wore that day could also be designated my best, it wasn't quite up to the level of the rest of my apparel.

I caught another cab, and we made a nearly straight shot up Pacific Avenue. When I climbed out a half block from the address, the meter read thirty-five cents. I handed the cabbie a half dollar. I still had ten minutes to spare. I decided that gave me time to case the joint, as they say in the moving pictures, and I took a slow walk along the sidewalk.

The O'Malleys had a whole block to themselves, all that land surrounded by a high stone wall behind hedges. One gate was on Pacific and another around the corner offering ingress from the Eastern side street. I stopped at that latter location for my first gander at the house itself.

I took it nearly in profile, but it was still a beaut. Mansion doesn't quite cover it, though I admit castle might be hyperbole. The front was burnt brick decorated with all sorts of trimming around the windows and the door and at the corners of the roof. The porch looked like marble, and it spread out ten feet from the front, with matching columns to support the cover which doubled as a terrace accessed by some French windows on the second floor. Being in San Francisco, there wasn't much lawn. The yard was mostly taken up with a great sweep of red gravel drive connecting the two gates and swirling around a fountain located about twenty feet from the porch. Assorted trees dotted the periphery in a thin strip of green hugging the wall and a flowerbed along the front of the house. The flora was all highly regimented and fit for photographs in *Better Homes and Gardens*. The afternoon sunlight transformed the splashing water of the fountain into a cascade of glittering jewels. Thinking it was a trick, I glanced back across the street, where, sure enough, the sky was scattered with wispy clouds and the light seemed dimmer. I decided maybe I was still slightly drunk. If it was a trick, it was a swell one.

The gate from the side street was closed, so I made my way slowly back around the corner and along Pacific to the main gate. It was open and twice the size of the other. Even the big new cars could probably come and go simultaneously and not have to worry about rubbing sides. Passing through, I saw I'd missed out on my opportunity to see my supposition tested; the gravel drive was crowded with vehicles.

I wondered if I was crashing a party. I counted six cars in all, ranging from an aging green pre-war DeSoto to a sporty silver coupe without a lid. In between were a Hillman Minx, a high-end Hudson, a Ford sedan, and a yellow, nearly golden Chrysler Highlander, also without a top, that managed to win my heart the moment I laid eyes on it. It was parked over near the side gate, so I sidled up to the little coupe first, admiring the elaborate triangular grill work adorning the front. Ah, those crazy Italians.

"What're you doing?"

The voice came from nearer the house, and I looked up to see a man I hadn't seen before, probably because he'd been hidden in the thick foliage of the flowerbed. His raiment identified him as Chauffeur, though its style and age did not match the prestige of the house. I noted some repair work done to a tunic sleeve and one leg of the trousers. Someone capable of affording a brand new Alfa Romeo probably wouldn't have tolerated it. I figured he could be matched with the DeSoto all right.

He left the camouflage of the hedge to come toward me, a scowl lining his weathered face. His eyes, saggy and a bit wet, were dwarfed by a nose that looked like it had been pushed in with an unsettling regularity to which it had finally grown accustomed. His mouth was wide and thin-lipped, and his scowl revealed the tips of some seriously stained bridgework. He was shorter and a bit heavier than me, and though his cap covered much of his head, his hair looked to be mainly devoid of any color.

"Just admiring the view," I told him, doing so. I stood beside the coupe and whistled approvingly at the leather interior.

He stopped about ten feet from me, and his scowl worsened. "You're the shamus."

"I am *a* shamus," I allowed. "I don't know about *the* shamus. I've heard tell of others."

He spat a big wad of something down next to the front wheel of the DeSoto. "I've been waiting for you."

"Huh." I checked my watch. "According to this, I'm a few minutes early."

"Yeah, only I—"

"Hey! What's this?" Another voice interrupted him, not mine.

A large car shed stood off to my left, separated from the house by the gravel drive. Of its three big double doors, the pair at the near end stood open. A man was coming out, rubbing his hands on a rag that didn't look any too clean. He was a young fellow in coveralls over a sweaty T-shirt, wearing work boots that looked well-worked. A cigarette dangled from his lips; another unlit one rode behind his ear. He had dark hair, nearly black, cut close, with a remarkably low hairline above his bushy eyebrows. His face was simian, with a sloping honk and jutting jaw. His big protruding ears really added to the illusion of a trained monkey striding toward us.

"I thought you was told to wait in the kitchen," he said.

I didn't think he could have been addressing me, but, by the way the old chauffeur ignored him completely, I didn't suppose he was addressing him either.

Chauffeur said to me, "I want a word with you."

Monkey boy stopped about ten feet to the side of us, like we were mapping out a triangle in the gravel. He didn't seem to notice I was there, however, and he squinted angrily at the chauffeur. "What the hell are you doing?"

Chauffeur glanced over at a small office attached to the car shed, passing right by the younger guy like he didn't even exist. "What do you say we step in there?"

These two characters interested me no little bit, but I said, "I'm expected at the house."

"Yeah. It'll just take a minute." Chauffeur started toward the shed.

"What the hell?" That was from Monkey boy, who I figured, in fairness, was probably some sort of mechanic. He stepped into the chauffeur's path and reached out toward the old guy's shoulder.

I barely saw it, even though he must have taken a good swing. There was just a jerk and then a loud smack as the chauffeur's palm met the side of the mechanic's face. Both cigarettes went flying. Monkey boy staggered a step to the right, more surprised than hurt I imagine, though the smack echoed around the walled yard. Then I saw him bare his teeth, his heavy brow moving down as he threw a wild fist up at the old guy's head.

Wild as it was, it might have connected had the old man not weaved. He was smooth and cool. Just as his mangled nose suggested, this was a fellow who had been exposed to his fair share of flying fists. Pivoting with the grace of a Golden Gloves boxer, he snaked his left arm up in a tight arc and grabbed hold of the kid's T-shirt. He pulled Monkey boy up straight and brought his other hand back across the simian face, offering a taste of hairy knuckles. Then, in quick procession, he doled out three more slaps while the mechanic stood there, either too shocked or too dazed to do anything about it.

Despite being sharp and stinging, the slaps were—like most slaps—more to prove a point than inflict any real damage. The only reason the kid fell was due to his pulling back trying to get clear when the old man let him go. Monkey boy dropped his keister down hard on the gravel and sat there looking up with his mouth open. Chauffeur glared down at him, finally acknowledging his existence with a look of pure disgust, then cocked a leg. The mechanic scrambled quickly, getting himself upright and tearing in the opposite direction of the car shed. He disappeared around the side of the house.

Chauffeur turned to me with the disgusted look still lingering on his homely mug. A moment passed as he glared, apparently trying to decide. Finally he started toward the shed again. "Come on."

I followed him across the yard into the dark little room that was cramped with shelves and workbenches and every sort of automotive tool imaginable, but offered no place to sit down. Another open door in the opposite wall led to what appeared to be a bedroom. The old man closed the door we had entered through, then produced and lit a cigar with trembling hands.

"Christ. I been waiting three years for that."

"Yeah? What is it, a shakeup at the livery union?"

We were standing a few feet apart in the middle of the dirty floor. After disposing of his match, he squinted at me. From his expression, you'd gather I had some secret code hidden in the lines of my face and he was determined to decipher it. "You know that kid got a waiver?"

I shrugged. "Lots of guys got waivers. You go around offering them all slaps like that, you'll ruin your hand."

"Huh." He seemed to grow even more suspicious. "What about you?"

"What about me?" I inched my shoulders back. I wanted him to make no mistake. If he tried slapping me, he'd be the one on his keister.

At that, he didn't actually back down. He just offered me the sort of snarl that said we could table the question for the time being. When he thrust out his big hard hand, it was to offer a shake. "Sergeant Wayne Holmsby, ninth infantry."

Not anymore you're not, I thought, shaking his hand anyway. Now you're just a grizzled bird who goes around slapping poor saps who got deferments. What I actually said was, "Declan Colette." I'd left all the rest of that madness behind, and there it would remain.

Holmsby had a grip, and he tightened it. "Enlisted?"

I'm not one to go in for that tough guy routine, and if you buy that, I have some swamp land we can discuss later. I gave Holmsby back about twice what he offered and watched as he realized his mistake. "Yes, sir."

I let him go, and he retreated a step, half-turning in an attempt to hide the fact that he was massaging his right hand with his left. "I could see that."

Bullshit, I thought. I'd seen more than a few pantywaist enlisted men indistinguishable from that monkey boy mechanic outside.

"What I should have said," Holmsby continued, "is that he bought a waiver, or had a waiver bought for him. Probably on account of the son. Probably they were queer for each other."

"You don't say? You see them holding hands?"

He reared up at me. "Do they look like I seen 'em holding hands?"

I nearly gave him a taste of *my* palm right then. He needed it. He'd obviously been holding something in and, rather than purging himself, his roughing up the mechanic had merely made it worse. He had spittle on his protruding lower lip.

"What did we need to come in here for?" I asked.

He rubbed a fat finger along his lip, then dried the finger on his tunic. "I don't like this business. It don't look right." He paused to give me another look, or maybe to offer me time to respond, but when I didn't he told me, "I was wanting a look at you. I took a stab at that other shamus, but he ain't our type. He snubbed me. I think he might be part of the fix."

"Whoa, brother, you're a mile ahead of me. There's a fix?"

"What are you, smart? Sure there's a fix. They're gonna pin it on the colonel, ain't they? All on account of them letters."

"You're still speeding, Sergeant. Which colonel? What letters?"

"Where have I been cooling my heels all day? That's right, Portsmouth. They had me inside this morning, and they kept the old man most of the day. It ain't right. Before the war, the coppers never would have dragged the colonel in, but this family..." His voice trailed off as he stepped closer to the single window, which was neither curtained nor shaded but dirty enough that it didn't need to be. He glanced through the glass, and his scowl came back in force, like he hated the burnt brick of the mansion's facade. "These bozos get him so tied in knots. I thought we was through with them after the wedding. But no, he had to go on writing to the girl."

He jerked around to face me again. "Listen you. What's your part in this? Which one are you for?"

"For?" I let him see that I didn't follow. "Mrs. O'Malley invited me here."

He looked down at something, scratching his chin. "Her." He said the word without a lot of feeling, so I couldn't tell if he approved or not. "I don't get her. She was all right when she was Addy's girl. They used to go out on his boat, y'know? I used to drive 'em down to the pier."

I played a hunch. "Yeah, but Addy's dead now, isn't he? And she's—"

He came at me in a surge, with that same fat finger extended toward my chest. "You leave him outta this! He was a fine boy. A good boy. He never—"

He stopped mid-sentence, his words hanging in the air. I let them hang, thinking he should know I noticed. Finally I asked, "What did he never?"

Holmsby shook his head, backing away again. "Look at you. What happened? The fellow who loaned you that suit didn't want to give you the hat, too?"

"Don't start in on me, Sarge. I don't belong to your union." I got a cigarette going for myself. "What's eating you?"

"I told you! This whole business! What do they think—"

The outer door opened suddenly. A tall, square-shouldered fellow with wavy brown hair stood there, his hand on the knob. I recognized George Kelly even without the uniform. He looked startled and confused, but that quickly gave way to consternation. "What's all this?"

Another fellow stood behind him, trying to peer over his shoulder. A youngish Negro I took to be the butler, Fenton. He was dressed the part anyway. George Kelly, having stopped to pose his question, took another step into the room. "What's going on here?" He looked from Holmsby to me and then back at Holmsby. "Wayne?"

"Just having a chat, Mr. Kelly."

Kelly turned on me, looking suspicious. I decided I had shortchanged him before; he was handsome even in civilian garb. Maybe more so. His hair was longer and stylish and some of that boyish earnestness was gone from his face. "Who are you?"

I offered my hand. "Declan Colette. I'm here at the request of Mrs. O'Malley. We have an appointment."

He ignored my hand. Almost. He very nearly looked at it, but he caught himself. "You're not likely to find her in here." I could see that he was embarrassed for me.

I kept my hand extended just to spite him. "No, sir. Mr. Holmsby invited me in to ask a question."

His eyes moved again, darting over at Holmsby and then back to me. "What question?"

I looked at Holmsby myself. He didn't seem the least bit troubled by George Kelly. One would have thought he ranked the man just a step above a mechanic. I shrugged, finally dropping my snubbed hand. "Just a personal query regarding the last race at Golden Gate today. Major Folly's Foal by a nose."

Holmsby was fighting a smile, so Kelly turned on him. "This isn't like you, Wayne. I thought you were told to wait in the kitchen."

"Yes, sir. Only I take my instructions from the colonel."

"Indeed." It clearly took some effort for Kelly to swallow that one. He stepped back out onto the drive. "This isn't like you." He shook his head at the chauffeur and then forgot him, turning to me. "You'd better come along, Mr. Colette. Everyone's waiting."

CHAPTER SEVEN

I suppose I should thank you," George Kelly said. We were walking across the drive toward the marble portcullis. He was a half-step ahead of me. Fenton, the butler, was a few steps behind, and several more steps behind him came Wayne Holmsby, the slapping chauffeur.

"Why's that?"

"You've done something I haven't been able to do for months— get them all in a room together without sniping." He offered the statement in a mild tone, without bothering to whisper, so I assumed he didn't mind the staff overhearing the joke. If it was a joke.

"Happy to oblige," I said.

He stopped, and so did I, allowing Fenton to move around us and up onto the porch while Holmsby slipped behind along the drive. Kelly had a foot on one of the marble steps, facing me. The corner of his mouth had a certain tilt, and his eyebrows were knitted. "I also suppose I should warn you." Having said that, he nevertheless took another moment to consider. He massaged his jaw. "They're pretty much laying in wait."

"Then I'm afraid they're in for a disappointment."

He looked away. He was either watching Holmsby's back or admiring the half-size Negro lawn jockey who stood about two yards the other side of the porch. It was a proud little monument to old-time bigotry, with a big red smile painted on its coal black face, holding up a large hitching ring like a grand prize trophy. The polished surface sparkled in the sun, and I wondered if they made Fenton shine it.

After a moment Kelly said, with much more volume, "Wayne, won't you please wait in the kitchen? Have Mrs. Dillon get you some pop or iced tea. It's hot out here." His tone was no longer the authoritative one he'd employed in the shed. He sounded like a concerned child beseeching a doddery grandparent. He also sounded quite exhausted by the effort.

Holmsby had stopped another few yards beyond the hitching post, standing with one foot in the flowerbed. I estimated it was the exact spot he'd been standing in when I first laid eyes on him. He showed us his cigar. "She don't like me smoking in there, Mr. Kelly. I'll go along shortly."

Kelly glanced down at the toe of his brogue on the marble step. "Listen, Colette. If you would rather not stay, I can explain to them. I know how to handle them, and, believe me, you don't want to face them all like this."

I gave him a sympathetic smile. "You're probably right. I spent most of the night down at police headquarters, and my manners leave something to be desired at the best of times. But I like to keep my appointments."

Considering how the last appointment I'd had with a member of his clan had turned out, it occurred to me that he might think I was trying to be rudely ironic. But I'm not sure he even noticed. He had seemed hopeful at the start of my statement, then by the end was back to looking tired and glum. He patted his breast pocket and then his hip pockets. He looked up at me, nearly in pain. "Spare a smoke?"

I gave him one without grumbling. Even lit it for him. Some guys in my income bracket might have minded his bumming a cigarette off them, seeing as he lived in that house and probably drove at least one of those cars in the drive. But I knew he asked because it never occurred to him that supplying oneself with smokes might be a hardship. Had the situation been reversed, he would have given me two without a second thought.

He started up the steps, beckoning me along with a jerk of his head. Fenton, who had stood waiting, opened the door for us and also took my hat. After that crack of Holmsby's, I was glad to be rid of it. Kelly led me across a foyer bigger than my entire apartment— including the attached toilet—to a set of open double doors. The room beyond was probably the size of an entire floor of my apartment building.

It was a two story chamber, decorated in high class Edwardian, not antiques. Most of the sitting furniture was arranged a good pace away from the walls, probably to spare any occupants the trouble of shouting at one another just to be heard. Two long sofas sat in a row, with a table between them and matching tables at either end. At ninety-degree angles to the sofas were two sets of high-back easy chairs, comprising three-quarters of a square with the open end facing a large, unlit fireplace. The wall opposite the fireplace, behind the two sofas, was made of floor-to-ceiling windows, several of them open with their light white curtains billowing lazily. The view looked out across an expanse of lawn, a tiled patio with more furniture and a swimming pool that was not square at all, but formed of great curvy overlapping circles.

They *were* all waiting. Everyone from the photos, except Miss O'Malley's dead beau, of course, and a few extras besides. Lana herself was perched on the end of the nearest sofa, her face looking more pinched than ever, with my old friend Joe Lovejoy standing behind her like a bodyguard. On the next sofa over, all by himself, was an aged bird I didn't recognize, but from the style of his attire and the nature of his mien, I pegged him as Jasper Reed, Lawrence O'Malley's former attorney, Adam Reed's father, and Wayne Holmsby's boss— the colonel. He had silver hair and silver eyebrows and a very well-kept silver mustache. But the bags below his eyes sagged half way down his face, and he looked like he might never smile again. That's what becomes of old guys who spend all day getting hammered by the cops.

The succubus stood at a wet bar on the far side of the fireplace, probably mixing some potion or other. She alone didn't look up and over at us as we entered. Morgan O'Malley, who had been seated in one of the easy chairs with its back toward the door, got up and took a step around his chair, coming toward us.

"Listen, I need a word with you." What he needed was a comb run through his ginger hair, and possibly some cold water splashed on his heroic mug. He was dressed in an off-white suit without a tie, his white shirt open at the collar. He looked not only ready for an afternoon out on the patio, but desperately in need of it. Michelangelo could come another day.

I didn't get to answer him, as George Kelly, still leading me forward, said, "Not now, Morg." He took me over in front of the fireplace, where we stopped and he said, "Miranda, this is Mr. Declan Colette."

She looked up and over as if she hadn't noticed us enter, nor heard O'Malley's request for a word, and it was all right there, just like in the photographs, only more so.

First, I noticed her hair, which the camera had not managed to capture at all. Sure it was black as night, but it was also every other color too, like the wing of a raven stretched out in the sunlight. She wore it long, below her shoulders, in a simple Veronica Lake wave. Only black. Did I mention it was black?

Her face was white, nearly alabaster, and as smooth as the lawn jockey's grin. The red lips seemed to explode across the bottom, even though she kept her mouth small, somewhere between a pucker and a pout. Her eyelids fluttered slightly as she looked at me, rose a bit as if she wanted to be sure, then came down to significantly less than half-mast as she turned and offered me her hand.

"You weren't the disturbance Fenton mentioned?"

George Kelly had somehow positioned himself between us, and I nearly had to knock him aside to get my hand over and into hers. "No, ma'am. Just an innocent bystander," I said.

Her grip was warm and sure, everything you'd hope for but not what you'd expect. She managed to give me the feeling, while she was holding on to me, that she was actually holding on and it mattered because in a moment she might have to let go.

"How do you do?" I asked.

She tightened her lips slightly as if I had committed some social misstep, and she removed her hand from mine. "Thank you for coming. Can I get you a drink?"

I glanced at the bar, saw bottles of both Sazerac and Paul Jones, and told her the latter would be fine with lots of water in a tall glass. Meanwhile, the old bird on the second sofa worked himself to his feet, an operation requiring a cane and heavy reliance on an arm of the furniture. The struggle was somewhat more understandable once

I saw the result. Unfolded, he stood about six foot four. Sadly, he weighed perhaps a buck-fifty, wet. His shoulders were as narrow as his waist, but they had very little stoop to them, even after what I estimated had to be about sixty-five years and a full day with the police.

"Was it Wayne, George?"

George Kelly stepped behind me toward the others. "It was nothing, Jay. Everything's under control."

After my glances at the bar and the member of the bar, I found myself gazing down at the hand Miranda O'Malley had shaken. I felt a queer tingling in my palm. So I glanced up at her, at the flowing shoulders under the silk dress. She was concocting my beverage like a skilled mixologist, neither hurrying nor struggling. Bourbon, ice cubes, seltzer, and a cherry. In that order. I figured in a pinch, I could get her a job tending bar anywhere.

Jasper Reed took a step toward the door through which Kelly and I had entered. With him erect, the cane seemed little more than a prop. His legs and feet worked fine. "I had better speak to him myself. If you will excuse me, Miranda, Lana."

Lana O'Malley spoke up for the first time. "I want you to stay, Uncle Jay. You promised to support me in this. If he won't cooperate..."

She didn't finish the thought; she didn't have to. The way she looked at me as she said the word 'he' left little doubt to whom the pronoun referred. And if I refused to do as I was told, I would be sent to the dungeon, probably to be slapped by that chauffeur until I learned my place.

So, maybe they really were all laying in wait for me. It wasn't half so imposing a notion as it might have been if they'd given a bit more consideration to the seating arrangements. It was clearly not a united front; they were too spaced out. With the exception of Joe Lovejoy and Lana O'Malley, no two others had less than six feet between them. Morgan in his easy chair closest to the door, Lana on the first sofa, Jasper Reed perhaps ten feet the other side of her on his sofa, and Miranda nearly twenty-five feet away at the bar. Although, after handing me my drink, she did glide over and take the nearest easy chair, only eight feet from the second sofa.

But the old lawyer was ambling toward the door by then. "I'll return shortly, my dear."

George Kelly took one final stab at stopping him. "Really, Jay, everything is handled. There's no need." Either the old bird was all but stone deaf, or he was ignoring Kelly. He proceeded out through the doors with neither another word nor a backward glance. Kelly went to the bar to stub out the cigarette I'd given him. "You've met everyone else, haven't you, Colette?"

"I believe so," I told him. Then I nodded at Lovejoy. "You're Lowell, right? Jim?"

Lana nearly launched herself, but Lovejoy managed to get a calming hand on her shoulder. That girl was all about the soothing touch. He didn't acknowledge me, but said, "Really Mr. Kelly, if you want I can talk to him privately. I'll have this whole thing sorted in no time." Then he did look at me, offering the type of sneer that made me think he might really believe the gibberish he was peddling.

Personally, after the day I'd had, a few minutes alone with Joe Lovejoy in a soundproofed room, or even a room where the noise wouldn't disturb anyone who happened to overhear it, sounded like more fun than I deserved. I'd even have been willing to tie one of my arms behind my back to make it last longer.

But it was not to be. Mrs. O'Malley swept her arm in a graceful arc. "George, get me a cigarette? Won't you sit down, Mr. Colette? I know our appointment was for six, but I promised them they could speak with you first. We've had a very—hmm, I nearly said *trying* day, but I doubt that would begin to cover it. We're all in something of a state of shock. And Lana and Morgan and George and Jay were all curious about your connection to my niece. Sit here." She indicated the easy chair between her own and the sofa Reed had abandoned. That put me opposite Morgan O'Malley, who glowered at me from beneath his disheveled head of ginger hair.

"You're not curious about my connection to your niece?" I said to Mrs. O'Malley.

"I'm curious about a great many things." She took the cigarette Kelly offered her and affixed it to the end of a jade holder, perhaps six inches long. She put that between her teeth, and Kelly provided a light. The way she was settled in the chair didn't strike me as indicative of any emotional turmoil. Her legs were folded up and to the side, exposing her bare feet. Her toenails were painted green or purple, it seemed to depend on how the light hit them. But the green was neither sickly nor reptilian; it was deep and luxurious, like emeralds or more jade. And the purple was dark and regal. The effect reminded me of peacock feathers.

She looked at me through a swirl of smoke. "You and I shall speak privately." And then, she gave me the impression she might smile. "When they feel they've ridden you enough."

"Oh, joy."

"Damn it, Colette, watch your manners." That was from Joe Lovejoy who took several steps along the back of the two sofas in my direction.

Kelly, crossing in front of me toward the second sofa, frowned at him. "Thanks, Joe. I think we agreed I'd start this." That deflated Lovejoy's sails a bit, and he slunk back to his place behind Miss O'Malley's shoulders. Kelly claimed Jasper Reed's seat, sort of the way he'd claimed Jasper Reed's job as Lawrence O'Malley's attorney. A fresh cigarette bobbed between his lips, and he sucked on it a good three times gathering his thoughts. "Why did you arrange to meet Ramona?"

I reached up to scratch the back of my neck. "Really? That's no way to start."

He seemed incredulous. "What do you mean?"

"Just that," I said, shrugging. "Are you a trial attorney? That's probably a neat trick in a court room, but no one swore me in, and I am under no obligation to tell the truth. So was the hope to catch me in a lie early? I'll happily oblige. I called her up to discuss French literature. Discovering a mutual interest, we agreed to meet. But where does that get you? You are who you are, so I assume the cops were not completely tight-lipped about facts." I got out a cigarette and prepared to light it. "Start over. Rephrase."

He was sitting forward on the sofa, his elbows on his knees. He lowered his face and rubbed it with several long, rough strokes of his palm. "You did arrange to meet her."

"Fine. You're bushed." I looked up at the others. "Frankly, I'm surprised you all wanted to do this today. Tomorrow would have been better. Has anyone slept?"

Morgan O'Malley got up suddenly and crossed to the bar, a hike of at least thirty feet in that room. Though he didn't tarry, it took some time and gave the rest of us something to look at while we waited.

"Listen," Kelly said. "We just want to know if she was in some sort of trouble. We want to understand."

That surprised me, and I took a moment to look him over. Even allowing that he was exhausted, it struck me as a ridiculously inept question. What sort of lawyer was he, exactly? But he seemed genuinely bereaved. Hurt and helpless. His eyes were full of moisture, and his palm had smudged his cheek nearly purple.

I exhaled a cloud of smoke. "Fine. She called me up and arranged for me to meet her at Eisley's deli. She wouldn't say why. I went there at the appointed time—"

Lana O'Malley nearly shouted. "There! He just confessed it. He agreed to meet her, even though he knew it was..." Joe Lovejoy had his hand on her shoulder again, and she placed hers atop his. "What did you say, Joe? It was *unethical*! He never should have agreed to meet her when he knew she was *her* niece—"

"I didn't know anything about her." I didn't shout, just said it like the simple truth it was.

"Liar." Morgan had leaned his back against the bar, bent a few degrees at the waist, his ankles crossed. He had his left hand in his pocket, clutching a fat lowball glass in his right. The liquid was so dark, I knew it couldn't have been diluted with anything, not even an ice cube. He looked as intrigued as he did mad, though he was sticking out his lower lip at me and still holding his head like it weighed about ten pounds too much.

I shrugged again. "As I said, this isn't a court of law. And your calling me a liar just points out what a waste of time the whole thing is. Any one of you probably knows twice as much about this affair as I do. If I was interested, which I'm not, I'd suggest we'd all be better served by letting me ask some questions. Alibis, for instance."

"I'm certainly not answering anything," Lana O'Malley told me, turning away.

"And I don't recommend any of the rest of you do either." That was from Joe Lovejoy.

"You," I said. "Haven't you been snooping around here the past few weeks? Where the hell were you when that poor girl—"

Lana faced me angrily. "Shut up! Shut up at once!"

"Yes." Miranda O'Malley was unfolding out of her chair. She rose, slowly and gracefully, a dark flower in search of the sun. "That's plenty. I apologize, Mr. Colette. I never should have agreed to their being here. If you'll follow me."

I had risen already, and Kelly also nearly leapt to his feet. But it was Lana who spoke. "No! I want to know what he told her. It's ridiculous to just believe...He was going to blackmail us. Tell them Joe!"

Yeah, I thought, *tell us, Joe*. But Kelly, without glancing over, barked, "That's enough, Lana!" He then appealed to Mrs. O'Malley. "Miranda? Do you want me to come along?"

She didn't favor him with a glance either. "That won't be necessary." She walked toward a door opposite the ones through which I'd entered, leading me deeper into the labyrinth.

The ice cubes jangled in my glass, and I thought I'd like another, but Morgan O'Malley was still guarding the bar and didn't look predisposed to fix me up with anything except maybe a black eye. I drained the last few drops and set the empty glass on the table between the two easy chairs Mrs. O'Malley and I had been occupying. Then I went after her, sparing myself any fond farewells to the rest of those sorry souls.

CHAPTER EIGHT

The room she led me to was about half the size of the one we exited. It only had two normal sized windows facing the front of the house, and both were heavily draped. A few pieces of furniture had been scattered around, but I was left pondering the room's purpose. There appeared to be a daybed at the far end, and a desk against the right wall. But another wet bar was centered between the two windows.

Mrs. O'Malley went directly to the bar. "Paul Jones, you said?"

"Yes, please." I trailed along behind her, watching the sway of her hips. They didn't put me in mind of Billie Holiday; there was no slow jazz in them, no deep blues. But I do acknowledge being aware of something primal in the reaction they stirred. I said, "Is that natural? I mean for Mr. Kelly to try and horn in like that."

She started mixing up two copies of my drink, tossing me a tiny laugh to let me know I was being silly. "He wasn't horning in. My, you're certainly a different sort of detective than I'm used to."

"Have you much experience with detectives?"

"Absolutely none, until recently. I meant you're nothing at all like Joe. You're much more like the police."

"*Joe?*"

"Yes. Joe Lovejoy." She made a vague gesture back the way we'd come. "The detective from the Cobb Agency."

"Oh! *Joe!*" I said it like I hadn't actually known to whom she'd been referring. I thought I should point out how remarkable I considered it that she called him Joe as opposed to, say, *Mr. Lovejoy*, or *the other detective.*

Finished with our drinks, she handed one to me. Then she extinguished the smoldering remnants of her cigarette and got another from a collection on the bar. She didn't reach for the gold-plated lighter in front of her, but she glanced back over her shoulder to see what kind of a gentleman I was. I think I surprised her by being there.

I struck the match I had ready, got her started, then, having a fresh butt between my own lips, did me as well. Before I could shake out the flame, she closed her hands around my fist, pulling it back toward her. She puckered gently and blew.

She shouldn't have done that. A woman like her, so fully possessed of the self-awareness required to go on being a woman like her—she'd doubtless sussed fast enough that her usual toolkit wasn't equipped for me, but at least until that moment she'd been something of a kick. The match trick was just sad. It cheapened the whole effect.

"I need your help," she said.

There's a type of man unable to resist a damsel in distress; I call them men and count myself among them. We've all got our inner Saint George, aching for the dragon. The trouble was she had nothing of the waif about her, not her shape, her clothes, her hair, and certainly nothing in the way she moved. *Maneater* was writ large in the ebb and flow of the silk along the small of her back. It was spelled in slinky script across each lowered eyelid. She flashed her smoky emerald irises at me, sparkling jewels, barely visible. That was her. The signal she sent out had nothing to do with 'Save me before I get hurt.' It was 'Act fast, my man, because if I have to do things myself, there will be blood.'

I didn't tsk her, but I wanted to. Instead I said, "Mind if I sit down?"

She led us to a cozy grouping of two well-stuffed easies and a chaise lounge at the corner of the room. All of them felt quite close together after the vast expanse of the previous chamber. I took one of the chairs, and she perched on the lounge, her elbow lodged on the pillow end and her slightly folded legs stretching off to the other side. One bare foot lay casually atop the other, as if everything she did wasn't calculated for maximum effect.

She must have seen me taking it all in. Her voice was amused, though she somehow managed to keep any trace of it off her face. "I can't help feeling you're laughing at me." As I said, self-aware.

"Less now."

She took a long drag on her cigarette, then let the smoke out slowly, not blowing. It lingered in a wispy cloud around her head. "You've got sense. I appreciate that in a man...now and then."

"More now."

She laughed. It came from deep in her throat and barely made it past her lips. "What did I say that amused you?"

"You need my help."

"You don't believe it?"

I shrugged, exhausted, and sat back. "You called me here for something, I suppose."

"You spoke to my niece on the telephone."

"Yes. As I said. We talked."

"But what about? I don't understand."

"That makes two of us." An ash stand was between the two chairs, but no table. The closest surface was a small square of polished cherry near the head of the lounge. I killed my highball in three easy gulps and leaned forward to deposit my empty glass on the box. I flicked my excess ash into the stand and crossed my legs, ankle to knee. "I imagine you talked with her on occasion. You know how she could be."

"She was a silly seventeen year old. Overindulged by her aunt and uncle and..." She let it hang, studying something that only she could see, which apparently floated in the air between us. "I can't believe she's dead." She widened her emerald eyes. "You didn't...see her down there today?"

"I had no standing. I was just a guy whose name was on a piece of paper in her pocket. I'm sure they'd let you see her. I don't recommend it."

She shivered, and I watched it go all the way down to her naked toes. She made motions with her hands as if she wanted to embrace herself, but she opted instead to polish off her own drink. She offered the glass across to me. "I don't suppose you'd make me another."

"No." That earned me nothing but a barely noticeable kink in her left eyebrow. I told her, "You have a butler and, presumably, a maid or two. If there's a button around here that calls them, I might be persuaded to push it for you."

She arose, graceful even in annoyance. Or maybe she wasn't annoyed. When she spoke, making her way across to the bar, her tone was quite businesslike. "I don't believe Ramona didn't tell you why she wished to meet. It isn't—wasn't like her. And it certainly isn't like you." Reaching the bar, she set to work. "I suspect you may even have met with her."

"Sure. The police felt the same way. Unfortunately, the people at Eisley's confirmed I occupied one of their outdoor tables from approximately three-thirty to four-thirty. Alone. I certainly might lie, not just to the police but especially to you. However, I couldn't afford to buy off the entire deli staff. Half of them are Jews. As to our phone conversation. I thought we covered that. Oh, boy, could she talk. And she did. Just not about what was eating her."

"Then why would you agree to meet?"

"She appealed to me. She liked my name, said it sounded French. She was hopped on France."

"Yes, my husband did some...work there. My first husband. He doted on her. And she loved him as only an adolescent girl could."

"Did he write her often?"

She'd had a cube of ice on its way to her glass but dropped it. Her shoulders tensed. Her back was to me, but I figured my question had earned a far bigger reaction than even my earlier refusal to make her a drink. "What do you mean?"

"Nothing improprietous," I said, taking a stab.

By then she had recovered. She completed her work and came back toward me. "I told you. They were devoted to one another. I imagine they exchanged letters regularly." She resumed her perch, telling me pointedly, "Nothing *improper*."

"Good to know. And after your first husband died, Miss Wyman took up his father as a pen pal."

Better prepared for the possibility that I might not actually be an imbecile, she handled that last statement almost perfectly. She toyed with turning up a corner of her mouth. "So you are interested."

"I never meant to imply otherwise. Even when I said it straight out." My cigarette was down to a nub, and I smashed it out. I sat forward as I slipped another between my teeth. "I'm interested."

She considered. Her new drink had gone straight onto the cherry table-box-thing, untasted. So that had merely been a point of order, as in who gave the orders and who followed them and what might come of my questioning the chain of command. She fiddled with her cigarette holder, twisting off the last butt, even though she didn't have a replacement.

I held out my hand.

She gave the device to me, and I loaded it with one of my Camels, leaving me with two in the pack. That meant I'd need to depart soon or restock from her supply at the bar. And God only knew what frou-frou crap she had there. I put the tip of the holder in my mouth next to my own cigarette and lit both. She watched nearly the entire operation before telling me, "You have wonderful hands. Powerful. Adam had hands like that."

I used one of my powerful hands to offer her back her cigarette holder. "Can you control it at all? I know you've had a shock."

She ignored me, tasting her smoke before asking, "Do you think the police will find who did it?"

I sat back again, recrossing my legs, same ankle to same knee. Seeing the three inches of exposed sock made me wish I could afford a better wardrobe. Like the hat, the socks weren't quite on a level with the rest of the ensemble.

"They'll try. You have a name and the money to back it up. That'll interest the papers, and they'll prod the cops. They'll definitely try. God knows where they'll start. Do you?"

"Do I what?"

"Know where they'll start? What did they ask you?"

She bit her lip, looking away at that other invisible thing again. Then she looked at me. "I could hire you to find who did it."

"That would be swell." I tried to sound like I meant it. "Five hundred a day plus expenses. And cigarettes."

"Five hundred? But that's outrageous."

I shrugged before holding up my hands, fingers extended toward the ceiling. "For these babies? Powerful, remember? And besides, I'd need someone to open up. Say you, for example. And that wouldn't be easy on either of us."

"You don't believe that if I hired you, if you agreed to work for me, I wouldn't be completely candid?"

I shook my head. "There were too many negatives in that sentence. Like I said, you've had a shock. Though I appreciate the way you were extra precise about me working for you. As to opening up, I'd hope that at five hundred a day, even you wouldn't want to waste too much of my time."

"Can I write you a check? Say for a week in advance. What do they call it? A retainer. Twenty-five hundred."

"It's been a hell of a shock. Should I slap you? Would it help? I got a keen demonstration on how it ought to be done out on your driveway."

I half expected her to grab her drink and throw it in my face. I figured maybe that's what it was for. She kept her expression clean, but there was a glint in her eye. "You really won't help me?"

"That again. The day you need help."

"Then for Ramona. Do it for her."

I sighed, realizing I really wanted another drink myself. But damned if I was going to ask for it. I can have points of order, too. I rubbed my chin rather than let my powerful hand snatch her drink off the cherry box. "Why does Lana think you murdered her father?"

"What?" She was amazed and confused and tickled pink. It was one of her best performances so far. "That's insane."

"Sure, but why?"

"Why is it insane?"

"Why does she think it? I don't care whether or not it's insane. Unless Lana's insane, which...Well, why?"

"You'd have to ask her."

"See there? I don't doubt I could get it out of you, but for nothing less than a grand a day."

Proud of my snark, I sat there puffing away. She was looking something over, although it didn't appear to be that mirage that had entranced her before. Maybe it was my cheap socks.

"This was a mistake."

"Almost certainly. What's more, it's something you and Miss O'Malley can agree on. Though I believe she called it a waste of time." I stood. "I'll go."

"No." She held her hand out toward my thigh, probably as much a reflex as anything else. Old habits die hard. She was just far enough away that her fingers hovered about an inch from my leg. She tilted her face up and lifted her eyelids nearly three quarters of the way. Very emphatic. "Please."

I stayed there looking down skeptically at her.

She said, "She must have told you why she thought I was responsible."

"Lana? No. Miss O'Malley, her brother, Miss Wyman—they all told me remarkably little. That's why I'm being so extra patient with you."

"Damn, you're insolent."

"Mostly, I'm tired." I sat back down. "And thirsty."

"Take mine," she said. She covered her face with her hands, and she rubbed slowly up and down. It was quite similar to the move George Kelly had pulled earlier, only not so rough. "This isn't easy for me, Mr. Colette."

"Yes, I can see that."

She lowered her hands to watch me swallow about a third of her beverage. "I didn't murder Larry. It's absurd. Why would I?"

"Again, not my look out. I don't care if you murdered him. I asked why Lana thinks you did."

"She received an anonymous letter. But it *is* ridiculous. He thinks—" She stopped herself and, rather than let her know I noticed, I pretended to interrupt her by blurting out the first thing that popped into my head.

"From *Troyes*?"

"What?"

"The anonymous letter."

"Why do you mention *Troyes*? That's where my husband died."

I raised an eyebrow. "I thought he died here. In the bedroom."

She was flustered. I decided that was a real achievement on my part, though it wouldn't do. I shoved it aside with a wave of my powerful hand. Okay, I'll stop that now. But you must admit it was funny. *Powerful hands.* Tsk. Tsk. Tsk.

"So you do know about the letter," I said, playing up my savvy. It's not something I often get the chance to do, and I relish it when the occasion arises. "I just wanted to be sure. You know what's in it." I made it a statement, not a question.

"Of course."

"Well, how did Mr. Anonymous know all that?"

"All what? It's nothing but vague accusations. The author was naturally careful not to include anything that could either be proved or disproved. Lana's a fool to have shown it to you. I thought Joe had convinced her there was nothing to it."

"When did she show it to *you*?"

"She didn't, of course. Certainly not. We've barely spoken in months."

"Where did you get a copy?"

"Does it really…" But then she saw that wouldn't wash. "I have my resources." I believe she thought that *might* wash.

"I'll bet." I got to my feet again, beginning to feel like a yo-yo. I shook my pant leg down, embellishing the action with a shake of my head. "But you need my help. Where were you yesterday from three to midnight?"

She ignored me, focusing instead on sucking the life out of her cigarette.

I took a deep breath through my nose. "I'll call you. Or that old *Fraulein* who handles your phone. Maybe I won't. Don't get up. I'm not so turned around I can't find my own way."

CHAPTER NINE

I don't know how butlers do it. No warning at all, and he managed to beat me to my hat. He didn't pick it up, however.

"If you have a moment to spare, sir, Mr. O'Malley wonders if you might join him in the game room."

"He wonders, does he?" But I decided I couldn't take it out on the help. Especially not that stony-faced specimen. He was several shades lighter than the lawn jockey outside, but not nearly so proud of himself. His was that quiet, aloof dignity employers would mistake for obsequity. Still, of everyone in the house, I probably had the least chance of getting any info out of him. And he probably knew twice as much as any other. *Butlers.* I told him to lead the way.

He took me across the foyer in the opposite direction of how I'd gone before. We walked down a long, windowless corridor, then turned up another, exactly the same only darker, to a set of heavy doors. Morgan O'Malley was leaning against the wall, smoking.

"Thank you, Fenton," he said.

That's society speak for scram, and the butler left us. Morgan opened the doors, gesturing me to proceed him. I did, and I found myself in the dark heart of Africa.

It was another huge, double-storied room, this time made almost entirely of stained teak. Long low fireplaces lined the side walls, interspersed with the occasional tropical plant in a large vase, or, in a few cases, taxidermied animals mounted on pedestals. The heads of other specimens jutted from the walls, and spears, blowguns, and ivory tusks dotted the room. Native African masks, painted like long-faced Zulu warriors, glared down at us with hollow eyes.

Moving directly to a wet bar just to the left of the doors, Morgan said, "Paul Jones, right?" Apparently, based on recent events, that was society speak for, 'Thanks for agreeing to speak with me alone.'

I examined a rhinoceros head close up. It gazed down with sightless inscrutability from above the second fireplace along the left wall. The floor beneath was covered in the striped ivory pelt of a Siberian tiger. My scruffy wingtips were practically lost in the fur.

Morgan brought me my drink, nodding up at the big head on the wall. "Revolting, huh?"

"Huh, indeed. I wasn't looking at it from that angle. I think he looks surprisingly resigned." I tasted my beverage. He'd forgotten the ice, seltzer and cherry. I shrugged. "Not the sort of game I was expecting."

He pointed further along the wall. "There's a dartboard."

We both stood drinking a moment, him not looking at me or anything else and me looking from the rhinoceros to him and then sort of vaguely around the room. "How many of these are yours?"

"Not a single one. Even if I'd had any desire to shoot something, father wouldn't have allowed it. Well, I mean, he wouldn't have cared, but he never would have allowed me to display them here. This was his room. His triumphs."

"He liked to hunt?"

"I suppose. He enjoyed killing things. But really he liked showing off their pitiful heads. What is it Lear says? 'Allow not nature more than it needs. Else the lives of men are as cheap as beasts'?"

I thought he was saying it wrong, but just nodded like I understood. I'm not a big fan of quoters, generally, and I tend to have even less patience for those who do it poorly. "Was that the old man's motto?"

"No." His voice got drowsy for a moment, and I wondered how many straight whiskeys he'd had. He yawned and frowned up at the rhino. "And I take that back, about him enjoying killing things. He much preferred to see his victims suffer."

"And here I remember reading something about what a great humanitarian he was. A philanthropist. A real supporter of the war effort."

"He and the war did all right by one another." He shrugged, then seemed to wake back up. He looked at me. "You? Europe I'd guess."

"Very good." It's not a question I usually answer, but since he got it right, I figured he deserved something. "You went to the Pacific."

"Heavens no. Europe for me as well, though I never made it out of Merrie Olde. Special Attaché to General Willard F. McElroy." The name apparently left a bad taste on his tongue, and he had to wash it down. He grimaced. "I know what you're thinking."

"Typical army snafu? You never should have made it out of the states. A phiz like yours could have sold a ton of war bonds."

I expected him to laugh, but my crack only confused him. He retreated to the bar for a refill. My glass was still three quarters full, so I did a little work on that, then told him, "So yours wasn't then?"

"How's that?" He was pouring and didn't risk a look back at me. "My what wasn't what?"

"Your life," I said, toasting the rhinoceros. I corrected O'Malley's line for him. "Cheap as beast's."

That time he did laugh, lightly. "I hope it cost him a goddamned fortune."

His remark had a strange effect on me. Maybe it was coming as it did so soon after hearing Wayne Holmsby's accusation about the mechanic. Maybe it was that I don't like entitled millionaires. Or maybe it was that I'd been hoping he'd turn out to be every bit as heroic as he looked. And honestly, I can't say what upset me more— the possibility that his father bribed the war board, or the fact that he could disparage the old man for it.

"That's no attitude. I suppose if I had the resources I might be tempted to pull a few strings to keep the son and heir out of harm's way."

"You think that's why he did it?" He turned to me, leaning back against the bar. I imagined he did a lot of debonair leaning against bars. A smile tugged at his lips, but he drowned it with a quick drink. "What a charming notion. Sadly, by the time I left for England, my unsolicitous tongue had spewed enough sharp-toothed venom in father's ear that he wasn't overmuch concerned with whether or not I ever made it home."

That pinched me right between the shoulder blades. I offered him a pained look. "You need to stop that."

"What?"

"Mangling your Shakespeare. The poor sap's rolling in his grave."

"Where did you go to school?" He sounded like he was curious.

"F-Q-U—S-H-K."

He shook his head, giving me the sort of scrutiny that made me itch. I had to pretend to admire that poor rhino's head again. "But you were telling me about your father."

"Was I?" He tossed back some whiskey. "How did we get there?"

"I don't know. Europe and you riding out the Blitz at some country estate trimming a fat general's cigars."

His face darkened. "It wasn't quite like that."

"No? Did he occasionally exhaust his supply of cigars, forcing you to sally forth and secure more?"

"I don't get you."

I looked over to find him still studying me. I tried to weather it. "Do tell."

"Well, for starters, I don't think you're as rough as you pretend."

"Sure." I figured that made him half-right anyway. "It's a theory."

"And I still want to hire you."

"This is turning out to be a banner day. That's the second offer I've received this hour."

He looked down at his drink, forlorn. "So she turned you."

I had to give my head a little shake to get that to sink in. "Yikes! I thought it was just your sister." Swallowing the last of my drink, I started toward him. "Listen, bub. I'll help you out. And it won't cost you a blasted thing. Not one thin dime." I put my glass on the bar and reached for the Paul Jones. O'Malley sidestepped to give me room, but not much.

"All ears," he said.

"Get some sleep. You might not feel better in the morning, but you won't feel worse. And it'll help if you get it into your head to quote any more Shakespeare."

He swirled his glass, then tossed back the dregs. Just as he was about to speak, a door opened.

It was not the door we'd entered through. There was a short ledge along one wall, accessed by a spiral staircase. At the top of the stairs was a door leading to somewhere on the second floor. It was that which opened. Jasper Reed ambled out onto the landing, blinking down at us.

"Oh, Morgan. I'm sorry."

O'Malley, who had been standing quite close to me, took a casual step back, probably by reflex. He looked up, bewildered. "Uncle Jay."

"Sorry to interrupt. I can't seem to find anyone."

Leaving my session with Mrs. O'Malley, crossing through that room with the large windows, I'd spied Lana, Joe and George Kelly out on the patio. I shared that info.

"And Mrs. O'Malley?" Jasper Reed asked.

"She had not joined them."

The old man didn't thank me or otherwise acknowledge my assistance. Having dispatched my information, I got the impression that I ceased to exist for him. He blinked another few times at O'Malley. "Do you mind if I pass through?"

Morgan shrugged and Reed started slowly down the spiral stairs. As stated, he was not an invalid, but he was certainly fading fast. His face looked even more saggy and pale than it had half an hour before. He made it nearly two thirds of the way before slipping. Even then he'd had the forethought to keep a good grip on the railing, so he merely fell against it and sat down on the next highest step. Both O'Malley and I lurched toward him. I got there a bit ahead, mounting the second step. I reached out to take hold of the old man's arm and help him to his feet.

He proved he was fast then, and I barely got my arm up in time to stop the handle of his walking stick from bashing my crown. As it was, it clonked pretty impressively against my forearm. I stepped back down, leaving the old bird sitting there.

"Uncle Jay!" O'Malley slipped past me to help the old man up. "What the devil did you do that for?"

Reed got back up to his full height and pulled down the ends of his vest. "I apologize, Morgan."

Morgan! I backed up another few steps, rubbing my arm. No need to present him with a tempting target. If he tried anything else, I was likely to return the favor, and I didn't want that on my conscience.

O'Malley walked Reed down the last few steps. The old man didn't say another word. He left through a door at the far end of the room. It took him a while, and we watched in silence. When we heard the faint click of the latch, O'Malley looked at me.

"Are you all right?"

I grinned, not feeling it but putting on a game face. It wasn't the pain so much as all the hard proving of points going around. "Sure." We moved back to the bar.

"I've never seen anything like that."

"Murder upsets people."

He shut his eyes. "Murder. I can't believe it."

My drink was only half made, and I pulled his empty glass over beside mine to prepare both. I went full-board, with plenty of ice and seltzer. I couldn't find any cherries. "You can't believe it. You were in my office yesterday telling me your stepmother murdered your father."

"Yes, but that was…" Only he didn't seem to know what it was. I handed him his drink, and he gaped like he couldn't figure it out either. "Did she really hire you?"

"At least you're not claiming she turned me anymore." I was leaning on the bar, facing him. For a change, he was standing up straight with about a yard of parquet floor between us. I was surprised that he struck me as far less intimidating than he had. Then I realized he was looking down and slouching, and, well, let's face it, at least half of what was flowing through my veins was not Declan Colette, but Paul Jones.

"She made me an offer," I said.

"She certainly was fond of Ro, as fond as she could be of anyone but herself. Listen to me." He took a drink and then made a face. "Why would you do that to good whiskey?" Then he took another bigger drink, draining half his glass. "You really don't think this might just be a coincidence. I mean, why would someone set out to murder a child?"

"'Set out to' carries a lot of baggage. Considering how it happened, maybe it was spur of the moment. As to coincidence, sure. Like how it's a coincidence that drinking all this whiskey makes us drunk."

"I'm not drunk." He tilted his glass to his lips again as if determined to rectify the situation.

Of course, he *was* drunk. He was just so used to it, he didn't recognize the fact anymore. "I didn't accept her offer," I told him.

He had his head cocked way back, the glass still lodged against his lips. He tapped the bottom of it, intent on wringing all the ruined whiskey off those bothersome ice cubes. "Good. I'm not as rich as the rest of these people, but I figure I can afford you."

I sneered. "You're not drunk. I quoted her a rate of five centuries a day."

"Which is ten times your normal fee." He finally decided he'd done his worst to the glass and aimed his gaze back at me. "We didn't just walk in off the street, yesterday. I know a little about you."

"Well, we'll see. How are you at answering questions?"

"I've been doing nothing but for most of the last twenty-four hours."

"Then tell me about the letter."

"What letter?"

I growled and nearly said something I would have had to skip putting down here. "What letter, he says. *The* letter. The one Lana got, the one I'm wondering why you didn't mention yesterday."

"I don't care about all that now. I want you to find out who killed Ramona."

"You O'Malleys are all batty." I slammed my glass down on the bar in disgust. "Nuts. I begin to suspect that should you all wake up and decide to start talking to one another, I might could go home and get some sleep."

"Calm down. It was an anonymous letter hinting—broadly—that Miranda had something to do with father's death."

"Who sent it?"

"What? I said it was anonymous."

"You said. It's the things you people don't say. Why didn't you show it to me yesterday?"

He showed me his palms instead. "She had it with her. Stop trying to be tough."

"Nuts again. It's my rough pretense." I pulled away from the bar and took a step toward him. He stepped back, confused. I said, "Maybe I ought to slap you. I offered one to your stepmother, but she passed. Maybe I should give it to you. Between that old bird trying to clock me and watching that chauffeur do a number on your boyfriend out front, I'm slap happy."

He was at least an inch taller, and my threat reminded him of that fact. He pulled his shoulders up and back and clamped his heroic jaw tight. Still, as good as he was, he couldn't do anything about his eyes,or his cheeks.

I tsked him. "Look at you blush. Pathetic. How many Germans did you actually kill?"

The ice was rattling in his glass. He wanted to order me out or slap me first or something, only he wanted it all too much to try for any of it. I didn't wait. For one thing, I was giving him the shakes and if it ever started spreading, I feared he might end up on the floor in a fit. Also, I'd gone too far. I knew it the instant the words were out of my mouth. I don't enjoy being a bully, though I appear to be built for it and, more and more of late, it seems to come naturally.

I cut for the door. When my hand touched the knob, I paused to offer him a last look. "Be at my office at ten in the morning. Bring that letter."

He had taken over leaning against the bar, half turned so that I got him in profile. His chin looked even more impressive from that angle. He still had his jaw clamped; all the muscles from his ear to his collar bulged beneath the skin. He didn't answer me—he couldn't have. His Adam's apple just jerked up and down as if a spring had come loose. He brought the tumbler to his lips with a shaky hand. He tried to drink, looked down at the naked ice cubes in disgust, then threw the glass against the wall.

CHAPTER TEN

I made it out and home, where I stripped and showered again before climbing back into my bed, this time under the sheets. It was nearly nine. After some guilty hemming and hawing, I dialed Gig, but didn't get him. The office said he was home, and home didn't answer. He was probably at dinner somewhere. I hadn't even considered eating after everything I'd drank, but sitting in bed I did weigh the option. I ultimately scrapped the idea because it would require clothes.

I called my service and sat examining the nice blue bruise on my arm while a girl read my messages. Walter Cobb had tried me again. He'd reverted to please call, dropping the important. Probably, Joe Lovejoy hadn't had a chance to report. I also got two more messages from the sap at the *Chronicle*. I filed those with his previous one.

I considered calling Inspector Ackerman. The report I'd made of my conversation with Ramona Wyman hadn't been strictly verbatim, and I doubted I'd provided her direct quote referring to 'that letter.' My visit to the O'Malley manse had actually netted me a few interesting tidbits, in addition to a headache and the hematoma. For instance, the girl's phrasing struck me as significant. Then I thought about all the things the cops were doing that I couldn't, like an autopsy to pinpoint the time of death or charting tides to zero in on where the body had been dumped, and decided my reinterpretation of a fact would hold until morning.

I went to sleep.

I dream about drowning a lot, though I'm a keen swimmer, and sometimes it's a nightmare, and sometimes not. That night it was until a pretty blonde mermaid with a lavender scarf swam up and took my hand. She told me, "The ocean is wide and deep," and led me down to her city made of coral and sunken battleships. She and her sisters cavorted there with a thousand drowned sailors. Someone was calling my name, only I couldn't hear very well on account of all the water. When I tried to answer, my mouth flooded and water tore down icy and hard in search of my lungs. The dream became a nightmare again, and I woke up gagging.

It was seven-thirty a.m., and I figured that even with my shortage the night before, ten hours was plenty, especially if the mermaids weren't going to play nice. I did what I do first thing every morning: roll over, swing my feet to the floor, sit up and light a Camel. I like to perch there at the edge of the bed, puffing the smoke and flexing my toes in such a way as to get the blood circulating properly. I've heard other people do things differently. I can't imagine.

That day my ritual was cut a little short because enough of the whiskey had made its way through my system by then that my belly demanded food. But I didn't rush my grooming. I subjected the form to a thorough wash and the phiz to a meticulous shave. I even trimmed my nose hair and swabbed my ears. Digging through my sock drawer, determined to find a good pair, I nearly stopped to consider why I was being so attentive to a process I had long since whittled down to taking ten minutes tops, but then decided it was best not to ruminate. I brushed my teeth twice.

I grabbed breakfast at Jack's and made the office by nine. Nearly every morning, I check my messages the minute I walk in the door. There being none that day, it took approximately fifteen seconds. Clearly, I'd need to find another way to pass the time. I began by straightening the client chairs. I grabbed a rag and dusted the file cabinet and the safe. When the telephone rang at about nine-twenty, I realized I had moved all the items on my desk to one side to polish the glass top.

"Declan Colette's office." Sometimes I answer that way. Honestly.

A man's voice told me, "I thought we understood one another."

I was not so distracted that I wasn't able to identify its source as good old Joe Lovejoy. "I can't imagine what I might have said to give you that idea."

"Cobb ain't happy."

"Ain't, he says. Are you slipping or just trying to adopt a rough pretense? I've been told—"

He cut me off. "We tried to play nice, Colette."

I sat down in my chair to straighten my desktop again. I deposited the dust rag in the bottom drawer. "Any time you want to come down here and play it another way, feel free. Or name a time and place."

He called me an idiot, which I admit did not reduce me to a quivering heap. "You think Cobb can't shut you down? How about Marty Velasco?"

Velasco is a mid-level racketeer who operates a nightclub and illegal gambling joint in Marin. "How *about* Marty Velasco?"

Lovejoy made a noise between a snicker and a guffaw. "You have no idea. This case goes deeper than you imagine. Stay clear or else."

I wanted to laugh right back at him, but it was too pathetic. "You're boring me, son. Now, go play. I have work to do."

That time he called me something worse than an idiot, and recommended a course of action anatomy has rendered impossible. "I warned you. Don't say I didn't." Mercifully, he hung up.

I glanced around the room. The window was open, and the curtains undulated slowly. The walls looked bare to me all of a sudden. There was one framed item over the sofa: my operating permit. On the wall with the window hung an electric clock. It occurred to me that something attractive on the wall behind me might not be a bad idea. And why had I never considered a plant? I got up and went out and down the hall to the public toilet. I brushed my teeth a third time.

At ten o'clock, I was trying to get the three magazines in the foyer to fan properly atop the small table. Not that anyone would want to read them. The newest was from March. I had tried sitting in my chair smoking, but that wasn't going to work. At ten-ten, I was standing by the open window, practicing tossing my hat across the room and getting it to catch on the coat rack. At ten-twelve, I heard the elevator ding for the third time and leapt to get settled in my chair.

Unlike the two previous dings, this one was for me. The outer door opened, and he strode into my office a moment later.

I was leaning back in my chair, my feet up on the corner of my desk, my ankles crossed, a cigarette hanging jauntily from the corner of my mouth, and I looked up at him like he was the last person in the world I had expected to see. "You're late."

His ginger hair was combed neatly to one side, and he had gone with nice blue-gray slacks of light cotton. He had on a sweater vest, a ten dollar tie, and no hat. These kids today. Control of his expressions had not quite returned to the level he'd exhibited that first time we'd met. His cheeks ripened as he stood and looked at me. "I nearly didn't come."

"Sure. That's natural."

"What is? My almost not coming or my saying that?" He ran his hand through his hair negating in a moment all the hard work he'd apparently done on it. He was talking fast, like he had sat somewhere building up his nerve, and now it was unwinding like a top. "Because it's a lie, of course." He moved jerkily over between the two client chairs and then took the one on his right. He plopped down into it hard, like it was his turn to prove a point. There was more to his soliloquy. "I don't even know why I said it. I tried to convince myself I might not come. I wasted a lot of time and plenty of good bourbon on it. But the more I drank, the more inevitable it seemed."

"How much have you had today? Liquid courage, I mean."

He looked up at me, his eyes wide. "You just…you're brutal. Is that attitude supposed to help? Keep me from lapsing into shock like—" He swallowed something hard. "Like that slap you offered yesterday? I saw those tricks during the war. It struck me as bunk then, and it strikes me as bunk now. And brutal. Give me a cigarette."

"Say please." But that just confused him, so I dug out my pack. "You people. Why don't you carry your own?"

"I usually do. My mind was a bit distracted this morning. I…I think I have a pack in my car. Probably." Taking the cigarette I offered, he did produce his own expensive, gold-plated lighter, which made me think he might not have been lying about normally carrying his own. He lit up and sat back, relishing that first puff. He closed his eyes, then opened them and perused my desk. "Why don't you keep some out? For clients. My broker has a Faberge dispenser he keeps right about here." He leaned forward to touch my desktop near the front about a foot from the corner. "Three different brands of cigarettes."

"Sure. Faberge. It would match the couch."

He sat back, examining the cigarette I'd given him. The smoke or the tobacco or maybe just having a toy in his hand that he could fiddle with had done the trick. His words weren't tripping over themselves trying to make it out of his mouth. He took a slow breath and let it out. "I like that couch. You'd be surprised what an impact seeing that thing had on me. Lana wasn't at all keen to even come in here after getting a look at your hallway out front. But the instant I saw that couch, I knew we'd found the right place."

It was my turn to be confused, so I backtracked. "I thought you said you were on an English holiday during the war."

"No, that's what you said. Trying to be rough. And I haven't had anything to drink today."

"Want some?"

"No. Damn it, I couldn't. Not after yesterday." He attacked his hair again. The problem was that he was shoving it against the part, and it was falling down in a scattered mess across his eyes. "I don't think I stopped drinking after the police left. And you came. I think I thought you were going to help." He glanced up at me through his bangs.

"Is that why you called me Tuesday night?"

"Called you?"

"Yeah, Tuesday at about ten. I got a message you had called."

He seemed genuinely perplexed. "I don't know—oh!" It hit him. "Yes. I mean, no. I was calling to apologize. For Lana and…and what happened. It was nothing. I'd completely forgotten I'd telephoned you. That's strange?" He put it up to me like a question.

I shrugged. It didn't strike me as too remarkable in light of all that had happened since. "You sure you don't want a shot of something?"

The corner of his mouth went up. "It's not even ten-thirty."

"What time did you start yesterday?"

"Nine. Maybe. Maybe eight-thirty." He took another deep breath. "But that was different. Yesterday was a nightmare. The police were brutal."

"The police were brutal. I'm brutal. Brother, you have no idea. This thing's just leaving the gate."

He slid lower in his chair, propping his arms on the rests. His hips were nearly riding the front edge of the seat cushion. He looked disgusted about something, but whether it was murder or the twin brutalities of me and the police, or maybe just his drinking, I can't say. He wasn't much of a smoker either. The cigarette spent more time smoldering between his fingers than it did in his mouth.

"I'm not really that weak. At least—God, I hope I'm not. It's just they all decided so long ago that I was unfit for…so much of life. Those things weren't for me. I wasn't to be allowed in. I guess I'd gotten used to breezing along the periphery of everything. My life wasn't real. Now it's…" He hesitated.

"Real?"

He gazed at me again, shaking his head. "Don't laugh at me. I may very well still be drunk."

"Are you normally that type of drunk? The philosopher?"

"I'm normally the fool. Drunk or sober. Ask anyone."

"Sure, now you sound like a whiny rich kid." He no doubt thought that brutal, but I meant it. I sat forward. "Did you do what I asked? Did you bring the letter?"

"Asked? Is that what you call it?" He dug a folded paper from his breast pocket. "Yes. It wasn't easy. Joe said you and he had discussed it and agreed he would take the lead. He didn't want me to—what's so funny?" He stopped in the process of handing the document over, apparently put off by my laughter.

"Nothing." I quashed the chuckles and took hold of one end of the paper. "Nothing is funny at all."

He didn't let go of his end. I could see he doubted me. "Then why are you laughing?"

"That Joe." I gave the paper a tug, prompting him to release it. We both sat back. "Sometimes he gets confused."

O'Malley flattened his tie to his chest and then reached up to comb his fingers through his hair the right way this time, pushing his big curtain of ginger bangs back across the top of his head. He was looking at something on the edge of my desk. "I don't know. He seems pretty slick to me. Too slick. Lana's—" He stopped himself with a visible jerk and swung his gaze up at me.

I tried to make him think I wasn't paying attention. I'd opened the document in my hands and gave it a thorough look. It was plain stationery, eight-by-five, yellow, with no date nor addressee nor salutation. About halfway down the page someone had typed:

What was in the drink his wife gave him the night Lawrence O'Malley died? Why had the glass been removed and washed before the police arrived? Why had the entire staff been given the night off? Two men dead. How many more shall follow?

Naturally there was no signature, but without trying to prop myself up, I think I knew immediately who had sent it. And it wasn't just a hunch or intuition; it was keen observation and the fact that at least one person the day before had let on that she knew too.

I asked, "How did this arrive?"

He fidgeted, trying to get comfortable with something. "Regular mail. The envelope had no return address and was postmarked at the local branch. The police told us all that. Joe dusted the envelope and the letter for prints and examined them under a microscope for any—what?"

Another fit of the chuckles had taken hold of me and again I struggled to master it. "It's the comedy. You're killing me."

"I don't understand. Are you implying this is all a hoax? That we're simply too foolish to see it?"

"No. That's not what I am implying. And I shouldn't be laughing. It's very unprofessional."

He looked like he agreed with me but let it slide. He sat there ready for my next question.

I supplied one. "Is any of it true? Was the glass washed before the police arrived? That's the sort of thing that usually rates some investigation. I don't recall reading anything about it."

"Well, no. How could anyone have known? There was some alcohol in his blood, they said, but no sign he'd had a drink there at the house. He had just come from his club and was going to bed."

"And Mrs. O'Malley denies making him a drink?"

"She didn't need to. She wasn't there. No one was there. She and George were at the Shanty." That was Marty Velasco's joint in Marin. "I know they were because I was there too."

"So the three of you alibi each other."

"I guess so, if you want to call it that. We were there from at least nine until well after one o'clock."

"You came and went together?"

"Not in the same car, no. I took my own car." He twisted in his seat again. "You do know that I don't live in that house?"

"But you might have swung by and picked them up. Or vice versa." I pulled a few flakes of tobacco from my lower lip, considering. "What about your sister?"

"She never goes. She doesn't approve." He had answered just as open and willingly as he had any previous question, but then something occurred to him and he grinned at me. It was a jaunty grin, full of snide rebuke, but still one hell of a grin. "Of course, she'd need to be a loon to have killed our father and then spent the last two months trying to get someone to investigate his murder."

I grinned back at him, more manly and pure I hope, but wanting him to see that I could play. "She might have hoped to frame your stepmother. Stranger things have been known to happen."

His grin devolved into a disapproving frown. "Except she loved the old man. Someone had to. And she was mostly indifferent to Miranda before this happened."

"What," I said, "were her feelings toward Adam Reed?"

His head pulled back. "Adam Reed?"

"Yeah, Mrs. O'Malley's first—"

"Yes." He interrupted me, returning the favor. "I know who he is. Or *was*. Adam got killed in France. What the hell do you drag him in for?"

"I didn't." I tapped the anonymous letter on my desk with a fingertip. "This does. 'Two men dead,' it says. Do you suppose it's referring to someone else?"

"No, but—" He looked down and then off to the right, but whatever he was searching for seemed to elude him.. He shook his head at me, perplexed. "What was the question?"

"What were your sister's feelings about him? Only let's broaden it. What were your feelings about him? And your father's? You call *his* father Uncle Jay."

"Sure." He was nodding, slowly at first, gradually building momentum. He had shifted his eyes down and left, but I didn't get the feeling he was being evasive. He was just trying to see it all clearly enough to put into words. "My father and Uncle Jay were business partners. I mean, he was the family retainer and all that, but they made a lot of money together. During the Depression. Before that too, I guess. But especially during. Especially after my mother died." He looked up at me suddenly. "Can I tell you something?"

"I thought you were."

"Something secret. It may not be true, but I think it is."

"Truth is overrated when it comes to secrets."

"Well, hell. If we're going to be melodramatic."

I thought my line had been pretty good. But he sat shaking his head at me. He was done with his cigarette, and I gave him another without his having to prompt me. I didn't want him to get any more distracted. He lit it, then brushed his lower lip with the tip of his thumb. "I think Uncle Jay was in love with my mother."

That actually disappointed me. I suppose I figured in families like his, the kinks were bound to stretch way back. I shrugged and nodded both.

He squinted at me as if he didn't quite trust my reaction. "My aunt, my actual aunt, mother's sister, told me once that they fought a duel over her." Then he lightened up and shook his head. "Naturally, I looked into that but never found anything to back her story up. But I do think Uncle Jay loved her—mother, that is."

"What did your father say?"

"Come now. Do you really suppose we had that sort of relationship? I spent most of my childhood away at school."

"What did Uncle Jay say?"

He chuckled. "I should ask him. Maybe I will. I guess I always figured that bringing it up would be bad form, seeing how he lost."

It occurred to me that never having seen a picture of his mother, I couldn't go willy-nilly along with his assumption about who had won and who lost. Of course, it also occurred to me that stating that thought aloud might be in bad form.

I got myself a cigarette and leaned back in my chair, hoisting my feet back up onto the corner of my desk. I had on a shiny pair of two-tone brogues and felt like showing them off. It was a wonder I didn't tip over backward. "That was a fascinating tangent. But I haven't forgotten about Adam."

He waved a hand casually. "I don't know what you hope to find out. He was two years older than Lana and nearly five older than me. She liked him all right, I suppose, but they never had much in common. He was athletic. I had a bit of a boyish crush on him. I admit I wept when I learned of the accident. I suppose I shouldn't have admitted that. But it's true. I had several friends perish in the war, but that one hit me hard."

"So the two of you were close?" I felt my Adam's apple sliding up and down, like something was lodged in my throat. A few tears was his idea of taking it hard?

He smirked, mainly at himself I gathered. "Not really. Our schooling overlapped slightly and having a successful and popular upperclassman as a benefactor didn't hurt my first two years. Although I suppose it was something of a nuisance to him. Of course, George took a more active interest in my welfare."

"The three of you went to the same boarding school?"

"Of course." He said it like it was the only natural assumption; which maybe it was. I admit to having no idea. "Adam and George were a year apart, and I was four years behind George."

"Which brings up another sticky problem for you and I to settle. Why did you pretend you couldn't recall how your father and your stepmother met? She was married to 'cousin' Adam."

He flashed his grin at me, then he reined in his mug, getting serious. He sat forward, propping his forearms against the edge of my desk. "That brings up two sticky problems. First, stop calling her that. I don't care what you call her. Why not Miranda? It's her name. But she was never my stepmother. I used to like her quite a lot. I never understood why she married my father. I was on holiday in England at the time you may recall." He had started this speech in a playful tone, but as he progressed, his resentment built. "And I didn't pretend anything. Yes, my father had undoubtedly 'met' her when she wed Adam, probably before that. He may have seen her socially afterward. And, of course, even then most men would have noticed her, and my father was certainly a man. But how they ever met in terms of uniting in holy matrimony is completely beyond me. And, honestly, of no particular interest."

I cocked my head. "What do you mean, you used to like her quite a lot?"

His grin came back, gradually this time. He sat back, halfway to horizontal again, his arms on the arms of the chair. "I like how you do that." He eyed me a moment, squinting slightly. "She was fun and fresh before the war. We all were, weren't we? Adam's death hit her very hard, like Ernie's hit Lana. And since father's death..." He looked confused again.

"And since father's death what?"

"No. It's nothing."

Pressing him would just shut him down, so I leapt instead. "Tell me about the accident."

His eyes grew wide. "What accident?"

"Adam's accident. In France." I nearly said, *The one that made you weep*, but decided that would simply be more brutal bullying.

"Amazing." He pointed at my desk. "You don't even take notes. The first week, Joe wrote down nearly everything anyone said."

"That's why Cobb can charge the prime rate. What sort of accident was it?"

"A sniper hit the jeep he was riding in. They crashed. Adam was shot twice, in the neck and in the back, but survived several days. He made it to a nearby village and died there."

"*Troyes*."

"Maybe. I thought George said it was something like Fulne. But I could be mistaken. Either way, a nowhere place. Adam had been staying at *Troyes*. I do know that. I got a letter from him there."

"He was clearly a prolific writer."

O'Malley shrugged. "Well, he and George were MI. They didn't move around as much. Well, Adam didn't. George, it seems, always managed to find himself in the thick of it. Determined, like always, to carry the lion's share of the burden on his own poor shoulders."

Deciding I liked this George Kelly fellow less and less and didn't want to hear any more about what a hero he was, I dropped my brogues back to the floor and sat up. "Listen, I know you don't live there at your father's house, but—"

"It's Miranda's house now."

"Sure. I know you don't live there, but can you get me back in? I'd like to try my hand at a little detective work. Yesterday was…well, yesterday. Honestly, I expected to find the place crawling with cops. You folks must really have pull. Can you get me in?"

"Well, I doubt it would involve any serious smuggling. They've never barred me from the place. Why not?"

"I'm glad you think so. You may be surprised how murder changes things. But if you're willing, I'd like to try."

He was studying me. "What exactly do you want to do?"

"I want to see Ramona Wyman's room. It's on the second floor?"

"Of course."

"West wing."

He pulled his head back again, narrowing his eyes. "Yes."

"Somewhere near that game room we were in yesterday?"

He thought about that a moment. "That side of the house, yes. Not directly adjacent."

"No, it probably faces the front, with a window overlooking the drive. Say about thirty feet to the west of the front door."

He offered me a skeptical frown. "Is this a mind-reading trick? It's pretty impressive."

"No, my boy, that is detecting. Only it's probably a day too late. We shouldn't waste too much more time." I arose and made it halfway around my desk before he even started to get up.

"What do you hope to find?"

"Clues. Though I expect to find nothing. Which can, of course, be a clue."

CHAPTER ELEVEN

As I was locking the door to the hall, he asked me, "Is your receptionist on vacation this week?"

I said yes in a tone of voice I hoped might discourage any additional inquiry. It may have worked too well. He was completely silent during the ride down on the elevator, not speaking again until we hit the sidewalk where he said, "Shall we take my car?"

I consented, seeing as the option was to walk nearly three blocks to the garage that housed mine, and we headed south down Pierce and around the corner to where he'd lucked into some space at the curb.

Knowing his predilection for fast cars, I half expected the Alfa Romeo to be sitting there, but it was even better: the Highlander. It looked completely out of place in that neighborhood, glistening like gold bullion. As we approached, two Negro men who had been standing near the hood, admiring it, backed off. Trying to be sociable, I nodded at them and one nodded back, but the other just squinted, eyeing us skeptically.

Once we were in traffic, O'Malley glanced in both his mirrors and told me, "This is a very colorful neighborhood you've set up shop in."

I was watching my own mirror. After he turned up Divisadero, I asked him to take a left on to Pine. To his credit, he put the operation in motion even before asking me why.

"Just curious," I said.

Sure enough, the brown sedan three cars back made the turn as well. I suggested he make another left on Presidio and then, almost immediately, another onto Bush, heading back toward Divisadero.

He suddenly sat up, gaping into his rearview mirror. "Are we being followed?"

"Sure." I sat back with my arm propped up on the door. Between the struts and the plush plaid interior, that Highlander offered a swell ride. I tilted my head back to let the sunshine splash across my face.

O'Malley was frantic. He was twisting his head around and back on his neck, staring into the mirror and trying to look back over his shoulder, sometimes simultaneously.

"Watch the road," I told him.

"But who is it?"

"Who do you think it is? It's cops. Forget it."

He ignored my suggestion. "What do they want?"

"I suppose they want to find out where your hideout is, and whether or not you're going to murder anyone else. Don't be silly. Let's go to your—Mrs. O'Malley's house."

But he lucked on to even more curb space and took it with a sudden crank of the wheel.

That brought my head up and I looked around. "What are you doing?"

"I'm going to ask them what they suppose *they're* doing." He actually looked like he might. He shut down the engine and was about to open his door.

"No," I said. "That would be, to quote your sister, 'worse than useless.' It would embarrass whoever's driving, and they would resent it. Worse, their boss would resent it. Don't forget, you're not as rich as the rest of the people involved in this thing, and you can bet they've got tails too." I sat back again, relaxing, hoping to lead by example. "Besides, we already snubbed our noses at them. They know we know they're there. Or rather here."

They were currently passing us, not having O'Malley's curbside luck. It was a Ford, probably mid-thirties, so nondescript it stood out a mile. The two men in the front seat were looking determinedly ahead. I watched them out of the corner of my eye, but O'Malley turned his head and glared.

"Let's go," I said.

He didn't start the engine. He sat there gripping the wheel with both hands, staring at the dash. Something was building. I could see it, but I didn't feel particularly inclined to spur it along. During our silent trip down in the elevator, I suspected he might have been struggling with something. Whatever it had been had clearly returned.

"Listen." He gasped the word in a sort of explosive exhale. "There's something we need to clear up if you're going to be working for me."

"Hold it." I didn't gasp but interrupted calmly. "I work for myself. I may do a job for you, for which you will remunerate me. Though, if we're going to make it official, I think I should have you sign something. Just a simple—"

"Yes, yes!" He smacked a palm against the steering wheel. "You said something yesterday that I think you should explain."

I nearly remarked that I had said several things the day before which a more polite individual might feel compelled to explain if not apologize for. Did he have a list? But I only waited to see which particular thing it was.

"You referred to my *boyfriend*." His head sunk lower, until he was staring at the floor between his feet. He looked like a dog who had been whipped once too often. "I want you to tell me what you meant by that."

I took a breath, wondering what he really wanted. There were at least three possibilities as I saw it. If he was the sort of man for whom a boyfriend was simply out of the question, he shouldn't even have brought it up. That sort of man might laugh or be shocked by my insinuation at the time, but he wouldn't bother to protest a day later. That meant that he was either the sort of man who could conceive of having a boyfriend but currently lacked one and hoped to leverage that lack into a blanket denial, or he had a boyfriend and wanted to find out just how much I knew.

I tried to act cavalier. "Which part didn't you understand?"

He twisted his head around so that he could glare at me. I saw fear in his eyes, but a certain menacing glint too. The dog still had some fight left in him. He even snarled at me. "What did you mean?"

"You must have heard about Reed's chauffeur slapping that mechanic."

No matter how good he was with his face, he couldn't have feigned that amount of confusion, not on top of everything he was already feeling. "I don't know what you're talking about."

"That chauffeur, Holmsby, who works for Reed. He and the mechanic that lives in that garage at your family's house had a bit of a run-in just as I arrived yesterday."

He was sitting back up, looking even more confounded. "But what does that have to do with anything?"

"Well, someone hinted that you might have a particular fondness for the boy."

He screwed his face up in such a way that I felt he was attempting to show me a textbook example of what shock and dismay looked like. "Hector?"

"Is that his name? The mechanic?"

"Who would tell you something like that?" He shook his head. "Hector and I barely know one another. I had moved out long before he came to work for father." He aimed his gaze at me again, and it was all fight now, no fear. "Who told you that? What did they say? It was Marty Velasco, wasn't it!"

I cocked a brow. "No, as a matter of fact. But let's discuss that a moment. Marty Velasco has come up several times today. What is his connection to this thing?"

"What thing? If it wasn't Velasco, then who?"

"Not so fast. Tell me about Velasco and your cousin's murder."

"That's ridiculous. What would Velasco have to do with it? Who told you I was involved with Hector? I demand to know."

That made me grin. "This is what they call a stand-off, I guess. Take me to the house."

He started the engine. "It's ridiculous." Apparently, he wanted to emphasize that fact. "Hector isn't even attracted to men. He's a womanizer. Father nearly fired him last year when he found a woman had spent the night in Hector's room."

I shook my head, wondering if he had any idea of how much he'd just said. I pretended I didn't realize either, following up with a more innocent take on his statement. "But he didn't fire him. Apparently your father *was* fond of him. Another thing I heard was that your old man bought the kid a deferment."

O'Malley had maneuvered us back into traffic, heading north on Divisadero. "Yes, I've heard that rumor too. But it's false. Hector didn't get a deferment. He was reassigned early on because of his injuries, and my father did pull some strings to get him as his official driver, but there wasn't a deferment. George sent the paperwork to me, hoping old Billy Mac might be able to grease the wheels. We were Supply Services."

"What were Hector's injuries? He looked alright to me. Even getting whipped."

"He hurt his leg, but I think it's completely recovered now. Mainly it was his back. From the accident, I suppose, and from carrying Adam all that way. It was about nine miles."

I sat up suddenly and grabbed the dash, turning on him. "What the hell?"

He looked around frantically. "What is it?"

"He carried Adam! You mean to tell me he was in the accident that killed Adam Reed?"

Realizing our demise was not imminent, O'Malley allowed himself a sigh of relief. "Well, yes. He was Adam's driver. After the crash, he carried him on his shoulders nine miles to the village. With a bum leg."

I sat back, flabbergasted and not afraid to show it. "You people! How many times have I been accused of dragging poor Adam in? Hector the goddamned monkey boy! If I'd known that yesterday, I might have stopped him."

"Stopped him from what?"

"Not him, the other him." I growled some choice language I'd heard, mostly from sailors. "Just drive."

CHAPTER TWELVE

L ooks like you weren't the only one with the idea." O'Malley steered through the large gate and up the red gravel drive. We couldn't go very far as once again the way was blocked, this time by two patrol cars and a dusty old rambler that certainly didn't live there. Two uniformed policemen were conversing beside one of the patrol cars. They looked over at us as we parked. A police van had been positioned right up next to the car sheds in the corner, and several plainclothes men were at work there, apparently going over the vehicles.

O'Malley and I climbed out of the Highlander and started toward the house. No one paid us much attention until we reached the porch, when George Kelly stepped out of the front doors.

"Ah, Morgan, good. I've been calling you. The police want to examine our cars. Yours too. They may be at the bungalow, but I suppose these fellows can take care of it here. Lieutenant Dent is right inside." He gestured us in. "Hello, Mr. Colette."

"Mr. Kelly," I said, as we all moved into the foyer and he closed the door.

He hadn't been kidding about Dent being right inside. The lieutenant was seated on a wooden chair about five feet in. He had his hat in his lap, but jerked up onto his feet when he saw me. "What's he doing here?"

Both O'Malley and Kelly looked somewhat taken aback by the question, and the latter asked, "I beg your pardon?"

That reminded Dent to rein in his bluster, and I was keen to see whether he'd be able to manage it with me standing right there, ready to traipse all over his toes. He swallowed something and looked at Kelly and then me and then Kelly again. "I'm sorry, Mr. Kelly. I mean this gentleman here, Declan Colette. Who called him?"

Kelly made a face, letting us all know the question had never occurred to him. He looked at me like he hoped I'd enlighten them, though he told Dent, "I'm sure I don't know. Mr. Colette and my cousin just arrived. I was under the impression you wished to examine Mr. O'Malley's car. Can your experts outside do that here? It's the yellow Highlander parked in the drive. We'll wait in the salon." He started forward again and O'Malley and I followed.

"Wait a minute!" Dent was mangling his hat in his hands.

Kelly pivoted on his heel. He managed to be simultaneously aloof and friendly, an admirable ability when you consider it. "Did you need something, Lieutenant? I'll call Fenton."

It was one of those situations where I was bouncing up and down on the inside, wanting so badly to share some of the sweet venom on my tongue. But Kelly's condescension had already cut the old hound off at the knees, and I would only spoil it by descending to Dent's level.

The lieutenant was choking again. That gave the rest of us nearly enough time to reach the other side of the room before he finally managed to squeeze something out. "I…I want to talk to him."

Kelly performed another graceful half turn. "What about?"

Dent goggled. His lips moved a moment without producing any sound. "I want to ask him some questions."

"Indeed. The warrant was strictly to examine the automobiles, Lieutenant. It said nothing about entering the house nor accosting our guests. I'm allowing you to take the shade through forbearance." He said all that sounding like twice the attorney he'd been acting the day before, but then he softened his tone slightly. "Would you like a beverage? I'll send Fenton out."

He led the way through a door under the stairs, traversing a short hallway that brought us to a medium-sized room that looked like a nice dining room probably would in any other home. A round glass-topped table was positioned at the center, surrounded by half a dozen matching chairs. For them it was probably the third most casual breakfast nook.

"What's he doing here?" Kelly addressed O'Malley with the air of someone who assumed I didn't know the language. Apparently my brief elevation to the status of guest had merely been to jab a thumb in the eye of the police.

"He wants to see Ramona's bedroom."

"What on earth for?" Clearly, the idea was not only shocking but also slightly nauseating. "The police were up there all night."

"I don't know." O'Malley ran his fingers through his hair again. Neither he nor Kelly had hats, and since no one had taken mine, I had it in my hands. I used it to make a plaintive gesture, figuring it was time to remind them I did speak the lingo.

"What's your objection to me having a look?"

O'Malley showed me that was a bad idea by joining his cousin in completely ignoring me. "He's investigating Ramona's murder," he said to Kelly. "I've hired him."

"On who's authority?"

That took both me and O'Malley by surprise. The rich guy wore it better of course. He adjusted his shoulders and raised his chin, practically daring Kelly to take a swing at it. "I wasn't aware I needed anyone's authority. I don't need yours, certainly. I'll discuss it with Miranda myself if you think she might object."

Kelly wilted, propping himself with one hand on the back of a chair. I don't mean to imply he'd lost some silent power struggle, merely that he realized he was making a fool of himself. He rubbed his face with his other hand. "No, it's fine. I'm just dealing with the police and...Fine. Go ahead."

O'Malley told me to follow him and was about to start off, but I took another stab at Kelly. "If the police are checking the cars, they must have a reason. Did they say anything?"

He wished I would just go away, it was there in his tired eyes and his sagging chin. "Just that they assume she was taken in an automobile to where she was...where her body was placed into the ocean."

"And you said the cops searched her room last night. Did they take anything away?"

"No. At least they didn't show me anything. Or mention it. Florence was there the entire time. I insisted."

"Florence is the maid?"

"Mrs. O'Malley's maid, yes." He looked at his cousin. "Morgan, I have so much to do."

O'Malley stepped back over and took hold of my upper arm. He didn't tug, however, and I managed a final question. "Where is Mrs. O'Malley?"

"Out by the pool." Kelly was going. "I'll send Florence up. This is your responsibility, Morg." He left.

O'Malley turned me, let go, and led me in the opposite direction, back further into the house. "He's not holding up very well," I said.

"Can you blame him? He's single-handedly kept this family together the last ten years. And now look at us." He certainly managed to sound broken up about it, seeing as he'd been disowned.

Our path twisted and turned. At one point we passed a window that overlooked the back grounds, and I caught a brief glimpse of Miranda O'Malley lying on a lounge beneath an umbrella. She had on a swimsuit, hat and glasses, and from what I could tell had not been wet. She was so still she might have been asleep.

Another turn brought us to a heavy door, which let us into the game room. I didn't say 'Ah-ha!,' but I admit I felt it. All the cheap beasts around, many of whom had their maws gaping in silent roars, didn't say anything either. They just watched us with their glass eyes as we strode loudly through the silence. We went up the spiral stairs and through the door at the top. A left turn led us down another short corridor toward the front of the house. Finally O'Malley stopped and indicated the door directly in front of us.

"Here it is." He stood there looking at me.

I hoisted my eyebrows. "What, are you afraid of fingerprints?" I grabbed the doorknob and twisted. "The cops were already here."

I stopped just through the door and surveyed the landscape. There weren't many surprises. Like the rest of the house, it had no shortage of acreage, with enough floor space for four energetic couples to foxtrot without colliding. A double bed was against the wall to my right with an armoire and dresser opposite it. The wall directly opposite the door, at the front of the house, had two tall windows with flower-print drapes. Between the two windows was a small secretary and chair.

That seemed like the logical place to start, but I went across to the right window first. It was open about six inches, and I tugged it up the rest of the way. The view was of the drive and, to my right, the car sheds. The two uniforms were now over at the Highlander, discussing its merits. That baby deserved the attention and got it. The men I assumed to be scientists were still at work going over the Minx. No sign of Hector the monkey boy mechanic. I angled my body forward, leaning out through the window to look down. That had me staring at the top of some large oleander bushes. About fifteen feet to my right was the top of the lawn jockey's red cap. Another fifteen feet was the porch. I figured if I went down and searched the flowerbed around the oleander, I'd probably turn up some cigar ash. Fortunately, the cops were too hopped up on the cars.

Apparently it hadn't been a fear of leaving fingerprints that had given O'Malley pause. He was still standing in the hall. As I straightened up from the window, I asked him, "You superstitious?"

"No." He frowned. To prove how brave he could be, he took a single step forward to lean against the door jamb. His arms folded across his chest, and his eyes glowered at me from beneath a furrowed brow again. Luckily for him, he had the type of face that looked good even wearing a glower.

I proceeded to the desk, examining the chair briefly before sitting in it. Again I stopped to survey the layout before touching anything. It almost always pays to be cautious. Assorted tools: pencils, pens, scissors and ink, and a stack of stationery was on the back shelf. Three rows of cubbyholes filled the space below the shelf, so I began opening them one by one. I found lots of surprises among the contents, but nothing that merits mention. Ramona Wyman had been a rather typical seventeen-year-old girl. My most remarkable finding was that so many of the little drawers were empty.

"Oh, Florence."

I turned at O'Malley's voice and saw that he too had pivoted to greet a new arrival. She was an older woman, probably topping fifty, with tied-up gray hair and a simple, somber uniform. Her features were rather large for her face, and her skin looked sallow, like she had subsisted for too long on nothing but boiled potatoes. Her eyes were a light shade of silvery blue and tended to bulge. She nodded at O'Malley and stopped a few paces shy of the door.

"Mrs. O'Malley wishes to speak with you, sir." Her accent still put me in mind of the Rhine, but I make no claim to having a precise ear.

"Me?" For all his threatening Kelly with going to her himself, the idea suddenly appeared to render O'Malley incapable of swallowing.

I sat back and put my hands in the air. "Shall I stop?" I made my voice loud and deep, hoping to give him, if not perhaps a verbal slap, at least a healthy nudge.

It worked as well as I could have hoped. He spun back around to look at me, confused. "No." He forced down whatever had been blocking his throat and squared his shoulders. "No. Keep going. I'll explain to her."

He strode off down the hall as I went back to exploring cubbies. After a moment, I realized that the Swiss maid had entered the room and stood next to the armoire, observing me.

"I'm Declan Colette," I told her without stopping work. "We spoke on the telephone. You're Swiss."

She didn't say anything. She'd folded her arms, but then decided against it. She angled her torso to see what exactly I was doing.

"Did they tell you to watch me and make sure I didn't plant any evidence?"

Again that earned me nothing at first. Finally, quietly, she told me, "No."

Her tone inspired me. "Did you watch the cops?"

"Yes."

"And they didn't take anything?"

"No."

She was reticent, but I felt I might coax her along if I played it right. I had no doubt that she'd been instructed not to leave me alone, but she didn't exactly sound like she was going to hinder my progress. Or, if she was, her heart wasn't in it.

I felt like I had finished with the desk and wanted to explore the dresser and armoire, but I also didn't want to spook her. I turned slowly in my chair, twisting my lips and showing her an arched brow. "Then I'm confused."

I lost some ground. She stood up straight again and then leaned back. Her eyes narrowed suspiciously. She wasn't dumb.

I shrugged. "It's just I can't find Miss Wyman's diary. Didn't she keep it here at her desk?"

Her suspicious look turned smug and disappointed. She folded her arms again and turned her head, unable even to bear looking at a chump who would try something so patently phony.

Ah, well, you can't win them all. I glanced over at the window. "You must have known Ramona since she was a girl." No response. "Probably she could be bratty. I remember her telling you something about a hat—the other hat. Did you help her with her wardrobe?" She might have been alone in the room. "Surely you want the person who hurt her to get what's coming to him."

I got up and went toward the armoire, and she nearly jumped to get out of the way. As smart as she was, apparently she wasn't completely immune to nerves. I opened the cabinet and glanced at the wardrobe. Expensive and modern duds all, but like the contents of the cubbyholes, about what you'd expect. At least a dozen sweaters were folded up at the bottom, and the two drawers below held socks and assorted undergarments. The five drawers of the dresser showed me more of the same.

Atop the dresser sat various knickknacks and an assortment of low-grade jewelry along with a miniature chest containing higher class trinkets. There were hair ribbons of every color imaginable. At the back stood a five-by-eight photograph in a gold frame. It showed a blonde girl of about twelve standing next to a man who looked like a giant in comparison but was probably not much more than six feet. He had dark hair, no hat, and two bars on his uniform. They both smiled at the camera, and she was holding on to him like he was scheduled to depart and she wasn't willing to let him go.

It would have been a wistful photograph even if both its subjects hadn't since met with violent deaths. Just looking at it made my eyes itch. I turned to the maid. "Miss Wyman must have had her own bathroom. Is that where she kept her makeup?"

"Miss Wyman's aunt did not allow her to wear makeup." Her tone indicated that she approved of the edict, and her own face cinched it. A little rouge and some lipstick would have done the old gal wonders.

I cut for the door. "Still I'd better check."

She took an abortive step to head me off, but I stopped, sparing her the need. She said, "There is no makeup."

"Yeah? And no diary. But the cops took nothing." I let her see that the idea didn't appeal to me. I wasn't dumb either.

Florence turned away again, directing her attention toward the door. That put the back of her head pointing at the bed.

"Ah, under the mattress? Classic." I moved over to the far side of the bed and shoved my arm between the mattress and the springs. I slid it all down the side feeling nothing, so I lifted the mattress for a look. "Huh."

The maid turned back around, shocked.

"Sure," I said, deciphering her expression. "But I would have been surprised if he missed it."

"The police took nothing."

"I know." I dropped to one knee and took a peek under the bed. Unlike a typical teenager, she kept nothing there. I looked around the room again. "Miss Wyman told me she had a letter from France. And her aunt said she probably had several. Where did she keep them?"

More silence, but when I looked up, the old woman was chewing her lip.

"They would have been special to her. Probably she kept them together, in a box. Someplace safe."

More lip chewing. Then she abruptly crossed over and opened the armoire. She dug down through the folded sweaters stacked at the bottom, expecting to find something, and then reacting poorly when she didn't. "It *was* here."

"Good. He was thorough. I like that."

She turned on me. "I assure you, the police took nothing! I was here always when they were."

Still kneeling beside the bed, I turned my head slowly, letting my gaze do a near two-seventy sweep. When it hit me, I was glad I was down as otherwise I would have had to kick my own sitter for not spotting it at once.

I went back to the dresser, snatching up the gold frame and turning it over in my hands. I undid a small clasp at the bottom and slid out the thick cardboard backing. I shook the frame and the photograph dropped on top of the dresser. But just the photograph. I shook the frame again. It was empty.

As I had been manipulating the latch, Florence had taken a lurching step toward me, her hand outstretched. "*Nein.*" She had limited her objection to just that, however, so I ignored it until I saw that I was either too late or wrong again.

"*Nein* indeed." I slid the photograph gently back inside the frame, inserted the backing and swung the latch into place. "Are you on the level about the makeup? That means, are you sure? Miss Wyman wasn't allowed to keep any?" I looked at her.

Florence shook her head, bewildered but unbowed.

"Not even, say, a lipstick? She might have kept a secret stash. Maybe you didn't know."

That flabbergasted her. "How can I say, then? If I did not know?"

"True. But I take it you think not. Probably you kept a close eye on her. Someone had to." Having gotten her started talking, I was keen to keep it going. "What did she do for fun?"

"Fun?" She said it in such a way that I wondered whether I might need to learn the German translation. It didn't appear to make any sense to her.

"Yeah, you know, how did she spend her free time?"

"She attended school."

"Sounds like a blast. How about after school?"

"She studied." I started to say something again, but she shut me up with a curt nod. "She also swam, took horseback riding lessons, and, some months ago, performed a small part in the school play."

"How did the boys treat her?"

Her hands clasped in front of her hips. "There were no boys."

"That's what she wanted everyone to believe," I said, mostly under my breath.

"I assure you, there were no boys. During the school year, there had been a boy, part of a group of friends, but it was quite casual and…" She paused as if contemplating the right English word, but it escaped her. "It ended with the semester. I do know."

"She talked to you about it?"

"Her aunt. They were very close."

"Sure. Yesterday her aunt even thought about hiring me to find out who killed her. Now she sends you up to spy on me."

"I am not a spy."

"That's what your cousin Fritz said right before I put a bullet in his brain."

She said something else then, something in her native tongue that I could not decipher, except that her tone left me relatively certain she was not complimenting my shoes.

I told her, "No, you're right. *That's* what he said."

I sighed and gave the room one last look. Not that I expected to find anything. In fact, I'd already found what I'd expected—nothing. It wasn't evidence, but neither did it disprove my initial suppositions. I only wondered what had set him off? Why wait four years? And why drag a teenage girl in if you couldn't ultimately trust her?

The old witch had not made an exit after cursing me. She stood stiff and tall in the middle of the floor with her yellow hands tightly clasped in front of her waist. Her gaze was on me, but not so much scrutinizing as daydreaming about how I might look flayed. As is pretty SOP, my fast tongue had left me feeling a bit remorseful, so I apologized for what I'd said.

She turned up a corner of her withered lips. "*Du bist ein Schwein.* Just like the Germans who *did* kill my cousin. And my brothers." She aimed her gaze down at the rug then, although I suppose it wasn't the rug she was looking at. Her tone grew even more severe. "*Alle Männer sind Schweine. Schweine haben aber ihre Nützlichkeit.*" The faint hint of a smile she'd been playing with faded completely as she glared at me again. "You ferret in the mud—*der Schmutz*—that others will not. You stink of it."

My inclination, naturally, was simply to shrug her insult off, especially as I savvied only about half of it. But something in her tone and her evil eye had worked its way under my skin.

She said, "Do you think that I can not see the darkness in you?"

As a matter of fact, I believed she could. She pierced me with her sharp eyes. I felt exposed,not just naked but actually flayed. Sliced open like a cadaver on a coroner's slab. Maybe she was a witch. I wanted to throw wide my arms and beg her to reach in and rip it out of me, all of it, the good and the bad. I'd rather be empty than carry it around any more. It was eating me up, eating me alive.

But of course she wasn't a witch. Witches don't exist. Just like succubi don't exist. And there's nothing inside of me but me. We were just two bitter souls alone in the room of a dead girl.

The noonday sun was pouring through the window I'd opened, splashing across the floor and filling up the room with heat. I tugged out my handkerchief and applied it to my neck. Florence watched me do that, then spoke slowly, quietly, like someone might be lurking outside the door.

"She wished to learn to drive." She swallowed, choosing her words carefully. "Madame did not approve. Nor Mr. Kelly."

I squinted at her, working hard even to translate her English at that point. And then I felt my right eyebrow creep slowly up my forehead. "Huh. He defied both Madame and Mr. Kelly? I wouldn't have thought he had it in him."

She sneered, as if suddenly she could smell the schmutz. "He doesn't. He's a terrible coward. Afraid even of a small child."

CHAPTER THIRTEEN

She led me down via some hidden stairs, and we found O'Malley seated in that third-rate breakfast nook. He still looked forlorn, but I could spy no new battle scars from his recent encounter with his father's widow. The ginger hair was mostly corralled, and his jaw was only half clamped. He swung his gaze up at me as I approached.

"Did you find anything?"

"No."

He thanked the maid for bringing me and, after she'd left us, sighed all the way down to his ankles. "Can we go now?"

"Sure. But is there another way out? A way that doesn't take us past that bloodhound in the hall?"

He nodded and started off with me at his heels. The first half of the trail was the same we'd followed to Miss Wyman's room. As we passed the window overlooking the patio, I noted that the lounge chair was empty. As was the pool. Mrs. O'Malley had moved elsewhere. Seeing that gently undulating water made me long to jump in myself. Following my flaying upstairs, my skin felt as if it didn't quite fit.

In the kitchen, a large, aproned woman stood snapping peas into a bowl. As he went by, O'Malley kissed her on the cheek, putting a small smile on her rosy lips. But he said nothing and neither did she. Then we ducked into a short hallway and out a door into the sunlight.

We were at the west side of the house. The car sheds were located in the northeastern corner of the grounds. It didn't seem likely we could make our way there unnoticed, but I tossed out a hopeful suggestion anyway. "How about a brief word with Hector?"

His eyes widened at the prospect, but he didn't immediately say no. He ran his fingers through his hair, then closed them into a fist. From his expression, I concluded he was reviewing maps in his head, trying to suss out a route. With our backs to the kitchen door, the front of the house was to the right. Directly in front of us was a cute little herb garden, tucked up against the stone wall, bordered by a picket fence. O'Malley stared at a pint-sized scarecrow lording over the plot. He pursed his lips and puffed out his cheeks. Then the air escaped in a sudden gust and he said, "This way."

A concrete path stretching in both directions had been laid in the grass, and he led me around the back. It turned out to be a hike. Maybe a safari. The path split at the southwest corner of the house, with a left turn leading toward the patio and pool. We took the right fork, heading into some shrubbery and trees near the perimeter wall. We passed another shed that looked like a gardener's headquarters at the back of the grounds, but encountered no fellow explorers. A few times we went off the path, forging through gaps in the foliage, but once he decided upon a route, he never second guessed himself.

At the southeast corner, we came upon a shady gazebo with worked iron benches. I asked him to hold up and he slowed to a stop, turning back to face me.

"We need a plan."

"A plan?" He was bewildered and clearly growing damned tired of it. "What do you mean a plan?"

I pointed north, up alongside the house. We could barely catch glimpses of the drive, the sheds and the activity scattered round there. "I mean for the cops. I just want to ask Hector a few questions, but you saw that Lieutenant. He won't like it."

O'Malley told me what the lieutenant could do, something not quite anatomically impossible, but certainly distasteful.

"Sure. You're new to this whole murder business. Cops don't take to such suggestions. Even coming from spoiled rich kids like you. Maybe especially from—"

He cut me off by offering me a similar suggestion.

I grinned. "I like you better sober. Yesterday you were a bit soggy. Today you've got some iron."

"The plan is you stay out of sight while I demand to know what is going on with my car. They'll expect a spoiled rich kid to do that, won't they? Then when I have all their attention, you slip into the carriage house." He drew another breath and stared off toward our destination. "I hope Hector's even there. I haven't seen him and didn't think to inquire. Oh, well. Come on." He started off.

I fell in behind him thinking it wasn't a bad plan at all. Certainly he'd hit the target as far as what the cops might expect from a spoiled rich kid. He kept going with his new impressive line of reasoning by explaining, "There's an entrance to the garage from the back. Between the building and the wall."

As we neared the corner of the house, I increased the distance between us to about ten feet. He waved his hand low, down at his side, signaling me to stop. I did. A swath of flowerbed and lawn, perhaps fifteen feet wide separated the house from the perimeter wall. The narrow concrete path I was on wound through the middle, slightly closer to wall. I stepped between two trees, allowing me to surveil all of the carsheds and a portion of the drive reaching just past the end of the police van. The personnel had moved out further into the drive, and O'Malley, without slowing, strode in that direction and quickly out of sight.

"Who's in charge here?" He made it sound good, like any lord to the manor born. I heard his shoes crunching on gravel a few more steps, then he stopped. Apparently someone answered him, though not well, because he repeated himself with the noteworthy air of someone who doesn't appreciate the necessity. "I asked who is in charge! That's my car, and I don't recall giving anyone permission to lay their grubby hands on it."

I sighed. Gig had mentioned he'd flopped in Hollywood, but it certainly wasn't due to any unwillingness to commit. Once I felt he had corralled all the attention, I made my move, weaving between the narrow trunks of the Buckeyes. Pausing at the side gate, I took in the scene on the drive.

O'Malley was gesticulating but not overdoing it, demanding to know when he'd be allowed to take his Highlander and depart. Two plainclothesmen were trying to explain. Two others, as well as the two uniforms, were all enjoying the show. Dent had not yet appeared, and I hoped the client wouldn't escalate the program to such a degree that someone might feel compelled to summon him.

I walked past the gate. In case anyone looked over, I figured skulking would have warranted more investigation than simply walking like I was doing something I might indulge in any day of the week. The car sheds were not quite attached to the perimeter wall, just as O'Malley had explained, and I slipped behind them into a gap about a yard wide.

A short path ended at a structure that extended from the back of the car sheds to the wall. I opened an unlocked door and entered.

I found myself in a vestibule about the size of a coat closet. Another door was directly facing me, and I peeked through into a toilet, complete with a commode and shower. To my left, another door led out into the first shed, which still housed the Rolls, and which still stood open to the drive. The opening was mostly blocked by the police van, however, and I stepped quickly over to another door that let me into the small room in which I'd conversed with Jasper Reed's chauffeur, Wayne Holmsby.

I'd barely got the door closed behind me when a sour tenor wondered, "What now?"

I looked over through the open door to the bedroom, where Hector the monkey boy lay stretched out on his bed, smoking and perusing a magazine. When he got a good look at my face, he bolted up.

"You!"

"Me?" I shrugged. "Were you expecting me?"

He took two steps toward me like he had intentions but stopped once we were in the same small chamber. "What are you doing here?"

"Just having a look around." I pretended to do so. "Your employers have certainly spared no expense ensuring your comfort."

"Get the hell out of here. You ain't even a cop."

"Ouch. Personally I think I'm at least twice a cop. Maybe two and a half times a cop. In fact, Mr. Morgan O'Malley hired me to investigate Ramona Wyman's murder."

"Hip-hooray for you. I work for Mr. Kelly. Get out."

"Huh. I would have thought you worked for Mrs. O'Malley. You were showing her niece how to drive a car."

He tried to play it, but wasn't quite up to the task. He snarled and tossed his head back. "Says who?"

I shrugged again. "Doesn't matter. I'm more interested in how much time Miss Wyman spent here. With you. Say back here…" I made a move toward the bedroom. He was blocking the door, and I knew it would not end well, but something about him annoyed me. It didn't help that he reeked of smoke and sweat and axle grease. He reached out to grab my lapels with his oil-stained hands.

"What the hell?"

I got a decent grip on his left wrist and twisted. Not enough to crack anything, just enough to angle him around and out of the way. When I stepped on the back of his knee, he folded like a beach chair, kneeling in the doorway facing the jamb. All skin and bone, how he ever carried that giant I saw in the picture up in the dead girl's room, I couldn't figure. Nine miles on a bum leg. It was a wartime miracle.

Just to scare him, I barked, "Where's that lipstick?" It worked so well, he grabbed a wrench from one of the work shelves and swung blindly backward, slamming the end of the tool hard against the middle of my thigh. I lost my temper then, a little, and ran my fist into the back of his head, sending his face into the door jamb. There was a small splash of blood, and I saw at once it was a wash because he panicked and took to hollering.

I hauled him up and tossed him back into the bedroom. He sprawled atop the bed and rolled over to glare up at me. Blood threatened to leak from a cute gash over his right eye, but it wasn't worth half the yowling he was letting loose.

Figuring I had nothing more to lose, I started improvising. "You greasy punk. You think I leveled with the cops? Mona and I did meet, twice, and we had a long talk all about you and that letter."

"You're crazy! And so is she. I told her—"

And then it was a case of the universe flicking me on the nose and saying *easy come, easy go*, as whatever he was about to say went back down his gullet when the outside door swung open, and a gruff voice demanded to know what the hell was going on.

"He attacked me!" The mechanic aimed a long, bony finger at me.

I put my hands in the air and backed away three steps. That returned me to the work room and nearly put my back to the shed door I'd snuck in through. One of the uniforms had led the charge, but a plainclothes and the other uniform were right behind him. They looked appropriately belligerent and more than a little befuddled.

"What's going on?"

Hector bounded up off the bed and into the back doorway. He shook his greasy hand at me again. "That malook attacked me! He slammed me against the wall."

The cops didn't seem to follow. The one in front had his corrugated forehead cinched tight. He glared at me. "What? Who are you?"

I shrugged my already hoisted arms. "I just wandered in here by mistake. And this kid got spooked, I think. He came at me with that wrench there." I nodded to the tool which lay in the middle of the floor where he'd dropped it after I tapped his head.

"That's a lie!" Hector came further into the room, rubbing the side of his head with one hand while keeping the other aimed at my chest. "This is that shamus was here yesterday poking around. He came in here to attack me!"

Of course, at that point I knew that eventually I'd end up face to face with Dent, and nothing I said before that reunion much mattered. I clenched my fists and took a step forward. "Why you lousy snake..."

The mechanic leapt sideways to escape, crashing into the work shelves and then rolling along them to take up a position behind the nearest cop's shoulder.

I pointed at him. "This guy brought me in here. He said for twenty bucks he'd tell me who killed her."

The cop actually twisted his fat head around to toss the kid a stare. "He said that, did he?"

"No, I didn't say that!" Hector goggled, and I couldn't blame him. "He snuck in here, Goddammit. I was—"

Then the bellow I'd been waiting for came from out on the drive. "For Christsake, Flatly, what's all this?"

The plainclothesman furthest out was shoved aside, and a large hand gripped the shoulder of the uniform blocking the door. Dent forced his way into the room. He stood beside the other uniform and glared all around. Seeing me, he said a single, deep, heartfelt word that needn't be repeated. Without averting his eyes from mine, he growled, "What's going on in here?"

The uniform said, shaking his head, "I don't know, Lieu. We heard somebody hollering for help and when we come in, this one," he nodded at me, "looked set to show this other one what was what."

"He did, did he?" Poor old Dent's upper lip started twitching.

But the uniform wasn't finished. "Only, he claims this one," he nodded at Hector, "invited him in saying he knowed who killed the girl and would spill for twenty simoleons."

The mechanic's voice rose so high it was nearly a screech. "That's a lie!"

It *had* been a lie. A foolish, useless lie I'd tossed out for no particular reason other than I felt like cracking my own head against the door jamb for balling things up so bad. "It isn't." I shoved a hand into my pocket. "Look, I got the cash all ready for him."

Dent ignored me. He indicated Hector with a dismissive wave of his hand. "Take that one around back and find out what he knows about the Wyman girl. I'll take Colette—"

I interrupted, politely. "The Wyman girl? Did I say the Wyman girl? That *would* be a lie. No, no. He said he knew about that girl down in L.A. What do they call her? The Dahlia. The Black Dahlia. This kid claims he saw the whole thing!"

The mechanic gasped and forgot to close his mouth afterward. Dent glared at me a moment, then decided to ignore me some more. He barked at the uniform. "Get him out, I said!" He looked around for the other uniform. "And you, Flatly, cuff Colette and put him in a car. I'll take him down myself, and by God he'll tell me everything I want to know."

CHAPTER FOURTEEN

W hat do you think you're doing?"
On one hand, the answer to that question should have been fairly obvious. A uniform was leading me across the gravel drive toward one of the police cruisers. My hands were cuffed behind my back, and my hat was barely hanging on my head because the man had not been particularly gentle in binding me. But I grinned at O'Malley just the same to thank him for noticing.

He confronted Dent. "This man is in my employ! What do you think you're doing? Release him at once."

"Yes, sir." Dent confronted O'Malley with his hands in his pockets and his shoulders so far back you'd think he'd just been awarded the key to the city. "This man is under arrest, and I plan to—"

"Under arrest for what? On what charge?"

"Attempting to disrupt a police investigation. Snooping." And then, as an afterthought, he added, "Sir."

"Of course he was snooping. That's what I hired him for, you idiot."

O'Malley being new to the whole thing, I couldn't blame him too much for calling Dent an idiot. Just a look at that mug would be plenty for most men to arrive at the same conclusion. But even idiot cops don't take kindly to being called names. "He's under arrest as a material witness. He's coming down to police headquarters."

"I don't know what that means, but you're not taking him anywhere. He's working for me."

"I don't care who he's working for. He's under arrest. Now, sir, I'll ask you to step aside."

O'Malley did step aside, toward the porch. "Don't move. George is a lawyer. We'll see about this."

As O'Malley went to the door to muster reinforcements, I turned to the uniform holding my arm. "Buddy. The sun's in my eyes." He had been rather enthralled with the conversation between his boss and O'Malley, to the point I suspected he'd nearly forgotten I was there. He obligingly reached over to straightened my hat. Chalk one up for the brotherhood of man.

We could hear O'Malley shouting in the foyer for Kelly and Fenton interchangeably. But Dent told the uniform to keep moving, and I was at the side of the cruiser with the rear door opened and waiting for me when O'Malley and Kelly came striding out.

"What is all this, Lieutenant Dent?"

"I apologize for bothering you, Mr. Kelly. I'm placing this man under arrest. And if you object, I'll want to know why."

"Well, I can't object until I know the reason." He smiled warmly, like they were old friends. "My cousin mentioned something about material witness."

"That's as good as any. He's a troublemaker, see? And you can thank me for taking him off your hands."

So, maybe calling Dent an idiot had worked out after all. Combined with his natural inclination to lose his head in my vicinity, his resentment of the remark was leading the old fool to make all manner of mistakes.

Kelly pounced. "Well, which is it? Troublemaker or material witness? The two seem somewhat mutually exclusive to me. And naturally I am disinclined to allow you to cart off one of my employees in handcuffs without a proper explanation of the charges."

"Oh, he's working for you, then? I understood he was working for—"

Kelly cut him off smoothly. "He's in the family's employ."

"Yes, sir. Only, if I may…" He paused, looked down at something, then rubbed his chin. Looking back up, he hoisted his brow. "How much do you know about this character?"

"I'm not sure I follow."

"For instance, did you know that he was court-martialed? He barely escaped a dishonorable. He was—"

Kelly cut him off again, not quite so smoothly. "The war is over, Lieutenant. I'm assuming that since he has a license, his war record isn't in question, and I find your airing of these allegations in so public a forum most heinous. It may even be actionable. Under the circumstances, I suggest you release Mr. Colette at once, finish up your business and depart."

Dent reared up, filling his chest with air. "And I suggest—"

"Tread carefully, Dent. It's our family that's suffered the loss here. And we have cooperated fully with your investigation. But I am nearing the limits of my forbearance. If you wish it, I shall be more than happy to telephone the commissioner's office and discuss the situation with him." Kelly dismissed Dent and told the cop at my elbow, "You there! Remove those handcuffs at once." And just as obligingly as he had reached to adjust my hat, the cop started to comply.

"Hang on," Dent said. He looked around, scowling, and his eyes lit on Hector and the other uniform off around the side of the car sheds. He started toward them. "You there! Kid. Come over here."

The mechanic came forward, though on his own or mostly thanks to the cop attached to his elbow I can't say.

Dent confronted Kelly. "This man is also in your employ?"

"Certainly."

"Well, look at him. Colette assaulted him." He addressed Hector, pointing over at me. "Didn't that fellow assault you?"

The mechanic nodded, dumbly. Dried blood showed above his eyebrow, but it was hardly a speck. He'd already sopped up most of the leakage with his bandana, and the flow had stopped.

"Well, you want to press charges, right?"

Almost simultaneously, Hector said, "Sure, I do," and Kelly said, "No."

Dent looked from one to the other, smelling blood in the water. "Well? Which is it?" He jumped at Hector, recognizing him as the weak link. "You want to press charges, kid? Just say it."

Hector looked over at Kelly, who gave no signal either way. Kelly didn't even look back. He just kept watching Dent. That proved to be sufficient. As the mechanic looked back to Dent, the last of the color drained from his face. "No. No, I guess not."

Dent was speechless. He took another two steps toward the mechanic, then pivoted on his heel and strode halfway toward me and my keeper beside the car. "Put him in, Flatly! By God."

The cop put a hand on my shoulder and applied just enough pressure to convey his desire that I enter the vehicle.

"If that's the way you want it." Kelly shook his head, clearly regretful that he should be forced to such extremes. "I'll speak to the commissioner."

"You do that, sir." Dent didn't look back, progressing around to the passenger's side of the cruiser and climbing into the front seat. My handler had put me into the back, behind the driver's seat. He closed the door and stood there, looking like a complete stooge.

The car was an oven. Dent sat glaring at the dashboard a moment, then shot a glance toward the house. Despite his threat, Kelly had remained on the porch. O'Malley was next to him, saying something, but Kelly didn't show any signs of hearing it.

Dent grumbled and dug in his breast pocket for a pipe. He got it between his teeth and struck a wooden match by scratching its tip down the dashboard.

I said, "For the love of Mike, man, roll down a window."

He responded in no less than a dozen syllables, all of which boiled down to "Shut your trap." The other words were merely color. He puffed on his pipe two or three times with the match shoved down the barrel. Once he was satisfied, he waved the match out, rolled down his window and tossed the smoking stick out on the drive. He sat staring out the front, puffing smoke.

I was perched uncomfortably, my hips shoved forward on account of my wrists being tied together behind them. I tried leaning back but decided it looked even worse than sitting up. There is simply no way to appear at your ease when you have been shoved in chains into the back of a police car.

"Are we heading somewhere, or is the idea to see how long it takes me to bake?"

"Shut your trap," he said again, only without all the excess verbiage. "Why'd you attack the Greek kid?"

"Attack, hell. I barely—"

He spun halfway around, snapping at me like a rabid dog. "Just answer the question!"

I adjusted myself in the seat, but gave up trying to be jovial. I like to tell myself I am a wit, and it's my charm and all that stuff that keeps me from spending the day bawling into my beer. But it was too damned hot, and he had gone too damned far. "No."

"No?" He couldn't believe it. "What do you mean *no*?"

"No." I turned my head to look out the window. Unfortunately, that cop, Flatly, was standing there and most of the view was blocked by his wide backside.

"You want to go down?"

"It's up to me now?"

"Answer my questions and we'll see."

"I wouldn't tell you my name." I leaned toward him, feeling the bile bubbling on my lips. "You said once you'd like to take me somewhere and find out just how tough I am. Well, let's go, pops. Put down that badge and your gun and let's see."

He watched my face closely as I said all that, then offered me a smug grin. "You don't like being reminded of how you ended your war, do you? I suppose I can't blame you. I wouldn't want folks to know I spent V-E Day in the loony bin neither. Only there ain't no shame in it. Some guys just ain't cut out for war."

"You mean like your boy who didn't even make it off the beach?"

I barely got that out before he was halfway over the back of the seat and whaling away at my head. Fortunately for me they were manic, wild punches. I rolled over sideways, ducking my head down against the door, trying to get my knees up between us—not to kick him—he was still a cop—but just as a shield. To Flatly's credit, he had the door opened fast and tugged me out of harm's way. I spilled onto the gravel as one of the plainclothesmen ran around to the other side and yanked open Dent's door.

It required three of them to keep the lieutenant from climbing over the seat of the car and following me out the back. They pulled him through the front passenger door, but as soon as he was on his feet, he thought he was still going to come after me. By then Kelly was standing over me.

"This is an outrage!"

"I'll say." I scrambled up with Flatly's help. "I was just complimenting the man on the aroma of his tobacco, and he went berserk." I addressed Flatly. "Be a good fellow and retrieve my hat." The cop bent over and snatched my hat up off the gravel, giving it a few considerate swipes to dispel some dust before returning it to my top.

Dent stood arranging himself, not just his disheveled clothes and hair, but also his temper. It was a struggle. He ground his teeth so hard, I could hear them. He'd lost his pipe during the scuffle, but I doubt he noticed. His glare was such that I knew he was more than ready to take me somewhere private without his badge and gun. I thought about sticking my tongue out at him, but it was too late for any sort of horseplay. We'd both gone too far at that point and, as strained as our relations had been previously, I knew they'd be far worse in the future.

"I'm beyond words," Kelly was telling everybody within earshot. "This is police brutality at its most despicable. Lieutenant Dent, I demand you leave these premises immediately."

Dent couldn't tear his eyes off me, but he told Kelly, "You demand, do you?"

But Kelly was neither biting nor buying. He stood there like my hero, facing off against the cops. "I do. And take your men with you. And count yourself fortunate that I am willing to let it go at that."

Without anyone instructing him to, Flatly, my handler, was getting the cuffs off me. No one tried to stop him. Most of the other cops looked around trying to figure out what to do. Dent stood there, murdering me with his thoughts and wishes. Finally he walked back over and climbed into the passenger's side of the police cruiser again.

Flatly climbed into the driver's seat and shut the door. He said something to Dent that I didn't catch, even though I was three feet away. Dent hollered back, "Just get me the hell out of here!" Flatly started the engine.

Kelly and I walked over toward the porch as the rest of the crew came back to life and returned to work. We heard assorted whispers, all variations of, "What should we do?" and "Do we finish up or scram?" No one seemed to have any answers.

Flatly steered his police cruiser out through the large gate onto Pacific and sped away. The scientists decided to finish up on the

Hillman they'd been examining. The sole remaining uniform said something to the O'Malley's mechanic, dismissing him, then moved over to join the scientists, probably on account of there is often safety in numbers. As Kelly and I reached the porch, I noticed that O'Malley was eyeing me right up until my gaze met his. At that point, he started looking at anything else.

Before anyone could speak, the front door opened and Miranda O'Malley stepped out. She was dressed in a print blouse and clamdiggers, with leather sandals on her feet and a scarf tied around her hair. An incongruously bedazzling bit of finery was dangling from her neck. I figured it was emeralds, cut large and cast in silver, with a few diamonds, a tenth the size of the green rocks thrown in for diversity. Her sleepy eyes were hidden behind large, dark sunglasses. She looked around at us as if surprised we should be standing there awaiting her.

"Oh. Morgan, George. Hello Mr. Colette. What happened to your face?"

I felt pretty certain my face was fine. Dent had grazed it a couple of times, but most of his wrath had spilled atop the back of my head and shoulders. Not to mention that he'd had neither leverage nor a proper arena to put too much into any particular swing. I tipped my hat to her. "Good afternoon, Mrs. O'Malley. I'm afraid I'm not used to all this sun."

She didn't smile. She might not have heard me. After delivering her question, she'd pretty much forgotten me, digging into the handbag she had hanging on her arm. "George, do you know if they've finished with me? I'd really like to get started."

Kelly replied absently, studying her with a suspicious slant to his brow. "Yes. I had them attend to the Bullet first."

"Thank you. Damn. I can't—oh, that's right. I gave them to Hector." She smirked at herself but shared it with us, all around, before starting forward. "Goodbye."

Kelly and O'Malley watched her go. From their expressions, a view that would have pleased most men was rather wasted on them. Kelly still looked worried and O'Malley, disheartened. I tried to cheer them up. "Well, I'd like to get started myself. I figure I've caused enough trouble around here."

Kelly directed his scowl at me, and I interpreted it along the lines of, "I hope you don't come back," or, "If you hadn't already had one thrashing and there weren't all these witnesses around, I'd enjoy having a go at you myself." Or maybe he just wondered where I got off addressing him so informally.

"Mr. O'Malley?"

Morgan didn't look at me. He aimed his sad, bewildered stare down at the porch, then over at the lawn jockey and then at Kelly. "They haven't started on the Highlander. They can catch up with me at the bungalow, you think, George?"

Mrs. O'Malley stopped halfway to the mechanic's room and pivoted on her toes. "Don't be silly. I'll happily give Mr. Colette a lift."

That hadn't occurred to me, but I admit I liked it. I told her, "Oh, ma'am, I can walk it easily enough."

She smiled mischievously. "I thought you said you couldn't take the sun. Let me get my keys." She twirled back around and ducked into the mechanic's shed.

Kelly sighed, looking out at everything and nothing along the great sweep of drive. "I suppose the inspector will come now, probably with another ADA. I won't get anything done." He glanced at me, not kindly, then looked over at O'Malley as he turned to the door. He didn't thank us, but we got the message loud and clear. He went back inside.

The client, which I supposed he was at that point, even if he hadn't yet signed anything, stood looking slightly nauseous. I offered him a bracing pat on the arm that had him nearly snapping his spine as he tried to dodge. I thought, *So that's how it is*, while saying, "I'll be in touch," and stepping down off the porch.

I didn't know which car belonged to Mrs. O'Malley, but based on the moniker the Bullet, I took a guess that it was the pretty little Alfa Romeo residing in one of the open sheds. Stepping up to the fountain, I lit a cigarette and hoisted a shoe onto the rim of the tile bowl. The garish contraption was about three times the size of my bathtub and presented a cavalcade of mythological fish piled atop one another nearly five feet into the air. At the top, what looked like half a dozen Chinese trout spit streams of water from their wide mouths. A very slight breeze carried enough of the spray over to mist me. Once I had the smoke between my teeth, I took off my hat and used it to fan myself.

"Mr. Colette."

I had tilted my head back, shutting my eyes to enjoy the sun and the spray, but when O'Malley said my name, I faced him. He had moved to the front of the porch and lowered one foot down onto the top step. He looked like he had decided something, and I figured I knew what. Words were clearly wrestling with one another in his throat.

But I never got to hear them. An engine revved and purred and gravel crunched as Mrs. O'Malley steered the silver coupe up along the other side of the fountain.

"Here we are."

She looked as suited to that machine as you might imagine. And as I made my way around to the far side, I spied something very like a smile on her face. I settled into the passenger's seat, perched so low I expected my rump to chafe on the gravel. My hat had been returned to my head but she reached over, snatched it up and dropped it into my lap.

"Silly."

She fed the snarling beast enough gas to make it leap forward. Gravel flew, and I leaned back against the seat and tilted forward again when we paused at the gate. I didn't swivel my head, but glanced surreptitiously into the side mirror. All the city employees were watching us. I couldn't see O'Malley, but I figured he would be watching too.

CHAPTER FIFTEEN

D o you drive?"
     We zoomed west along Pacific, heading further from my office. But I wasn't bothered; the wind felt great in my hair.

"Sure," I told her.

Lacking O'Malley's penchant for finding curb space, she nevertheless managed to squeeze in near the corner of Lyon. She sat simpering at me a moment, then reached over and took the hat out of my lap. "You aren't going to make me walk around?"

The Bullet rumbled, clearly distasteful of her leaving its stick between gears. I got out and made my way to the other side of the car while she climbed into the space I'd vacated. As I was getting settled, a dark gray Chrysler drove by, and she wiggled her fingers at it.

"You shouldn't tease them," I told her.

"Why? You do. You nearly gave that poor fellow a heart attack."

"Dent?" I showed her my hand, with all the fingers curled except the first two, which I held as far apart as possible. "We're like this." I put the car into first and looked for an opening to get back into traffic. "Were you spying from a window?"

"A little. It looked interesting. I told you yesterday, you're not the sort of detective I'm used to."

I tsked her. "Speaking of yesterday. What was all that about?"

"All what?" She had leaned her head back on the seat with her sunglasses aimed at the sky.

"The femme fatale show." I'd found my opening and taken it, turning left onto Lyon and heading south. Fully integrated with the flow of the other cars, I gave her a sidelong glance. "This is much better."

Turning sideways in her seat, she slid her right leg slowly up alongside her left. "How do you know this isn't the show?"

I shook my head, chuckling. "You're a silly idiot. Maybe you can't control it."

"I can control it fine." She climbed around, facing toward the rear with her hands on the back of her seat. Apparently she was looking for something. "Where did they go?"

I checked both my mirrors. "They'll be back."

In a sudden acrobatic twirl, she spun back around and settled herself properly again. "Can you lose them?"

"In this baby? What would be the use?"

"It would be fun." She put her hand on my forearm. "Impress me."

"Ah, rein it in and maybe I'll try." I dropped a gear and took a sudden right onto Clay. I figured the tail would probably swing back along Washington, and we might miss them. "It won't amount to much. There probably isn't another car like this within a thousand miles."

She made a face at me. "Smarty-pants. I happen to know of two in this very town."

"Huh." I decided to try flanking the cops by heading north, hitting the Presidio, then cutting for the sea. If they really had turned back to look for us at Pacific and Lyon, it wouldn't be a terrible strategy. The car handled like a dream, and I only popped the clutch a couple of times.

"I thought you said you could drive."

"Shut up and watch me."

When we reached the lake, she told me to take a right into the base.

"You want to go in there?"

"I want to go across the bridge." She sounded excited. "Wait'll you drive the bridge in my Bullet."

I complied, taking us through the tunnel and out on the bridge. "Hang on to my hat."

She did, removing her scarf with her other hand. The wind seemed to gather up her raven hair and lift her from her seat. I nearly grabbed hold of her myself, thinking she was apt to fly away. It was exhilarating—frightening and fun—and I resisted the urge to look out toward the ocean. I forced myself to watch the road, to concentrate on my driving and the girl on the seat beside me. She was taking so much pleasure in the speed and sun, I figured it wouldn't hurt too much to indulge myself in a small part of that joy. The ocean would still be there tomorrow, waiting for me.

Once we were across, I asked her where we were headed, and she told me nowhere. Then she suggested I take the first road toward the bay side of the peninsula, and we cruised into Sausalito. We made our way along the waterfront, up past the nearly desolate Marinship, then took side roads back toward the ocean.

A few miles west of Marin City, we passed an assortment of gay buildings tucked away from the road behind an orchard. A well-maintained dirt drive meandered back to them, but we did not take it, continuing westward through the rolling hills.

"You know what that place was?" She had her head resting back on the seat again, her face angled to soak up the sun. I hadn't been aware she'd even realized we were passing it.

"Sure. That's Marty Velasco's place. *The Sea Shanty*. Is that what we came to see?"

"Don't be smart. Have you decided to take my money?"

"Can't. I'm working for your stepson."

"Don't let him hear you call him that." She sat up and took off her sunglasses. Her eyes looked tired, and she squinted in the bright light. "I thought he might get you."

I didn't look over, but I let the side of my face show her what I thought of the remark. "You thought so, did you?"

She half-turned to face me, bending her left leg and tucking it under her in her seat. "I'm not really a silly idiot."

"Good to know." I drove on, waiting to hear what she had to say. When she didn't speak for a long while, I prompted her. "I didn't really think you were. I haven't decided what I think you are yet. Possibly silly, but definitely not an idiot."

"And you don't want to kiss me at all?"

I laughed. "*Want?* I'll do it if it'll help. You really have had a shock. A slap would probably do better."

"No. But I don't want a kiss, either. Pull over."

We were on a lonesome country lane between two vineyards with no houses in sight. Almond trees grew in single straight lines down either side of the road, overgrown and shady. I steered the car onto the packed dirt of the shoulder, completely off the asphalt and under the deep shadow of a tree.

She sat there a long time mulling it over. My hat was in her hand, and she was worrying the brim between her thumb and fingers. I removed it gently and set it up on the dash. As previously stated, I only have the two. She began fiddling with her sunglasses instead.

"Did he tell you about Velasco?"

I acted nonplussed. "He who?"

She looked at me, squinting some more. "You know he's been arrested three times."

"This will work better if you ease up on the pronouns. I assume Velasco has regular run-ins with the law. But arrests? I'd wager he parts with regular sums to ensure that doesn't happen."

She had clearly reached the understandable conclusion that the best way to appreciate my wit was by ignoring it. "Twice before the war, and once a little over a year ago. He isn't always as discreet as we would like. Though George has managed to handle things so far. That's why Larry threw him out—Morgan, I mean. He was at a party, and the police raided the place and he socked a cop."

"Really?" That surprised and impressed me. It was foolish as all hell of course, socking a cop during a raid, but not unimpressive. I was actually more surprised to hear he'd been arrested three times. Gig had told me there were no arrests on O'Malley's record. Of course, Gig had also told me O'Malley liked girls.

"So how does Velasco figure in?"

She gave me a world-weary look. "How do you think? He caught Morgan with his pants down back there at the Shanty."

"But George handled it."

"He's trying."

I looked across the road at the grapes and the almonds. "And you're telling me all this *why?*"

"I just want you to have the whole picture. And if Morgan really is in trouble, maybe you can help him."

"I assume Velasco wants money. I'm not going to be much help there. As rich as you all are, why wouldn't you just pay him?"

"Of course, we did. But now he must want more."

"What does he have? Pictures? If George was dumb enough to pay and not get negatives, he *should* pay more."

"I don't know." She certainly looked to me like she didn't. Her expression had a frightened, overwhelmed quality that did not suit her at all. "But he must have something."

"Well. Fortunately we're right here." I reached for the starter. "Let's go ask him."

She grabbed hold of my wrist. "What? Go to Velasco?"

"Why not? He's a businessman looking to turn a profit. Probably the main hitch in your situation is that no one ever tried to sit down and reason with him."

"You're crazy. He'd kill us!"

"Don't be ridiculous. You patronize his club. And he doesn't kill people. He takes pictures of them in compromising situations and then charges for it. Kill us. Pfft." I reached for the starter again.

"Wait! Please. Let me at least think about it a moment."

I sat back. "Fine. This is a nice spot. Think away."

She went into her purse for a cigarette and I held my breath, expecting to be asked to supply another one. But she surprised me not only by having a pack, but by also offering one to me. I pressed the lighter on dash, only to discover she hadn't the patience for it. She lit us both with her diamond-encrusted portable number.

After a nice, calming, smoke-filled breath, she asked me, "Is it true what that policeman said. Were you really court-martialed?"

"You *were* spying."

"I don't suppose you'd tell me why."

I shrugged, sliding down in my seat so that I could rest my head on the back edge. I held the cigarette in my left hand up on the door so that I could flick ashes into the road. Mrs. O'Malley was sitting up straight, her leg still folded under her, watching me.

"Sure. I was a Mess Sergeant, and I burned the colonel's toast once too often."

I heard a noise and looked up. A mud-colored Ford was heading toward us from the other direction.

"My. They might have hung you."

"No. The punishment for that is slow roasting over an open fire. They say it feels good once you get used to it."

The Ford sped up as it neared us. The driver had a hat pulled low over his eyes and his face turned far enough to the right I couldn't quite make it out. He didn't seem to see me at all, even when I waved at him.

"But you weren't convicted."

"I suppose that's the official story. Personally I'd prefer to change the subject."

I was watching the Ford retreat into the distance in my side mirror, feeling a sort of tickle begin deep in my belly. I put absolutely no stock in hunches as mine are so often wrong, but that time I wasn't so lucky. About three hundred yards past us, the Ford ducked right, then back into a wide U-turn, swinging around toward us.

Mrs. O'Malley, apparently completely unaware another car was even in the vicinity, was telling me, "Yes, I can see that you're not your favorite subject."

I sat up in my seat. "I'm dull. But this might be interesting."

"What?"

"I don't know. Maybe they need directions."

She looked back as the Ford revved its engine and barreled toward us. It slid past in a blur, and we heard the brakes applied suddenly and with force. The driver must have cranked the steering column. The car's near wheels came up off the pavement as it cut us off, missing the front of the coupe by about a foot. It stopped with its rear wheels on the pavement and the front wheels on the shoulder. Both the front and back passenger side windows were down, and men leaned out with guns. On the far side, the driver angled his entire torso out his window and leveled his gun toward us across the roof of the car.

Mrs. O'Malley didn't scream. She took my arm again, her other hand hovering over the jeweled necklace. All I heard from her was a faint intake of breath.

The men in the car wore bandanas over the lower halves of their faces, and the driver and the guy in back had hats. The front passenger, the one staring down the barrel of a Luger directly in front of me, had golden blond hair slicked straight back. His eyes looked young and clear and incredibly blue, even in the shade. A scar started in the middle of his forehead and sliced down into his left eyebrow. It had clearly come from a healthy cut, or rather an unhealthy one. It split his eyebrow into two distinct halves. Though I could only see a few inches of his face, I figured if it hadn't been for that scar he would have been playing a tough guy in pictures rather than on that deserted road.

For a moment no one spoke. We all just admired the tableau. Then the rear passenger door opened, and the man behind it climbed out. He told us to put our hands up. His barking breath caused his bandana to flap. I complied immediately. Mrs. O'Malley moved much slower. The man made a wide circle around to stand in the road to my left. He told me to get out of the car.

I did as I was told, keeping my hands high whenever they weren't absolutely required. The man waved his snub-nosed Colt, explaining I should turn around and put my hands on the side of the car. I did that too, thinking he meant to pat me down, but once I was leaning there, he simply told me to stay put and forgot about me.

I looked over at Mrs. O'Malley. She was on her knees in her seat, staring at either the Colt or the man wielding it. Her eyes were as wide as I'd ever seen them, her painted lips open in a small circle.

The driver of the Ford got out next, coming round the front of his car and over along the passenger side of the coupe. He told Mrs. O'Malley to "Stay put, kitten," at which point I was about ready to give up on those jokers. I figured I could probably take the Colt from the guy next to me without too much fuss, and the driver had pocketed his own gun. But the scarred, blond matinee idol with the Luger struck me as a wild card. He acted cool and composed, but you never knew just how twitchy a man's fingers might become once the action starts.

The driver reached out without any more preamble and closed a fist around Mrs. O'Malley's necklace. He yanked it off with a sudden jerk that elicited another gasp.

"I bet it had a clasp," I told him.

That reminded Mr. Colt that I was there, and he stepped toward me, growling, "No one asked you, buddy."

"I ain't your buddy, slick." I know it sounds like I was making fun of them, and I was. But the whole setup was ridiculous.

Colt looked over at the driver, who responded with a single nod and started back around to his place behind the wheel of the Ford. I felt a gun barrel stick me in the back and slide up over my left shoulder blade. The guy holding it was leaning in at me, whispering hoarsely through his bandana, "You ain't to follow us."

"Why would I do that?"

He laughed, and I sensed his arm angle upward. I managed to pull to the side just in time so that his fist and the handle of his weapon landed mainly atop my left trapezius. I sold it though, sinking down onto the dirt, rolling to my back and cowering against the rear wheel of the coupe. I tried to look frightened and hurt, though mainly I just felt mad as hell and devoted every ounce of willpower to keep myself from blowing out his knee with a well-aimed kick.

He laughed at me again, saying, "So long, tough guy," before bouncing back over and climbing onto the Ford. The driver revved the engine, reversed into the road and swerved around to head west, back the way they'd come.

I let them put a couple of hundred yards between us before bothering to get up. As I dusted myself off, frowning, I heard Mrs. O'Malley ask me in a breathless voice if I was all right.

"No," I told her, mainly because I don't consider being offended anything like all right. Not to mention my shoulder hurt some.

She caressed her chest just below the neck. "They stole my necklace."

"Yeah, I saw that." I lowered myself back into the coupe. "We should file a police report."

Her reaction told me that would make about as much sense as going sailing. "A police report? But..." She changed her tune. "Why didn't you do something?"

I smirked, using just a corner of my mouth. "Lady, you could see my hat sitting here on the dash. What was I supposed to catch the bullets in, my pockets?"

"But who were they?"

"How should I know?"

She showed me a shiver, not holding back at all. "Take me home."

"With pleasure."

I started the coupe and turned it around, heading back the way we'd come, in the opposite direction the Ford had taken. We passed Marty Velasco's place again, but neither of us bothered to glance at it. A few miles later, I turned south, not desiring another tour of Sausalito. A few miles north of the bridge, Mrs. O'Malley told me, "I recognized one of them. The one that hit you. He works for Marty Velasco."

I flexed my fingers around the steering wheel, and my jaw tried to crack a few molars. I drew some air in through my nose and let it out slowly, telling her, "Sure. Why not?"

CHAPTER SIXTEEN

I pulled into the red gravel drive and parked next to the fountain. The police scientists had taken their van and departed. Morgan O'Malley's Highlander was also gone. The other cars were lined up neatly near the car sheds. I killed the engine, then broke the silence which had dominated our return trip by asking, "Can you get yourself inside all right?"

Her scarf was tied around her hair again and the shades back in place over her eyes. She continued to stare at something on the bonnet of the coupe. "You won't tell anyone, will you?"

"Who would believe it?" I took my hat from her and climbed out. "Good afternoon, Mrs. O'Malley." I started toward the main gate.

She was still sitting there, stiff as a statue, when I turned onto Pacific. By the time I made it around the corner and passed by the side gate, however, she'd disappeared. I tried not to think about it. For one thing, she had offered me a ride an hour earlier, and there I was hoofing it with an aching shoulder and half a day wasted. Not that a little exercise wouldn't do me good. For one thing, it would allow me ample time to not ruminate and to not try and figure out what the hell she'd thought she might accomplish with that trick. I muttered to myself and scowled at things, earning quite a few appropriate looks from passersby.

At the office, I checked my messages—nothing—and called the client—no answer. So I smoked a cigarette. I avoided some more ruminating. I went to the window and sat on the sill, staring morosely down at the alley and not seeing anything. I called up Gig Barton at the *Clipper* and was told he'd call me back. I laid on the couch and had another cigarette, wondering what about that particular piece of furniture had so appealed to the client. I'd acquired it for two bucks at a used chattel shop down in the Mission District.

Gig called me back. "How goes the investigation?"

I settled into the chair behind my desk and flattened my tie. "I solved that yesterday. Just waiting for someone to offer a reward."

"I heard you were working for the O'Malleys." To Gig, that apparently meant Miranda O'Malley because he immediately followed up with, "Can you get me an introduction? I sat two tables down from her one night at the Storkey. Never managed to work up enough nerve to ask her to dance."

"Forget dancing, my man. You need to see her shiver. She has it down to an art."

"Oh yeah?" But I gathered my line confused him. He said, "Did you call for a reason? You got a quote for me?"

Having consulted a specific volume on my bookshelves the night before, I did have a quote ready: "*Our basest beggars are in the poorest thing superfluous: allow not nature more than nature needs, man's life is cheap as beast's.*"

"Christ. What is that, Keats?"

"Barbarian." I went to put my feet up onto the corner of my desk but stalled when a sudden pain pinched my thigh, right about the spot O'Malley's mechanic had landed his wrench. Between that, my forearm and my shoulder, I figured I'd need a vacation soon. I sat forward, propping my elbows on the desk and taking a long drag on my cigarette. "Listen, how are the various players set for alibis? No one tells me nothing."

"They exist," he said, a certain lilt to his voice. "Was there anyone in particular you were interested in?"

"Bad puppy. I'm just generally interested."

He sighed. "Miss Lana O'Malley had a late lunch at Saks with a name you might recognize."

"Yeah, don't say it."

He laughed. "They parted, and she met a girlfriend for shopping and then several others joined her at the aforementioned Storkey for dinner and dancing. So, she's out of it by most reckonings. As for your friend…"

"He is not my friend. And please tell me he is open."

"He claims to have spent the afternoon at the office of his employer, Walter Cobb. That has apparently been verified, though sketchily. Amazing how an office full of private detectives can't supply a concrete alibi."

"Well, if Cobb gives him the nod, the cops will go along."

"That seems to be the consensus. And what would his motive be?"

"You haven't seen her shiver. What about Morgan O'Malley?"

"He's even sketchier. He says he took a drive, then attended a pool party at a friend's house. But he won't name the friend. Apparently he doesn't like cops. Or rather, he likes snubbing his nose at them. How he's not in jail, I don't know. You and me, we'd be steaming under a lamp while big burlies caressed our cheeks. The book says some woman's husband would not approve of her sharing his pool with the O'Malley kid."

"Great theory," I told him. "You newshounds don't miss a trick. George Kelly?"

"He maintains an office downtown and was there until noon. Had lunch at his club then swung by the bank and the digs of a business partner. From three o'clock on, he was at his club. Dined there. Meant to drink after but got a call from Mrs. O'Malley about five-thirty alerting him that her niece had not returned from an outing. Now, as to the lady of the house—"

"Hang on. You heard about the family mechanic? Fellow called Hector."

"Sure. Papasomething. Greek kid. He chauffeurs Kelly. In fact, they primarily vouch for one another. He sat in the club staff lounge a while and rolled some dice with two other chauffeurs. Left with Kelly after the call came in. No one wants to swear to it, but no one has contradicted either."

"Okay. Mrs. O'Malley?"

"Home with her secretary, Florence Lange. Preparing to attend an opening at the De Young. Never made it. About five, she started panicking that niece had not returned from regular outing. Called George Kelly at his club as mentioned. Home all day and evening. Never unaccounted for. She is tightest of all."

"Well, that sort of thing is simple. Not like staging a roadside heist. *That* can get complicated."

"What?"

"Just gibberish. Last but by no means least, Jasper Reed."

"The retired shyster?" Gig was incredulous.

"Why not?"

"I just didn't know he figured in."

"Huh." I said it with feeling. "I heard the cops had him most of the day yesterday."

"Really?" It sounded like Gig was rifling through papers. "How did we miss that?"

I said it again, "Huh. Maybe he really *is* a criminal mastermind. All right my boy, you've been a wonderful help."

"Wait a minute! How does Reed figure into this?"

"I'm sorry, my stomach is rumbling."

"Hang on!"

"No time. Thanks again." I sent the telephone receiver back toward its cradle. Along the way Gig's voice echoed, calling me all manner of names not fit to print, like any newsman worth his salt.

I sat back and took a breather. My cigarette had burned down to a nub, and I smashed it in the ashtray. I considered lighting another, decided against it, and grabbed up the telephone again to try O'Malley's number. It rang five times before I heard the click. A soft, feminine voice asked me, "Hello?"

I pulled my head back, frowned, and glared menacingly at the numbers on the dial. "Mr. Morgan O'Malley, please."

"No. Mr. Morgan not here." Her accent was faint, but she spoke in the halting English of a non-native speaker.

"Do you expect him?"

"Yes, yes. They go dinner now. You call back."

"No," I told her. "Me leave message. You can write?"

She sighed, not exasperated, but rather indulgently like I was a silly child, only she was quite used to dealing with silly children. "Yes, yes. Hold please."

I held and listened to assorted sounds. Then she was back. "Message?"

"Have Mr. O'Malley telephone Declan Colette. At his earliest convenience." I waited, then inquired, "Did you get that?"

"No." She sounded quite honest about it. "You spell."

I spelled and also gave her my number. "Have him call me as soon as he gets the message. When do you expect him?"

"No expect. They go dinner. Be back soon."

"And you'll see he gets the message?"

"Oh, yes. I see."

I sighed, completely exasperated. "Thank you."

"Yes. Bye-bye." She severed the connection.

I hung up and looked around. Nothing I saw interested me much, so I locked up and went to dinner myself. It was only four-thirty, but I hadn't had any lunch. I ate half a chili size at Jack's, then gave up and walked down to the YMCA. I swapped my civvies for some shorts and an undershirt, admiring the twin bruises on my forearm and thigh. Then I spent twenty minutes attacking a heavy bag. I found that by pretending it had Dent's face on one side and that blond, scarred gangster's mug on the other, I had no trouble mustering the necessary enthusiasm. The bag never stood a chance. Had I got really creative and envisioned Joe Lovejoy's phiz somewhere in the middle, the bag probably wouldn't have survived.

In the steam room afterward, I enjoyed about five minutes before the place started crowding with the nine-to-fivers. That's not so bad until you get the fortyish fellows with the dapper haircuts and the trim physiques, advertising their wedding rings while simultaneously giving you the eye. And then sometimes one of them even strikes up a conversation and mentions something about what a great physique *you* have. At that point, your only options are to hit the showers or cause a scene. Well, maybe not your only options. But I usually take that as my cue to hit the showers, and that day was no exception.

I was back on the sidewalk by seven o'clock, and I ducked into a drugstore to check my messages. George Kelly had rang at five-forty-seven. That rated a frown but called for no other immediate action. More importantly, O'Malley had returned my call at ten to seven. I hung up and did the same for him.

He answered after three rings. "Hello."

"Mr. O'Malley, Declan Colette. I—"

"Oh." It was neither an exclamation of surprise nor joy. He also didn't sound particularly disappointed. The impression I got was that he had been engaged in some lively and pleasant debate, probably about something rather inconsequential, and my call had reminded him that he had more pressing matters that required his attention. "Hello, Mr. Colette."

"Yeah. Hello." I took a breath. "Listen, I have a question."

I didn't pose it immediately but apparently he expected me to. He didn't speak, and we listened to the echoing silence of the open line. Finally he asked, "Would you like to come here?"

"No." It struck me as a rather ridiculous suggestion. Then I reconsidered and softened my reaction. "No, there's no need to trouble you. But I need you to—"

"It's no trouble."

Standing in that dark booth with my back to the glass pane in the door, hearing all the pharmacy customers, the soda counter crowd, even the cars on the street, I wished I had gone back to my office to make the call. My thigh was hurting, and my shoulder was trying to feel worse. The workout and the steam had been only temporary salves.

"You're very kind, Mr. O'Malley. But I have an appointment." I paused again, and again he said nothing. After a moment, I broke the silence. "You dodged this question today, and I need you to be on the level with me. When I mentioned that rumor I'd heard about you and your father's driver, you assumed I got it from Marty Velasco. I want to know why you thought that."

He maintained his silence, and I suspected he was taking the time to formulate a response. But when he did finally speak, it was to say, "I'm not sure I understand."

I made sure he heard my exhale. "That won't do. If you want my help, you'll—" I stopped cold. "You do still want my help?"

"Of course I still want your help."

"Then you'll have to help me. That means opening up. Why did your mind immediately jump to Velasco? I think I know, but I want you to tell me."

He let me hear his breath as well, though I don't think he put as much effort behind it. "Because I knew you'd been out to see him."

"How did you know that?"

"Well, er, Joe, of course."

Of course. I wanted to be crystal clear. "Joe Lovejoy told you that I had paid a visit to Marty Velasco?"

"Yes. This morning. When I went to get the letter from Lana. He was there. Joe, I mean."

I tightened my fingers around the receiver, and clenched my other hand into a white-kunckled fist. I didn't speak.

O'Malley said, "You thought I was still under Velasco's thumb, didn't you?" His tone was daring me to admit it.

"No." I shut my eyes tight and didn't reopen them. "You were at some point though, right? A while back?"

"What does he say?"

"Velasco? He's cagey."

"He's a lousy bastard."

"Yeah. You still hang out at his club."

"Not as much. I enjoy roulette. And I'm not about to let that lowlife frighten me away."

I heard myself laugh, knowing it was wrong. "So your business transaction with Velasco concluded some time ago?"

"Yes. Six months at least. You know, you're kind of a bastard too. I shouldn't tolerate it."

"You shouldn't. You paid up and you got negatives?"

I heard another loud breath, in and out through his nose. "Do we have to go into it?"

"You think you're the only guy he shot pictures of? You probably aren't even the only guy you know. I just want to confirm that it is all over with. The negatives were destroyed? You know that?"

"Yes. I handled it. Well, George and I."

"Good ol' George," I said. "He telephoned me an hour or so ago."

"Why?"

"I don't know. I wasn't in and haven't called him back. I wanted to clear this up first."

He considered that a while. I found myself waiting with more patience than I would have predicted I still possessed. I relaxed my fist slowly. His voice came timidly, "Have you had dinner?"

"Yes. And so have you. Your girl told me."

"My girl." It was his turn to chuckle. "She'd love that. But you're wrong, we're having tapas. I have a lodger from Spain, and he's laying a feast. You're more than welcome to join us."

I was surprised at the virulent reaction his invitation stirred in me. I watched my fist clench, saw the knuckles go white again. I might have been some insane beast. My emotions seemed to ricochet back and forth like a dog who has been poked and petted so interchangeably, it can't tell the difference anymore. He called me a bastard, and I practically cooed. He offered me dinner, and I wanted to break something.

"I'll pass," I told him, forcing myself to breathe.

Not being there, he was naturally unaware of my bout of madness. "I do have a few questions I'd like to ask you."

"Sure thing. I'll be at my office no later than ten in the morning."

He chuckled again. "You're a funny duck, Mr. Colette."

"Not me." His latest assessment had me neither cooing nor railing. It just made me want to hang up. I thanked him for calling me back and answering my question, he told me I was welcome, and we ended the call.

I dialed George Kelly's number but got Fenton, who explained that Mr. Kelly was out. No one knew where, possibly his club or his office, both equally doubtful. I told the butler to make a note of my call and hung up.

CHAPTER SEVENTEEN

I was sitting on my bed, propped against the headboard, resting my eyes when the telephone rang. I jerked a bit, swiveling my head to survey the scene and size up the opposition. Finding none, I frowned and was about to wonder what had startled me when the bell sounded again. I leaned over and reached for it, causing the open book on my chest to tumble to the floor. My hand was halfway to the receiver before I spied the smoldering nub of a cigarette between my first two fingers. Seeing it there allowed me to acknowledge the searing pain, and I cussed and shook my hand, tossing the butt down alongside the book. The phone rang again and I looked at the clock. Nine-twenty. Almost certainly it had been eight forty-five a moment ago. I sat trying to figure how that might have happened, while the telephone bell pealed a fourth time.

"Hello?" I got the receiver up beside my head and leaned over the edge of the bed to make sure my carpet didn't catch fire.

"Mr. Colette?" It was a man I didn't recognize, not from those two breathless words nor the half dozen that followed. "Sorry to call you at home."

"Not to worry." I picked up the cigarette butt and put it in the ashtray on the nightstand. "Who'sis?"

"It's George Kelly."

I yawned. "Oh, hello, Mr. Kelly. You got my message?"

He was confused. "Your message? No. What message?"

"I returned your call. I spoke with Fenton."

"Oh that." But he said it in such a way that I deduced he wasn't quite sure. Neither was he particularly concerned. His breathing came a bit labored like he'd just run up a hill. "No. I—I haven't been…Mr. Colette, I must see you."

He actually sounded like 'must' was the right word. I sat up. "Of course. Would you like to come by the office tomorrow? Or shall I—"

"You misunderstand. I must see you now. Will you meet me?"

I had swung my feet over onto the floor, anticipating his request. Heavy breathers who phone late and interrupt your eye-resting seldom feel inclined to wait for morning. "Where?"

"I'm at…" It sounded like he pulled away from the receiver. I heard what I interpreted as the door of a telephone booth opening, and then street sounds, but faintly. "I'm at Third and Oakdale, in a—there's an alley half a block down Third. I'll be there."

"What's this about?" I stood and was strapping my wristwatch on. "Are you all right?" I grabbed my trousers from the chair I'd tossed them over.

"Yes. I—I think I lost them." He was back in the booth, gasping his words directly into the transmitter. "I'm not in great shape. Can you hurry? Don't—don't take a cab. Do you have a car? You can—"

"I have a car." I sat back down to pull on my socks. "Who did you lose?"

"Velasco's men. They—"

I cut him off with a very sweet oath. "Never mind that part. Get yourself into the alley. I drive a thirty-eight Lincoln. One of the old Zephyrs. You know it?"

"Yes, I think so."

"She used to be blue. Now she's sort of blue." I wasn't trying to make small talk, at least not for small talk's sake. I carried the telephone over to my dresser and was pulling out my armament, giving it a look. The only shooters I keep in my apartment are an ugly little belly gun that sleeps under my mattress near the head of my bed, and a Colt revolver, a forty-five that lives in my bottom drawer. The Colt's slow but very effective. It also has a kick and weighs far too much to carry in a pocket. Carting it requires a shoulder holster. I grabbed that and a box of ammunition.

"How long do you expect it will take you? I…I'm bleeding."

I repeated my oath. "It will take some time. Should I call an ambulance?"

"No!" He had nearly shouted, but then grew plaintive. "Please. Just hurry. I…I'm not shot. Or stabbed."

"Just get into that alley and keep an eye out. I'll be there."

"Thank you, Mr. Colette. I—"

"Yeah, yeah. We'll see. Go." I waited to hear the click at his end before hanging up. I finished dressing, and by finished, I mean the holster and the Colt, my shoes, a jacket and, finally, a handful of bullets for my jacket pocket.

I took a cab to my garage since I lodge the Zephyr in closer proximity to the office than home. Still, I slid behind the wheel a few minutes before ten o'clock. The night attendant knows me even though I seldom drive, and he offered some remark about my spending a night on the town. I grinned more playfully than I felt like doing and sped off into the darkness.

Traffic heading down toward the shipyards was predictably light at that time of night on a Thursday. Ten-fifteen found me slow cruising down Third, approaching Oakdale. I passed an alley and saw nothing but darkness in both directions, so I proceeded to the intersection and turned around. As I crawled north again, a figure stumbled out of the alley on my right, stopping just at the sidewalk and leaning heavily against a wall.

I turned into the alley, and my headlights swept over him. He brought his right hand up to shield his eyes, but not before I saw that someone had made alterations to his face. His cheek was apple red and more crimson traced a line from the corner of his mouth to the bottom of his chin. He leaned on his right shoulder, his left arm across his belly, guarding it. His clothes were somewhat disheveled, as was his hair, but neither looked as played with as his face.

I got out and helped him around to the passenger side of the Zephyr. He tried to thank me again and I brushed him off, also again. The fact is I was pretty disgusted. I got back in and started driving, down the alley and three right turns to get us back onto Third.

I didn't speak or really look him over except for the brief survey I'd managed getting him into the car. He sat with his shoulders forward, holding his belly, admiring the floor between his feet. His breathing was loud and anything but clear. The silence lasted halfway to my office.

"Don't you want to know what happened?" He sounded hurt that I hadn't asked.

I shrugged. "You fought back."

His look showed just how offensive he found my implication, which was funny considering the state of his face. "Of course I fought back!"

"Yeah, you and your cousin. You're not about to let some lowlife like Velasco scare you." Stopped at an intersection, I leaned over and opened the glove box. A half-empty bottle of Old Crow was in there, and I dropped it into his lap. "Wet your lips. It's not Paul Jones but it'll help. You got a handkerchief?"

He opened the whiskey and took a sip. That caused him to make a face and close the bottle tight. He didn't put it away though, just tucked it between his thighs. He produced a handkerchief from a pocket and wiped his chin. I was amazed that hadn't occurred to him until I mentioned it.

"Did she tell you what happened today?"

He turned his head slowly around so that he could scowl at me with his sour eye. "I can't believe you didn't stop it."

"Was I supposed to?" I lit a cigarette. Traffic was such that just a few looks in the mirror told me we weren't the object of any special scrutiny. Until we hit Army, the streets were mainly our own. Applying the glowing tip of the lighter to my cigarette, I noticed that the residual adrenaline had my hand shaking. Strapping on a shooter and speeding down toward the shipyards to save a man from a gang apparently had gotten me somewhat excited.

I took a nice puff and blew the smoke out into the windshield. It billowed back toward my face and I waved it aside. "I knew she brought me along for a reason, but I didn't think it was to stop it."

"What are you talking about?" His red face looked hot now as well as hurt. And his brow was tying itself in knots. He could deny it, but he had some inkling of what I was talking about. "She said they hit you and you simply lay there like a coward."

I chuckled. "One of them did get it into his noggin to try and tag me with the butt of his gun, probably an unfortunate adlib. It was one of the worst flubs in the whole comedy of errors."

"What are you talking about?" He managed to make it sound exactly like the first time, an impressive feat considering he had to know just how weak it came across. He braved another taste of the Old Crow.

I took a breath. "Where am I taking you? Home?"

"No." He looked around, considering the point. "Can't we...I need to get cleaned up. I can't go to my club."

"You're holding yourself kind of funny. You sure you don't need a doc?"

"I'm fine," he said, and then corrected himself. "I will be fine. I just need to clean myself up." He angled his head to sneak a peak at me, plaintive.

I kept my eyes on the road, chewing the question and some tobacco over on my tongue. "I know a place." I spit the tobacco out the window.

We rode the next several minutes in relative silence. He put away his handkerchief and took a third sip of the Old Crow. The taste seemed to be growing on him. I smoked my cigarette and wound through the streets, which grew less and less deserted as we made our way north. I found some curb space on Pierce a half block south of the Rooker Building.

"Wait here," I told him, getting out of the car.

"Where are we?"

I ignored him and got to the sidewalk and headed north.

There are actually two hotels on the same side of the street as my office. One, just south of the Rooker Building, is nicer and also an SRO. The other, two doors north, which rents rooms by the hour, is called the Lena Dorne. I went to the second place, passing the plain wooden door of a massage parlor called the Oriental Palace, which is nestled between the Rooker Building and the Lena Dorne.

The lobby looked and smelled like the waiting room in a hospital where no one ever wants to wind up. A row of recessed lighting ran along one edge of the ceiling, but half of it was not working. The furniture was modern and plain and designed to discourage sitting. No surprise, the room was virtually empty. The only occupant was at the far end, seated on a stool behind the front desk. A bare bulb hung over his head like a really bad idea.

I made my way over to him, asked for a room with twin beds and a bath and paid for a full night. Not that he cared much for trivial matters like length of stay or identification. He glanced at my signature on the register—John Hancock—but nothing about it caught his eye. He gave me a key and told me the elevator was off for the night.

I mounted the stairs, reached the third floor and matched the number on my key to one on a door. The room beyond it was a good deal cozier than the lobby below, but a little too creamy yellow. The beds had yellow spreads, and the one chair a yellow cushion, and the walls yellow paper showing what looked like tiny carnations. The paper was peeling from one corner near the ceiling.

I switched on the bathroom light for a look, deciding that not only would it have to do, but why did I even think there could be any question at that point. I left and took the back stairs to the ground floor, found the door to the alley and propped it just shy of latching. Then I went back up a flight, returned to the front stairs, the lobby, and the street.

Kelly repeated himself again. "Where are we?"

I kept right on ignoring him, pulling out and going around the corner and then turning into the alley. I stopped in front of the Lena Dorne's back door. "Go up and wash," I told him, handing over the key. "I'll get you something to wear."

He looked wary. "You can't go to the house."

"No. You'll have to slum it, I'm afraid. Fortunately, its dark and we're only a few blocks from home. Not much chance you'll run into many people you know. Go."

He sat examining the key and the numbered panel attached to it like he expected to find detailed instructions there.

"Go," I said again, but he only turned his head to look at me.

"You're...I've never..." He showed me a weak smile. "I'm glad I called you."

I showed him the side of my head, grimacing at the alleyway ahead of us. "I'm not. But we'll discuss that upstairs. Get out now."

He did, taking the Old Crow and limping through the door. As soon as I heard the latch catch, I sped off around the far corner and back onto Pierce. The same space was waiting, and I took it. Upstairs in my office, I got my last clean shirt and the only pair of trousers I keep there. These rich folks were proving a drain on my supplies: cigarettes and clothes and patience. It was fortunate for Kelly that he and I were nearly the same size. My rags might be a little loose around the shoulders and the waist and a bit short at the cuffs, but they'd get him home.

I sat and smoked a cigarette at my desk. The lights were off, and I waited for the dark and the smoke and the just plain sitting to help me unwind. I wondered if she had any idea of what she'd nearly accomplished with her silly little stunt. Then I decided I didn't want to think about it, and I closed my eyes and thought of the sea. When I had whittled my cig down to a nub, I dropped that in the ashtray, got up, stretched my tired and aching limbs, and carted my clothes over to the Lena Dorne.

"Who's there?" Kelly called when I knocked.

"Moxey's Drug," I told him, and he opened the door a crack to peek out.

He had showered and donned his shorts but nothing else. He'd draped a towel across his shoulders. He was in fine shape for a man my age. Not as muscular as me I feel obliged to point out, slightly softer around the middle, but he clearly kept an eye on himself. I thought he rated some time from my eyes as well, but kept to the task at hand and pushed my trousers and shirt toward him.

He backed into the room as I shut and locked the door. When I turned around, he was still standing there, looking at the clothes in his hands.

"Won't those do?"

His head came up, his expression startled. "What?"

"I realize they aren't up to your standard, Mr. Kelly, but times are hard."

"You think you're a joker." He didn't seem to appreciate it. Tossing my duds on the foot of the far bed, he stepped over to a long, low dresser against the wall. The Old Crow was sitting there, nearly dead, beside two tumblers. "I rinsed some glasses. You want a drink?"

"No, thanks. I never touch that cheap stuff. Stifles my wit." I sat on the bed nearest the door. "Tell me what happened."

He poured some whiskey for himself, hoisting the glass and looking at his reflection in the half length mirror mounted atop the dresser. There in the light, having had water sprayed over it, his face wasn't so bad after all. His left check was red and swollen and had clearly been tapped once or twice, and his upper lip had a single clean slit on the same side. But his left eye had escaped mostly unscathed, and his nose didn't appear to be broken.

He ran his free hand through his wet hair, sweeping it straight back. It was thick and wavy and didn't want to be pushed around. He gave up and drained his glass instead. I noticed that his knuckles were raw.

"Like I said, you fought back."

"I tried, I suppose." He smirked and looked down, returning his tumbler to the dresser but not refilling it. He stared at the whiskey bottle a while, then turned to me with a wistful look. "Why do you keep saying it like it was foolish?"

"Because it was. Look what it got you. As I tried to explain to Mrs. O'Malley, Velasco's a businessman. There's no profit in killing people. Or in roughing them up too much. For instance, if you'd just stood there and took it, they never would've strayed above the neck. Now you're gonna have a swell black eye to explain to all the fellows at your club. And a busted lip. I don't suppose you box."

He looked at himself in the mirror again and touched his belly, fingering another unhealthy bruise located just east of his navel. "I never got anywhere near Velasco, of course. He probably doesn't even know I tried."

"Sure he does. He probably just has no idea *why* you tried." He jerked his head toward me, and I tried to make my voice soothing. "I know, I'm not making any sense. Why don't you tell it from the beginning?"

He did, sparing a lot of details. After dragging the tale of our adventures in Marin from Mrs. O'Malley, he had contacted an attorney, Lester Benz, who had acted as a go-between for Velasco on another matter some months prior. Kelly admitted to being brusque with Benz. He also admitted to being distressed about recent events, and had demanded Benz arrange a face-to-face with Velasco. Benz had phoned back an hour or so later with the news an appointment had been set for seven o'clock. Kelly had arranged with his driver, Hector Papalia, and his butler, Fenton Barber, to stage a ruse to lose his police tail. Hector took Fenton, dressed as Kelly, in the Hudson sedan for a merry cruise. With the mechanic's coveralls over his suit, Kelly had slipped out the back gate and taken public transport.

"That's what I call fancy espionage," I told him.

He had got my trousers on and was closing the buckle on his belt, but he stopped to look at me. The suspicious squint of his eye told me he wondered if I was joking again. Air filled his lungs as he squared his shoulders, letting me know that he was beginning to reassemble his wits. All in all, it wasn't a half-bad play. A manly patch of brown curls bristled at the center of his chest as he flexed the muscles beneath them. "It was a farce. And when I got to Benz's office, three of Velasco's goons were already there. Benz claimed no one knew anything about a hold up. He made it sound like I was trying a frame. The conversation went downhill from there, and one of the men punched me in the stomach with something hard. I mean, harder than his fist." He touched the big bruise on his belly again.

I looked at the bruise and at the line of smaller curls that extended from the bottom of the aforementioned manly triangle, running down the center of his belly into the top of my trousers. I mean, my trousers he was wearing. I glanced back up at his face. "Where did all this happen?"

"At Benz's office in China Basin."

"How'd you end up down at the shipyards?"

"Like you said, I fought back. I tried. They knocked me cold, and when I came to, I was in a car. They told me they were taking me to Butchertown. I panicked and I—" He stopped and tossed me a quick embarrassed glance. Then he stared at the worn yellow carpet. "I threw up."

I laughed, not politely, and he glared at me.

"I suppose I had no business calling you a coward," he said. "I threw up on the lap of the guy next to me."

"Hell, it worked, didn't it? They pulled over, and that's when you managed to get away?"

"Something like that." He mustered enough nerve to show me a slight grin. "It sounds nearly heroic the way you tell it. Give me another cigarette."

I did. We'd already killed two apiece while he orated and dressed and paced back and forth in his bare feet. He'd also finished the Old Crow all by himself. Lighting that third cigarette, he tossed me a sidelong glance. "You brought a gun."

I imagine he'd noticed enough tell-tale signs as I drove and then sat listening to his story. As mentioned, the Colt's large and produces a sizeable bulge, but I peeled back my lapel to give him an honest peek.

He said, "We could go back there together."

"To that shyster's office? No offense."

"Why not? We could get the truth out of him."

"He's probably long gone. Besides, I'm a great coward, remember?"

He cussed at me in a way that I would not have expected him to know. Then he explained, "You know the reason I called you earlier this evening was to ask you to come with me. I shouldn't have said that in the car. Damn it, why can't we go back?"

"You're mixed up. You're dizzy from the booze and the blows to the head. Have a seat and let me explain things. I mean, the truth that you think you might get from Benz. Because I can pretty much assure you you already got the truth from him. He and Velasco probably have no idea about any holdup this afternoon in Marin."

He had sat down, but that brought him right back up onto his toes. "Are you calling Miranda a liar?"

I raised my hands, cowering just like I had for the bandits earlier, only letting him see by my face that it was a sham. "Don't start fighting with me. I'm a coward and I'm armed."

He called me another name and sat down again on the other bed, facing me.

I leaned back on my arms. "There was no holdup."

I paused and he waited, squinting at me. He took a drag, blew smoke and said, "Explain that."

"It was a set-up. At first I bought that the men were Velasco's. They came from the wrong direction and we were just a few miles from his joint, but none of that ruled it out. I figured maybe she had arranged a payment of some debt." Kelly clenched his fists into tight balls around the yellow coverlet on his bed, and I nodded to show him I sympathized. "She picked the spot we stopped at. It was obvious we were there by appointment. That's why I played along."

That right there, just to be open and honest for the record, was a lie. I mean that last line. I hadn't actually played along. While the pantomime unfolded, it occurred to me that maybe the reason I was there was so that I *would* try to stop it and possibly pay for my foolishness by taking a slug or three or four. But if Kelly had jumped up at my hinting his cousin might be a liar, I dreaded to think what he'd do if I let on that I suspected she'd tried to get me killed.

I sighed. "So the payment, or what I thought was a payment, went off without a hitch other than the fact that a stupid lug thought it might be nice to introduce his gun to the back of my head. And they drove off scot-free. But then halfway home, she told me that she'd recognized one of them."

I stopped to see if he followed, but he was still playing the skeptic. I spelled it out slowly. "If Velasco had been behind the holdup, why would she have told me?"

"Maybe she hoped you would confront him."

"Exactly. Like what you did. Only, if Velasco had been behind it, he wouldn't have been bothered by me calling him on it. He would have laughed at me." I took another breather, savoring my smoke and hoping he might tie up the loose threads himself. He showed no signs of any thread-tying whatsoever. I exhaled, disgusted. "But say, for instance, some hotheaded gumshoe comes to him accusing him of a crime he had no hand in, that could get a reaction. As you found out."

He sat mulling it over. His eyes were aimed off to my right, but swinging slowly around as if taking careful notice of every detail along their path. He pushed his lips against one another, pulling them in and out and side to side. The last cigarette I'd given him was smoldering on the bedspread; he'd nearly crushed it when his fingers had clenched into fists, and it had broken apart completely as he opened his hands again. I reached over to get it, not wanting to start a fire, when he suddenly lunged at me.

He knocked me back onto my sitter atop my bed. He went for the Colt, but I got my hands flat against his chest and shoved him off and he sat back down too. We both bounced up fast, and I beat him by seconds, but he came up swinging his fist at my head. I didn't much mind that. It would have required me to lean six inches forward and three more to the side to get my face anywhere near the path of it, but I caught his wrist and gave it a twist. Simultaneously I dealt him a swift solid short punch atop that manly patch of chest hair. It knocked the wind out of him and he gulped like a landed fish, making the same face and the same lame mouth movements you'd expect from a dying trout.

I twisted his arm some more, turning him around and bending his wrist up between his shoulder blades. He bowed over the bed, his face going down onto the rumpled coverlet. I planted my left knee in the small of his back and shifted a good portion of my weight to pin him down.

"What the hell was that about?"

He was still trying to get his breathing back on track. I'd hit him pretty hard, but it must have surprised him even more than it hurt him. Thinking I had a moment, I leaned down and crushed out his broken smoke under my thumb.

He tried to twist his arm free, but that proved impossible. When his voice came, it was a defeated croak. "Get off."

"Not 'til you explain to me what the hell just happened. People say I'm crazy. Hell, what were you thinking?"

He lay there another moment, not fighting me at all, staring at something off to our right. His breath came deep and loud, occasionally interrupted by a sort of strangled hiccup. Drool seeped out of his open mouth onto the yellow bedspread.

"Got hold of yourself?" I asked him.

He stared a bit more and then nodded as well as he could with the side of his face pressed against the bed.

I let him go but didn't sit down. I backed away around the foot of the bed I'd been sitting on, stretching the distance between us to at least eight feet. He didn't get up, but slid off his bed until his knees hit the carpet. His right arm unwound slowly to hang limp at his side.

"Well?"

He continued to lean against the mattress. "She didn't do it."

"Who didn't do what?"

He called me another name. I figured maybe he was having some sort of wartime flashback. I'd seen such things before. He told me, "Miranda didn't kill Ramona."

I cussed right back at him. "Who said she did? Not me. And why jump for my gun? The only thing that tells me is that you suspect she might have done it."

He sat back on his ankles and glared up at me. "You take that back."

I couldn't help but smirk at him. "Sure. Cause what you need right now is another beating. Look at you, you're about used up." I put my smirk away. "I know, its your job to protect them. It's what you've always done. But at some point you got to realize it may not be possible. They've sucked you dry. Maybe that's what they do to their attorneys—suck them dry. Hell, maybe that's what all rich folk do."

Turning his eyes down, he reached for the broken cigarette, lifting it delicately and wedging it between his lips. It was maybe the second saddest thing I'd ever seen, a grown man naked but for his borrowed trousers, kneeling beside that ugly yellow coverlet like a kid set to recite his bedtime prayers. The only thing that made it bearable was that the battered side of his face was turned away from me. And even in profile, I could still see him trying to suck on a crushed and cold cigarette.

I pulled out my pack and matches and threw them at him. They bounced off the side of his head and tumbled to the carpet. He looked down to see what they were and then went for them with the same slow, deliberate movements he'd been making.

"I tried to help you," I told him. And then, feeling the fury surge up again in my chest I took a step toward him like I was going to kick him. And I wanted to. Boy, did I. I held my leg cocked. "You went for my gun!"

Kelly didn't seem to notice. He got a fresh cigarette into his mouth and set to work on a match.

I lowered my foot to the floor. I watched him a bit longer, deciding he might have forgotten I was there. I sucked in some air through my nose. "I got you the room for the night." That didn't elicit any response, and I started for the door. As I was shutting it, I took a last look behind me. Kelly had settled on the floor, sitting back against the side of the bed. He was staring at something down by his feet and working methodically on doing away with my cigarettes.

CHAPTER EIGHTEEN

I went down and got in the Zephyr and drove. It felt like I drove for hours, but it was probably nearer fifteen minutes. Or maybe it felt like fifteen minutes but was actually hours. I made two stops: one early on, to resupply myself with cigarettes, matches and whiskey, splurging on a bottle of ten-year-old single malt from my good friend Jack Daniels, and a second on a quiet street in North Beach. Sitting there, I decimated the entire bottle of Jack. The problem with tossing the extra coin for the good stuff is that it goes down too easy.

Not that I didn't do other things to occupy my time. For instance, parked in North Beach, I engaged in a little game of spot the stakeout, trying to decide from among the other half dozen or so vehicles resting along the block which, if any, contained cops. I had narrowed it down to two, a Chrysler and a Ford, the former parked across the street and way down nearly at the corner, and the latter parked two cars back. Almost certainly the Chrysler had two figures hunched down in it.

Then, at about ten past twelve, the yellow Highlander cruised up and pulled into the driveway of a long low house set back on a lot across the street. My client got out and opened the garage door, steered the Highlander through, and closed and locked the door from the outside. He was in light-colored slacks and an open-collared shirt, with no jacket. A sack of what were probably groceries was in his arm. Going up the walk, he was sorting keys, and I couldn't make out his face, but I wondered if he'd got over his disappointment. Even if you have money to spare, it can't be easy to hear you've blown it on a disreputable private eye.

Just as he entered the house, another car came along past me, a black forty-two Olds that was in no hurry. A shiny Dodge I hadn't even suspected flashed its lights. The passing Olds flashed back and then sped off.

So not only did I lose the game of spot the cops, but I'd sat staking out an empty house. And all I had to show for it was an empty bottle of Jack. Deciding I was outclassed, I started the Zephyr and blew.

It seemed worthwhile to keep an eye on the mirrors since they may have noticed me sitting there and decided to investigate, but I didn't spot anything. Of course, that didn't mean they hadn't noticed and weren't interested; it might simply mean I really was outclassed or maybe just too damned drunk. Or both.

I got the Zephyr to my garage and tipped the night man a dollar to put her to bed. I walked back to my office and put the Colt and the holster into the safe. It occurred to me splashing cold water on my face might not hurt, except I'd paid a lot for that buzz, and it seemed a shame to waste it. Instead I went back down and out, made a sharp right turn, took two steps and stopped.

Neighbors tell me the Oriental Palace used to be called the Tokyo Palace, but then Pearl Harbor and Internment happened, and no one wanted to cop to being a Nip. Fortunately, for the actual Nips, most white folk can't tell one from a Chink or even certain Malaysians. So, the Oriental Palace remained in operation, same management and staff, servicing the non-stop stream of sailors that funneled through San Francisco on their way to get killed by kamikazes. Of course, they serviced marines who died on the islands as well, and probably some who actually made it back alive—but it was never those guys I thought about when I stepped through that plain wooden door under that buzzing neon sign.

The anteroom was tiny and painted sky blue, probably having taken its last coat back when the place was still called the Tokyo Palace. A dim light somewhere helped keep the room's secrets hidden and reminded the clientele to do the same. Making my way up a narrow lane between two surprisingly comfortable-looking sofas along either side wall, I reached a counter protected by thick glass. It being well after midnight, no one was stationed at the window, but there was a button over which someone had posted a hand-written sign explaining *Please Press Only Once.* I pushed it, heard a far off buzz, and let it go.

After a few moments, a curtain to one side of the counter was pushed aside and a woman moved into the protected space behind the glass. She was tall, in a cotton kimono with chopsticks shoved into the thick dark hair piled atop her head. "Good evening, welcome to the—" She saw it was me and dropped the B-movie accent. "Oh."

Sometimes I think one of the reasons I ever crawl into that hole is just so I can stand and let her look at me like that. It's a goddamned outrage. An unholy yellow Nip, with her dime-store geisha face paint and her ridiculous fake accent and her cheap plastic fingernails, snarling down at me like I was shit on her least favorite shoes. It made me want to put my fist through the wall. But, I suspect, sometimes its good to be reminded of one's place.

"Maybe tonight ain't a good night," she said.

I shrugged. "Well?"

She pressed a button on her side of the glass with one of her phony nails. I heard a quieter buzz in the door directly to my left. I pulled it open with a loud clank of the latch, stepped through into an even darker hall, and let it close behind me. The buzz died.

The dime store geisha came back through the curtain to join me in the hall. She was done looking at me and didn't even bother speaking. She started off and knew I'd probably be smart enough to follow. We went down, around a corner into a familiar room at the back.

She picked up a towel from a stack on some shelves in the corner and dropped it onto the padded massage table in the center of the room. I continued, apparently, not to exist for her, because she left without a glance or word. I undressed, draping my clothes haphazardly on the single chair, picked up the towel and tied that around my waist, then mounted the table and lay with my face wedged in the big hole at the end, staring at the dirty tile floor.

A while later, the door opened and closed again, and I heard someone moving around. Cabinet doors opened and closed; a match was lit and applied to an incense stick. The music, which sounded to me like a drunken halfwit plucking randomly at two strings, was turned up a notch. But nothing was said. It was the sort of establishment that made note of the peccadilloes of its regular clientele, and I had long since settled a preference for no talking.

Warm hands bathed in oil pressed firmly down just below my left shoulder blade. The hands were thin, with long, willowy fingers but plenty of muscle in the arms behind them. Another well-established preference was that I was no delicate flower and didn't want to be treated as such. Fingers dug into my flesh, pulling and stretching and squeezing.

Twenty minutes passed on my belly, then I was nudged gently over. I was relaxed enough by then that I managed to keep my eyes closed as the hands worked up my chest and out along each arm. They massaged my neck and my temples and the tight spots behind my ears.

Then came a pause filled with nothing but a few unhurried footsteps after which I felt the hands close around my right ankle. They worked slowly up the length of my legs, gliding back and forth from one limb to the other, sinking deeper into my muscles once they reached my thighs. A fingertip drew a slow circle around the spot I knew was the bruise Hector Papalia had been kind enough to give me. But otherwise that area was conscientiously avoided. The fingers dug their way down the interior of my thighs, flirting with the edge of my towel. I allowed my legs to be spread further apart. Simultaneously, I felt myself offering a silent request for more.

The knot in my towel was eased open and the flaps dropped to either side. One long hand slid all the way up between my thighs as the other moved over onto my belly and slipped softly down from there. Lips enveloped my flesh and a staggering sigh escaped my lungs. For several long minutes, me and that dirty Jap worked together toward a common goal, and I enjoyed the fact that my fellow soldiers had driven the bastards off the islands and shot them out of the air, and generally showed them what was what. It made me proud and angry and crazed. And it all seemed to find its center between my legs, there on that table in that dark room with the exotic incense assaulting my nostrils and that horrible distorted non-music accosting my ears, while a goddamned murdering Nip bent over me, bobbing its defeated black-haired head up and down.

And then everything stopped, and I wondered why. I hadn't finished. Lifting my head, I blinked into the glistering shadows.

"You okay, mister?"

He was the same handsome young man I sometimes saw out my window, working in the alley behind the parlor. Short, probably not quite twenty, skinny but well-muscled, with the same sharp angular features you saw in all those pathetic photographs of Jap soldiers during the war. Only he had been too young to fight, and he didn't have any trace of an accent. He might have been from anywhere around there—the Western Addition, Daly City, even Sacramento. The closest he'd ever been to Tokyo or Okinawa was looking at pictures of his grandparents in a scrap book.

My head went back, and the ceiling swam dreamily in my tears until I squeezed my eyes shut again. Jack was dying inside me, once again refusing to take me with him. I rubbed the moisture from the side of my face with the back of my hand, sick to my stomach at the display. I put my other hand on the back of the kid's neck and steered his mouth once more to its task. I lifted my hips, pushing down on him until I heard him grunt. I let go, but he didn't run away. He stuck with it, and so did I. My body melted away atop that table, dissolved to nothing but a ruined, weeping wreck, forcing myself to see it through to the end.

CHAPTER NINETEEN

Nothing woke me the next morning, so I slept until ten-thirty. Of course, the reason no one disturbed me is that they didn't know where the hell I was. Coming out of my stupor, it took me several minutes to suss it myself.

I'd made my way back to the room at the Lena Dorne. I could not immediately recollect it, but there I was, tangled up in sheets and a yellow blanket atop the bed closest to the door. The other bed was undisturbed, except for the slight tousling that had happened when I'd knelt on George Kelly's back. I jerked my head up for a quick survey of the premises, half afraid he might still be there, possibly beaten to a pulp in the corner, but then decided my mood the previous evening had been such that I'd have happily consented to letting him beat *me* to a bloody pulp. Either way, I was alone, and the more wakeful I got, the more I seemed to remember finding the room abandoned when I staggered back there.

I got up and availed myself of the amenities, such as they were, including the shower. Then I climbed back into my slightly sour suit from the previous day and examined my form in the mirror. I was looking as used up as George Kelly must have felt. Mostly I needed a shave, but that would require tools just then unattainable. I looked down at the available supplies, saw an empty bottle of Old Crow, two glasses and two room keys—Kelly's and the spare I'd clearly gone down for when no one had answered my knock the night before. The only thing of even proximate utility was one of the glasses which appeared to have a few drops of the Old Crow drying down at the bottom, but I decided trying to drink that at eleven o'clock in the morning would be even sadder than sitting half-naked trying to smoke a broken cigarette in the middle of the night.

I needed to say goodbye to the Lena Dorne, that was the main thing. Part of me thought I ought to burn the place down, but there was no telling where and how fast the fire might spread, so I denied myself that pleasure. I went down and out the back, through the alley and up to the third floor of the Rooker Building.

I stepped out of the elevator and headed down the hall, pausing because a young, husky man in a police uniform hovered outside my door. He looked at me and I at him as I closed the distance between us. I guessed he was probably older than twenty seeing as he was employed by the cops, but not much. He stood perhaps six-six, and weighed close to an eighth of a ton. His fresh beardless face was big and round, with a knot of tiny features in the center of it: a small, cupie-doll mouth, a tiny snub nose, two beady eyes so close together if I'd known him as a kid I would have dubbed him Polyphemus. Of course, he never would have got the reference.

Once again, my stopping before the door stenciled *Declan Colette, Private Investigations*, struck him as telling, as did my digging out a key. He sidestepped to stand directly in front of the door and twisted his little features into a look of surprise.

"Are you Declan Colette?"

I confessed, actually using that word.

"Not to me you don't." He reached out an enormous meathook and settled it on my left shoulder. "I'm here to take you to Inspector Ackerman. Come along."

I glanced down at his hand then up at his head. In addition to a Cyclops, he had the look of one of those boys who is an expert at following instructions. I asked him if I couldn't go in and change my shirt, maybe grab a quick shave. I offered as an excuse that I had been up all night on a stake-out.

"You look fine to me," he said. "And the inspector's been waiting. Let's go." He actually turned me that time, and I had about as much chance of resisting as the ant has of moving that rubber tree plant.

"How about you let me answer my phone?" It was ringing loud enough for us both to hear, but just in case his tiny ears weren't up to the task, I pointed out, "It's ringing."

We were walking by then, and he kept us at a fair pace. "It ain't been doing nothing but the last hour. Maybe you ought to hire a receptionist."

Once we were in the elevator, he let go of my shoulder and pushed the button. As he stood watching the floor display count down, I straightened my jacket and frowned up at him. I was in a mood to hit things again, rather than be hit, but he was still a cop, and, besides, I would have had to hit him three times just to get his attention. Also, he probably hadn't come on his own which meant when we reached the lobby he would have reinforcements, and I decided it would look more dignified to exit under my own steam.

Out on the sidewalk, my escort led me north past both the Oriental Palace and the Lena Dorne, toward another uniformed fellow enjoying the sun as he leaned on a patrol car. This second cop was older, about half the mass of the first and a born skeptic. He studied me as we approached, idly scratching the side of his big honk, then croaked, "Where'd you get this guy?"

"This is the guy," Poly told him.

"Oh, yeah? I didn't see him go in."

Poly made a noise like that proved something, waited while his partner stepped aside, then helped me into the back of the patrol car. He hadn't cuffed me, but was just polite and well-trained, rather like his namesake who had kindly invited Odysseus and his men into the cave for supper.

When the cops were settled in the front seat, Poly, on the passenger side, pointed a finger at his partner's cigarette. "Nah-uh."

Partner, who had probably twenty years on Poly and had made very little progress on his cigarette, offered a noise of his own but rolled down his window and tossed the smoke into the street. He then ignited the engine and steered us into traffic. Once we were well underway, he tossed me a glance in the rearview mirror.

"So, was he up there this whole time? Ackerman ain't gonna like that."

Poly had pulled from his breast pocket a notepad and pencil, both so small they looked like toys in his huge hands, and was utilizing the latter to make notations in the former. "He come off the elevator." He checked his watch and made another notation.

"Well, he didn't go in the front." Partner glanced over at the notepad and pencil. "What the hell? I tell you, Stuey, you'll make detective when the old man says so. You ain't doing yourself no favors acting like such a fussbudget."

Poly, or Stuey if I stick to facts, was reading over his notes with the tip of his pencil touching his tongue. He said, "Suspect came off elevator at eleven-thirteen. Confessed to being one Declan Colette. Placed in vehicle for transport at eleven-twenty-one."

"'Cept he ain't a suspect, is he? He's wanted for questioning. And what do you mean he confessed? Confessed to being *what*?"

Stuey crossed out a word, then scribbled something else. "Thanks, Dan," he said, "you're right. He's not a suspect." He kept studying his notes. "When I asked him if he was Colette, he told me he confessed he was. I figure he was attempting levity."

That nearly had me choking I was fighting so hard not to laugh.

Partner, or Dan, was not amused. "You figure, do you?" He shook his head. "Damn, it's hot. So, where were you, buddy? Hiding out on another floor?" He looked at me in the mirror again.

These two had the makings of quite the comedy routine, which is why I had remained so uncharacteristically mute up until then, but I said, "I came down from the roof. I flew in on wax wings, Icarus-like, only, as you say, it's damned hot."

"What is that? More levity?" Dan remained unamused. His window still down, he spat into the street, then sat scowling over the steering wheel as we rode alone in silence.

It was indeed hot. And my keepers hadn't seen fit to lower either of the rear windows. I sat back and loosened my tie, admiring the view and trying to figure a destination. We weren't headed toward the Hall of Justice. We'd gone north on Pierce but quickly turned east and then south. We dropped below Market and eventually wound up headed southeast on Sixth. I couldn't suss it and dug my smokes out of my pocket.

"Not unless you're wanting a sermon," Dan told me, watching from the mirror again. He tossed his head in the general direction of the big guy next to him. "This one don't abide such low behavior."

Stuey, having put away his junior detective tools, sat with his arm resting comfortably out the window. He didn't turn or otherwise acknowledge either Dan or myself, but said, "Do what you want outside. No smoking in the car."

By that time, I had a butt between my teeth and matches in my hand. I cussed, not loudly, but Dan shook his head.

"And watch your language, son."

I put the matches away but left the cigarette bouncing in my mouth as I spoke. "What, are you two some sort of new junior vice men?"

"It ain't me," Dan said, adding, "Balls," just to prove it.

Stuey shook his big head slowly, a prim pucker on his lips, pretending to enjoy the passing scenery.

I addressed the short, bristly hairs on the back of his neck. "What is it son, religion? Or do you still live with your momma and worry what you might have to tell her when she asks about your day?"

That got me nothing from Stuey, but Dan was finally smiling. He told me, "You can't rile him. Don't waste your time."

"Fine. Balls yourself." I tried to sound disgusted. The unlighted cigarette continued to dance on my lips. I decided to leave it there just to spite them. "Where are you taking me anyhow? I been damned agreeable up 'til now, never asked for papers nor nothing, but that's gonna change quick if I ain't even allowed to smoke."

Dan was still grinning; I'd definitely brightened his day. "Almost there. You can stand him another few minutes. I got him all day."

I muttered my response to myself, mainly because I didn't have one but wanted them to think I did. We were moving south alongside the bay, the cool air finally billowing through Dan's window and waking me up. The sweat that had beaded on my forehead began to dry up, and I dabbed at it with my tie.

South of the basin, we turned into an open lot overrun by city agents. Another uniform waved us in, but we parked almost immediately and Stuey climbed out and opened a door for me. I joined him on the packed dirt and did a quick scan, finding a fair mix of flatfoots, dicks, and scientists working over what appeared to be nothing more than a waste of waterfront real estate at first glance, but clearly was a scene. Stuey found something specific he wanted and took hold of my upper arm to guide me toward it.

About twenty feet along, another fellow ran up beside us, following with a grim, excited expression. It was Gig Barton, my reporter friend I'd supplied the clams to in exchange for dope on the O'Malley clan. He had a notepad and a pen ready to take down my statement. "Ah, Colette, why did you do it? Was it on account of the money? Or a crime of passion?"

Stuey might not even have noticed Gig, but I gave up a small appreciative grin. We kept walking east across the lot, toward the water's edge. That took us through a line of official vehicles onto more open ground, and I saw a single car parked very near the bay, a Ford sedan. Gig was held back at the line of cars, and I told Stuey, "You should have let me answer that guy. If he prints that, its libel. I'll sue."

Stuey wasn't biting, of course. Dan's assessment of his partner's susceptibility to being riled was proving damned solid. He was focused on our destination, a weary looking man in a gray suit discussing something serious with another fellow in a lab coat. They stood a few feet back of the Ford's rear fender, while activity went on all around them. Clearly, the car was the focal point. The front passenger door was open, and a handful of men seemed to be taking turns climbing in and out.

The weary guy was Inspector Ackerman, who stood holding his chin contemplatively, mainly listening. His hat hung way back on his head, allowing the sun to glint angrily off his high forehead. He saw us coming with about three yards remaining and said something to dismiss the lab rat before stepping up to meet us.

"Declan Colette," Stuey said, pulling back his shoulders.

Ackerman didn't speak. He looked me straight in the eye, leaning forward very slightly like he was trying to push me over with his stare. It didn't mean anything, of course, and certainly didn't rattle me. It was just a little ploy he'd picked up somewhere along the line, probably in an old book on interrogation tactics. I'd been questioned by him enough that I was not only used to it, but expected it.

"Where did you find him?"

The big copper released me and fumbled to get out his notepad. "He showed up at his office, sir. If you'll give me…" He paused to flip a few pages through his book. "Yes. Target arrived at his office at—"

Ackerman interrupted with a dismissive wave. "Never mind all that. The point is you brought him. Thanks, Stewart."

That was like Ackerman, to know a uniform's name and manage to brush him off without being completely dismissive of his efforts. It probably accounted for the fact that he was so highly regarded among the rank and file. That and the fact that he was good at his job. Myself, I had mixed feelings. He was a cop and wore his rather glum disposition like it went with his badge, but he knew his way around a murder. And wasn't above thanking you when he thought you'd helped him out.

Once Stuey was on his way, Ackerman frowned at my cigarette. "You need a light?"

I'd nearly forgotten the thing was there. The butt was not much better than mush, and I tossed it aside, digging out my pack for another.

"Damn it, Colette, this is a crime scene." Ackerman bent over to retrieve the discarded cigarette. He stood back up, looking around for some place to put it and then handed it toward me.

I took it, slipped it into my hip pocket and grinned around the new smoke in my mouth. "Sorry, Inspector, your boys caught me before I got any coffee."

"Where have you been all night?"

I went right on grinning, and hoisted my eyebrows too. "That's a question. Right here on a crime scene. What am I accused of?"

He glanced sharply back at me, squinting. We were nearly the same height, with him topping me slightly, though he was quite a bit thinner and a few years older. But not as old nor thin nor tall as his subordinate, my good friend Lieutenant Dent. Neither was he as unreasonable as Dent, though mainly because he had seen my work on the Hopkins and Fletcher murders as aiding in the furtherance of justice. Which, of course, it had. Dent had just seen my meddling as an humiliating exposure of his own lack of talent, which it also was. It helped that Ackerman's father had come up through the Pinkertons alongside Walter Cobb, and I'd worked both Hopkins and Fletcher under Cobb. I knew for a fact that Ackerman and Cobb had consulted surreptitiously on a few other cases as well.

The inspector told me, "You aren't accused of anything. But we've been trying to reach you since three a.m., and you've been unavailable at home or your office."

"Nevertheless, until you give me a compelling reason, my whereabouts and activities are my own business."

He shook his head at me. "Tell me about what happened yesterday at the O'Malley place."

I looked around at the faces of the men working. "Where is the old dog?"

Ackerman flinched, a real violent jerk that went right through his entire body, and I swear to God, I think his impulse had been to sock me. Color spread up his cheeks, and his eyes bulged slightly. Only his better nature spared us both. "I'm referring to the incident with Hector Papalia."

"Me too." I made a show of knitting up my brow. "What did you think I was referring to? Again, I'm reluctant to overburden you with useless facts. Perhaps if I knew why I've been dragged down here."

I tried to make that last part sound nonchalant, but Ackerman reached out anyway, taking hold of the same half of upper arm Stewart had used to lead me around. We relocated about ten feet further back from the Ford's bumper, and he leaned in toward me, saying, in a harsh whisper, "Why are you being such a pain? I don't give a damn about any feud between you and Dent. I'm questioning you about an open murder case that I believe you may have information regarding." He took a breath, rocking back on his heels for a quick look around to see if we had garnered anyone's particular attention. "You want to know why you're here? Fine, have a look."

He started back toward the Ford and gestured for me to follow with a wave of his hand. We moved over near the open passenger side door, not too close, and Ackerman instructed a lab rat to get out of the way. That offered us an unobstructed view of the entire front bench, which was lightly spattered with blood. The driver's window was more heavily coated in blood and various other bits. The most noticeable thing, however, was where the blood was not: a roughly human outline behind the steering wheel.

I peeked in, noted all that I've described, stood up, took a drag, exhaled, and squinted at the inspector. "Who was it?"

He was watching me, a very displeased frown stretching both ends of his mouth halfway down his chin. "Hector Papalia."

My lower lip went out, and I nodded like, of course, that made perfect sense. Of course, it made very little sense, but why should Ackerman know how dim I was?

The inspector put his hand on my arm again, not taking hold, but applying just enough pressure to indicate we should step further back. "Now. Tell me about your run-in with Papalia yesterday."

I took a moment to look it over, realized my lip was still sticking out, sucked it in and took another drag on my cigarette. "What do you think happened here?"

He folded his arms, planting his feet wide enough apart to let me know he was intractable, and stood there breathing through his nose. With Dent, I would have taken it as a dare, but Ackerman outranked the lieutenant in several ways.

"I went in to question the kid but got absolutely nowhere. He had some vague notion of getting physical, and when that went south, he started squawking. Then your boys broke it up."

His frown faded, and one corner of his mouth even hinted it might be coaxed into an upward slant. "You think I'm an idiot. What did you want to question Papalia about?"

I answered without much hemming or hawing, as that's usually the best way. "I was questioning anyone I could." I shrugged to show him how pathetically a lone PI compared to a legion of cops.

He flared his nostrils. "Tell me what was said. Both of you. Every word."

I shrugged, more naturally that time, adding a cavalier toss of my head. "I didn't take notes. But if you ask questions, specific as to what you're after, it might could help my memory."

He arched a brow at me, not an altogether uncomely affectation considering he was otherwise rather plain. "You're not working for Cobb on this one. Chances are you're out of your depth. And you went driving with Mrs. O'Malley yesterday and shook her tail. Did you get yourself in a fix? These types are way above you—me too. Spill it to me now. Better yet, you and me, we'll go see Walter and the three of us can straighten things out together. I don't expect you to trust me, but you trust Walter, right?"

He overplayed it calling Cobb *Walter* like that. I never referred to the old man as anything but Mr. Cobb. And did I trust the cagey snoop? He'd sent his lady-killer to warn me off, not merely a cheap move but also insulting. So, no. Despite the square deals we'd run in the past, Cobb was not topping my list of trusted consultants.

Ackerman took a final stab. "You've never had a homicide all to yourself."

Finished with my cigarette, I glanced around for a place to toss it, remembered we were in the midst of a crime scene, and lifted my left foot to crush the nub out on the sole of my shoe. That required me to stoop slightly, and I looked up at Ackerman with a whipped expression on my face. "I'll answer any question you want to ask, Inspector."

He took a breath as his expression hardened. "You certainly will."

He saw a plainclothesman waiting for a word, called to another uniform to locate Stewart and bring him back, told someone else he wanted an update from the scientists, asked another plainclothes to locate ADA Holloway, all of which resulted in a flurry of activity that ended up with me returned to the back seat of a patrol car while the unrileable giant, Stuey, sat in the front, reading a detective manual. I asked him if I couldn't even roll down my window and lean out with a cigarette. He told me no.

Though it hadn't been explicitly stated, I figured the idea was that I'd be taken down to the Hall of Justice and grilled. Only as soon as I got there, the clock would start ticking on such annoying details as my rights as an American citizen, so they were in no hurry, and I could wait for Ackerman to finish up with his crime scene. I still hadn't had breakfast or even a coffee, so sitting in a hot car with the windows rolled up and a pack of cigarettes singing its siren song from my breast pocket did not appeal to me. I took a few half-hearted jabs at Stuey, telling him how wrong I thought Ackerman had been to dismiss him before hearing the exciting details of my capture, but other than that one word answer to my suggestion about rolling down my window, he ignored me.

After ten minutes or so of one-sided conversation punctuated by various bouts of desperate silence, the golem's partner Dan came over to the open passenger side window. "Time for a break," he said.

Stuey looked up and out. "Huh?"

"Yeah, kid. It's union rules, you know that. Go have a—well, get some coffee."

"You know I don't drink coffee."

"Sure. But you need to get up and stretch your legs or something. The point is you can't stay here on duty. You have to take a break."

"The inspector told me to stay with the prisoner."

Dan leaned down to glance disparagingly at me through the window. "He's a prisoner now? Jeez, some guys." He stood back up. "Well, I'll keep an eye on him. You run along. Garabaldi found some footprints over yonder and was fixing to make a mold. Bet you'd enjoy seeing that."

Dan did indeed know his partner well. The young man tossed his manual up onto the dashboard and climbed out. "You'll keep here, Dan?"

"Didn't I say so?" But he didn't climb into the car. He pushed the door closed and leaned his back against it as the big kid took off across the lot. A moment later, the rear door across from me right beside Dan opened up, allowing Gig Barton to slide onto the bench next to me.

"Yeah?" I made no bones about my level of skepticism. "How much did that cost you?"

Gig grinned, pushing his cheaters up along the sharp ridge of his nose. "Dan's okay. Aren't you Dan?"

"I ain't listening," Dan told us, showing nothing but his back.

"Good man. Why don't you go not listen around the front, where you also won't hear?"

The old copper muttered an entire string of words his partner wouldn't condone, but stood up straight and shook himself. "You got ten minutes." He strode casually over to stand with a shoe on the front fender.

Sighing, Gig slid down in his seat. He looked mighty pleased with himself. He folded up his long legs, pressing his knees into the upholstery of the front seat grinning like the Cheshire Cat. "So spill."

"Spill what?" I was myself mildly pleased he'd wormed his way in to see me, and felt more than willing to pump him for any info he might have. But I made sure nothing but disgust showed on my phiz. You need to play these angles right.

"What first put you on to Papalia?"

"What makes you think I had any interest in Papalia?"

Gig looked incredulous. "You went there yesterday and started to rough him up and twelve hours later, he comes to the very spot he dumped the body and blows his brains out. I think—"

Any pretense I might have wanted to make as to my level of disgust was blown apart by real disgust. I cussed loudly and leaned forward over the seat toward the open window. "Dan!"

"Wait a minute," Gig said, confused and pulling at my jacket.

Dan came running back around the car. "For God's sake, keep it down! What's the matter?"

"Open the door," I told him. "We're done. We're getting out. I need to talk to Ackerman."

By then, Dan had leapt over and jerked the rear door open. I hustled out Gig, who continued to sputter and object, probably on account of the dough he'd squandered bribing his way in to the car. As I unfolded out onto the packed dirt, Dan goggled at me. "Where do you think you're going?"

"I told you," I said, getting a cigarette to my lips. "I need to speak to Ackerman. Take me there. Now. There could be a promotion in it."

Gig glared at me. "You are a..." What followed was a string of colorful adjectives that went on so long, Dan and I were out of earshot before Gig ever got to the noun.

As we passed through the line of official vehicles, I lengthened my stride, leaving Dan behind. Ackerman turned at my approach, and I asked him, "Why didn't you say he'd killed himself?"

He smirked. "It's not my job to tell you anything. Have you decided to talk?"

"Your assumption being that something I said yesterday led him to it?"

"I said talk, not ask me more questions."

I reached his side. He was nearly where I'd left him, and that meant I could see in through the open passenger door of the Ford. I asked him if I could poke my head in, and he told me okay as long as I remembered not to touch anything. I stepped over to the car, probably a model from the middle of the last decade, and stopped with my shins an inch or so from the running board. I put my head in but saw very little there in the way of clues, so I backed out just as carefully and returned to Ackerman.

"So you never suspected me at all. You just thought you'd play hard?"

"It troubles me that you were incognito for the better part of twelve hours. But, yeah, this looks like a real suicide, if that's what you mean. His .22 was in his hand and one shot was still in his skull, hence, the side window was still intact. His temple showed the barrel was close enough."

"No note?"

He narrowed his eyes. "Tell me what was said yesterday, Colette."

I complied, a near verbatim account of the dialogue in the small room next to the car sheds. As a bonus, I added a vague reference to how Mrs. O'Malley's maid had steered me toward Papalia. As a buffer, I held back the possibly misleading lie I'd told about actually having met Ramona Wyman in the flesh. "So, the conclusion is that he offed himself out of remorse?"

"Or fear of justice."

"Yeah, you say that with a straight face."

"Why not? It ties everything up, doesn't it? He was involved with the girl, and you can draw your own conclusions as to how far. Maybe she wasn't keen on going further, and he snapped. Then you come after him, and he decides the gig is up. That he comes here to do it says remorse more than fear to me. My oceanographer says this could very well be the spot he put her in the water."

A few things bothered me. "Who's car is this? Not one of the O'Malley's."

"No, it's his mother's car. He went there and back-doored his tail. She confirms he was agitated and seemed to be telling her goodbye."

"No signs of violence. I mean, other than the obvious."

"Sure. Someone banged his head. Right here." Ackerman touched the middle of his forehead, then shook his head at me. "Nothing else."

It was my turn to squint at him, and I did, gazing around the thin pillar of smoke leaking from my cigarette. "But you've got more. You like it too much."

He nearly grinned, but then remembered who and what I was. "Maybe Cobb is right about you."

That deserved no response and got it. Ackerman paused a moment, waiting, then said, "He had her purse in the car."

"Sure he did."

He squashed any hint of a grin. "The other thing Walter tells me is you never want to buy any story no matter how good it looks. Well, my ears are dry at the back. We'll go over everything thoroughly. But it might interest you to know that the lipstick you were so keen on was in the purse."

I shrugged. "It interests me more that if anyone had been in the car with him, say pointing the gun at his head and pulling the trigger, they would have got blood on them."

"Yes, there's that. And my guys say there isn't anything to show he wasn't alone."

"People today. The way you talk. So many negatives." I looked back over toward the city. "I don't suppose I need a lift back uptown. I can easily walk to, say, Third and Oakdale and catch a cab from there." It would be quite a walk, but hardly impossible, even after arranging to have yourself roughed up.

Ackerman was scrutinizing me. After all, he was not only dry behind the ears but a second generation snoop. He knew I was saying something. "You have anything to add?"

"No, sir," I told him. "Except for damn, I guess my job is done and I was set to pull in fifty smackeroos a day."

"Sorry about that." He let me know he was lying.

A breeze rolled in off the water. I puffed a couple more times on my smoke. We stood there, fully aware of one another yet unwilling to acknowledge the fact. We just gazed contemplatively into that blood-spattered front seat.

"Can I go?"

He didn't answer. He looked away, stepping back to join in with the other activity. He neither thanked me for my candor nor apologized for delaying my breakfast. He simply forgot me, which gratified me plenty, and I walked away.

CHAPTER TWENTY

I went home to shower, shave, and change my socks. It took about twenty minutes at my apartment, and the telephone spent at least half that time ringing. I ignored it. Collecting three new shirts, a pair of pants, and one of each piece of undergarment, I took a cab back to the office to listen to more non-stop telephone ringing while I restocked the bottom drawer of my file cabinet. I then walked to the garage and got out the Zephyr for the second time in two days, putting me well above my weekly average. With all the street cars and the parking hassles, it makes no sense to cruise around in the city.

But I was headed out. I needed to clear my head, and one of the ways I do that is to drive. The Zephyr isn't a convertible, but I rolled down the front windows on both sides, and once I hit the highway, I may as well have been back in Miranda O'Malley's topless coupe. The wind slammed my face, then ripped around the backseat until more air screaming along behind it forced it back out the open windows. My hair danced in the vortex.

I grabbed some lunch at a small spot I knew of in Pacifica, then proceeded down toward Half Moon Bay, riding the Devil's Slide, as they say. The coast is dotted along there with quiet, secluded little stretches of beach. It being a lovely day in August, both sides of the Slide were cluttered with haphazardly perched automobiles. At Pillar Point, I added the Zephyr to the mix and got out. I had replaced the Old Crow in the glovebox during my restocking chores, but didn't bring it along. The fellow who had introduced me to the Point a few years back had laid down a law that drinking wasn't to be allowed there. He had offered up some sort of hogwash reasoning for the rule, something about the Ohlone Indians and natural sanctity and maybe even the fact that he thought I drank too much, which I had scoffed at even at the time. I continue to conform. In fact, I consider the rule all the more inviolable now for the fact that he can no longer enforce it.

It's a bit of a hike from the roadside to the Point, through some winding trails around the base of a small hill. But on the ocean side of the hill, another secluded beach reaches north, looking out on some jagged rocks. The same guy who introduced me to the place also remarked that over the last two hundred years several ships had sunk in those waters, which is probably what kept me coming back, why I sat high up on the beach, huddled against the base of that hill, scowling out over the dark water toward Iwo Jima.

Part of the beauty of the long hike is it keeps most of the daytrippers somewhere else. The families with kids usually end up at the bay just south. But after only about a quarter of an hour, a young couple did stroll by. Not anywhere near me, they were barefoot and letting the waves tickle their toes, hand in hand and happy as drunken larks. I watched them a while, wondering certain inconsequential things such as had he asked her to marry him and why and had she said yes and why not? I also sized the fellow up as I am wont to do, deciding that even though he was a good ten years my junior, I could probably take him without working up a lather. A headshrinker once told me I judged pretty much every man I laid eyes on in those terms, mostly on account of my insecure ego's need to overcompensate. To that I say, Tsk.

Watching those two walk by, asking myself those questions which I'd never know the answers to, I began to consider, not for the first time, why I didn't just find a gal and marry. I could, of course. I like women fine and can talk to them better than most guys who enjoy their company in ways I can hardly contemplate. And, as I discovered once with a whore down in New Orleans, I can execute certain mechanics of male-female interactions when I set my mind to the task.

Of course, what kept me single was the fact that I knew I would never love my wife the way a woman I'd want to marry would deserve to be loved. Oh, I could love her and probably would even more once we started having little ones, but I've been in love once and know what it felt like. I'll never feel that for any woman.

But the fact is marriage would solve so many problems, also not a conclusion originating on the beach that day. Tying myself to a gal, bringing a passel of kids into the world together and devoting myself to taking care of them all would spare me the annoying distractions life kept tempting me with. Sure it was selfish, but once I was married…

And right there is when I answered a question that had been nagging me since the start of the whole O'Malley mess.

I arose, brushing the sand from my sitter, and stalked back to my car. Reaching the city, I found a telephone and placed a call to the home of Jasper Reed. A very punctilious gentleman explained that Mr. Reed was indisposed. I expressed a desire to stop by for a visit and was further informed that Mr. Reed was not seeing anyone. I said, well here I come, ready or not.

Where I came to was a tall, somber battleship gray Victorian at the end of one of those cul de sacs that twist into certain blocks up atop the hill in Pacific Heights. It was skirted by a trim and austere yard, with a small drive running down the left side of the building to disappear into the back. I found the Zephyr a berth at the mouth of the cul de sac and strolled casually toward the house, wondering if my warning had served its purpose and whether or not someone was watching out for me. No one appeared. On further reflection, I decided that would have made it all too easy anyhow, so I climbed up onto the porch and cranked the buzzer.

The door opened almost instantly, which encouraged me, revealing a middle-aged butler in a worn uniform, and behind his shoulder, Wayne Holmsby, whose livery had been swapped in favor of a cheap brown suit that doubtless had been quite snappy back before the repeal of Volstead. The butler, looking rather appalled to find me there, asked, "Yes?"

Before I could answer, Holmsby put a fat hand on the man's shoulder, told him, "I'll handle this, Jackson," and stepped out onto the porch pulling the door behind him.

Having seen the chauffeur excited, I had already stepped one foot back off the porch. I brought the other down as well. That served two purposes. First, it put about two yards of buffer between us, which his short arms would never have stretched if he got it into his head to start slapping things, and second, since the porch was elevated about eight inches, it allowed him to angle his gaze down at me, supplying him an extra boost of confidence I knew could only bolster my cause.

"You got some nerve."

"Have I? You wanted a word with me day before yesterday, and I acquiesced even though we'd never been introduced. Now I want a word with you."

I've always speculated that you can tell exactly how someone feels about surprises by what they do with their eyes. For instance, a person getting a surprise birthday party tends to open their eyes wide. A person getting a surprise visit from the BIR tends to narrow their lids to slits, possibly in hopes of shielding themselves from the pain. So, even though what Holmsby said was, "With me?" in a gruff tone designed to indicate what a ridiculous suggestion I'd offered, his eyes widened, and I knew I was in like Flynn.

"In private."

"What could we have to talk about in private?"

I shrugged, feeling rather smug but acting nonchalant. "Let's go somewhere and find out."

He expanded his chest, pushing back his shoulders and elevating his chin. "You think you can take me?"

Having glanced casually off at the lawn, I swung my gaze back around and gave him a quick survey from toes to top. "I know I can take you. I also suspect you could make me earn it. But I said I wanted a word, that's all. In private. You ever tried Pete's Place, down on Broadway? I'll buy you a drink."

He returned my look, doubled, seemed to linger on my shoulders and hands, then smirked down at me. "I got a private place in back."

"Swell."

He looked a moment longer, then repeated "Swell," not in any way trying to mock me, but like it really might be swell, once he figured out where to stash my corpse.

We went around the side of house to a gate that let us into a garden about five feet wide, and most of that taken up by a concrete pathway. We followed it the length of the house, beyond a small, wild backyard to the old carriage house on the alley. It was a one story structure converted to a single car garage and a quaint little cottage painted some years earlier in sky blue with white trim. Flowerbeds filled with Martha Washingtons adorned either side of the door we entered through.

The room was medium-sized and dark. The only light came from our right as we entered, through an archway that opened onto a kitchenette. The wall facing us had a single closed door which I later surmised led to the bedroom and toilet, and the wall on our left had a door that must have accessed the garage. The main central room had no windows except a small one beside the front door, but it was clearly set up as a parlor, with a comfy old sofa and a large easy chair facing off with each other but also turned to allow any occupants access to a battered Crosley standing against the wall.

I had stopped just a pace or so through the door, but Holmsby went a few steps further, removing his jacket and laying it neatly over the back on the easy chair. He faced me with another grin twisting his homely mug.

"Now. Tell me about how you think you can take me."

Stepping around him toward the center of the room, I admired the place, glancing appreciatively into the tiny kitchen and noting the comfortable furniture. "This *is* swell." I dug into my breast pocket. "Mind if I smoke?"

He shook his head, dismissing me rather than granting permission. Then, while I supplied myself with a Camel, he went to the sideboard and retrieved a fat brown cigar from a silk-lined wooden box. He came back toward me, snarling as he bit the end off the torpedo and spat it into a cuspidor next to the easy chair. I was lighting my own smoke by that time, but just as I made a move to offer fire across to him, he used his own lighter.

It required some heavy tugging to get that brown beast glowing. The old guy popped his lips open and shut, spewing ragged clouds of sweet-smelling smoke, while I stood watching him with my pale little Camel dangling from my own mouth, trying not to laugh. Once he had a sufficient burn, he pocketed his lighter, hooked his thumbs into the eyes at the bottom of his vest, pulled back his head, and grinned at me. Clenched between his teeth, the cigar jutted up at a proud angle. His eyes sparkled. His face glowed like he was three inches taller than me rather than four inches shorter. Freud would have lapped it up.

Since applauding struck me as cheap, I rewarded that performance by making a show of clearing my throat and lowering my chin, gazing timidly up at him from beneath a lowered brow.

"So talk," he said.

"Actually, my throat's a little dry. You got a beverage?"

That threw him off his game and he lowered his brow too. He squinted at me as if suspecting an angle. "What's your name again?"

"I'm Declan Colette. You're Wayne Holmsby, Sergeant—"

He cut me off with a flick of his round head. "That's right. And where were you? I don't recollect you saying."

"I didn't. Other than admitting to being a fellow enlisted man."

He used his hand to roll the cigar over and over between his lips. Judging by his eyes, I figured he had nearly discarded the notion I was pushing an angle, but he remained confused regarding my actual intent. "You're a cop now."

"You insult me. You know I'm not. I'm a shamus. Not *the*. A private eye working on the Wyman murder."

"For who?"

"Does it matter?" I asked that on the level but could see immediately it wouldn't fly. "Fine. I was hired by her cousin, Morgan O'Malley."

"The fairy?"

"Is that an accusation? You hinted the other day that Mrs. O'Malley's mechanic might be a fruit, but other folks tell me he chases skirt."

Holmsby looked away for the first time, glancing quickly toward the door then more languidly over at something near the sofa. "What do I know? I ain't never seen them acting queer."

"No, but I hear your boss helped Morgan out of a scrape back before the war."

That brought his eyes swinging back around to glare at me. "You leave the colonel out of this."

"No can do, Sarge." I made a show of not backing down, though I tried to let him see I wasn't happy about it. "In fact—"

"In fact, nothing." His big round body, already straining against the confines of that suit, seemed to swell up even more. "It looks like we're gonna have trouble."

I made a face. "Oh, don't get your dander up." Gesturing around, I told him, "The best we could do in here is break some furniture. You know, you haven't asked me to sit down."

"So sit." He growled that in a way most guides to etiquette would probably disdain, but I strolled over toward the sofa as if I'd been invited to do so by Emily Post herself. Holmsby asked my back, "You like beer?"

"Boy, do I." I settled myself on the sofa as he went through the arch into the kitchenette. I heard the sounds of an icebox being opened, beer bottles being uncapped, glasses tinkling. I reclined with an arm along the back of the sofa and my right ankle hoisted over my left knee. "This is a swell place. Sure beats the digs the O'Malleys put that monkey boy in over at the castle."

He came back bearing two bottles, two glasses, and a scowl. No tray, which I supposed meant he really didn't read Emily Post. "You know, you're a joker. Only you ain't funny. 'Cept your face."

I grinned around my Camel. "From now on, I'll leave the comedy to you."

He poured for both of us, emptying about half of each bottle into its own glass. The way he angled the glasses and measured the heads bespoke a certain level of expertise, as did his mottled crimson nose. Handing me one glass, he took the other and settled in the easy chair. He maintained his unfriendly expression, eyeing me like he anticipated some complaint about the beer.

I wet my lips, enjoyed the caress of the foam on my upper lip, then swallowed a very healthy sample. I sat back and recrossed my legs with the beer in my hand. "How long you been here?"

That actually seemed to befuddle him. "Here? You mean in this place?"

"Sure. Here." I gestured vaguely around. "Working for the colonel."

He showed me another smirk. "See there? That's two different answers. I been working for the colonel for about twenty years. I been living here about nine, 'cept for the time overseas. I used to drive a truck for a—for a beverage supplier that worked for the colonel and his partner. This was years ago, before you was in long pants."

I loved that answer for all the obvious reasons, but figured I should keep him talking having got him started. So I asked quickly, "You were born and raised here in San Francisco?"

"Near enough. Santa Rosa." He shook his head. "Don't play-act like you care about where I grew up."

I endeavored to keep my expression open and honest. "I thought I was being amiably inquisitive."

"So we're friends now." The set of his lips let me know exactly how appealing that was. "No. We ain't. And you ain't gonna trick me into spilling nothing about the colonel. No matter how slick you think you are."

"Yes," I told him, wetting my lips, "I can see you are far too astute."

He seemed befuddled again, brazenly so. "I don't know what that is. What is a stoot?"

I didn't find that funny at all and waved him off. "Never mind. I take it back."

All of which he found hilarious. He laughed so hard he nearly choked on his cigar smoke.

I eyed him suspiciously. "What did I say?"

He coughed and shook his head. "You're too easy. I may not be astute, but I'm no rube either. Save your flattery for the females. What are you doing?"

He posed that last question because I had settled my glass on the table and arisen. I removed my jacket. "I'd rather break furniture. On your feet so I can knock you down."

He got his coughs wrangled and squashed his laughter down into a smug grin. "I like you. Sit down. Want another beer?"

"No," I told him, settling once more on his sofa. I tried to still look flushed, though I admit I was feeling pretty smug myself. "I want to know why Reed took those letters from Ramona Wyman's room."

His grin deflated like a balloon. "Letters?"

"And her journal. Letters and a journal. You may remember he dropped them out the window, and the two of you carted them off in your car."

"You had a dream?" Trying to act unconcerned, his eyes flicked down at my hands again. "Where're you from?"

"Iowa."

"No kidding?" He didn't let it sound like a question. "And where were you stationed?"

I considered. "England."

"We come through there. Who were you with?"

I angled my head, admitting, "I'd rather not say," which scored me the suspicious squint I'd hoped for. "You won't like it."

"Ah, hell," he said, trying to get ahead of his disappointment, I suppose.

"I was M.P."

He crowed around the soggy nub of his cigar. "Jack-heeled thug! I should've knowed!" He popped the cigar from between his lips like a cork to offer me some more of his hacking laughter. "I wonder if you ever cracked one of my boys."

"Only if they got out of line."

"They did," he said, fondly, "but not too much, or I'd've cracked them myself." He suddenly pinned me with his eyes. "Listen, you hungry?"

I shrugged, not so much because I was or wasn't hungry, but because it was an intriguing question.

"I was gonna toss a T-bone on the grill. I can make it two. You like steak? Beryl might have a New York up in the kitchen."

Beryl, who I assumed handled the cooking up at the big house, did have a New York, but I ended up with the T-bone, medium-rare, on account of Holmsby thought it looked better and insisted. We also had a salad, prepared by me, following very precise instructions. I also set the small table in the cottage's kitchen while Holmsby attended the grill outside the window. He threw some asparagus down next to the steaks just before they came up off the flame, making for a nicely-rounded meal.

It was a strange turn of events, considering, and though I felt it at the time, I also felt that it was a welcome sort of strange, the sort of strange that's tinged with familiarity. I couldn't put my finger on what exactly, but something about that grizzled old pug put me at ease. I exhaled, and it felt like it was the first time I'd really done so all week.

Part of it might have been that I wasn't expected to talk or think much, just do what I was told and let him worry about it. Not that he seemed worried. He spent most of the time regaling me with increasingly unlikely war stories, most set in the months leading up to D-Day, usually involving ridiculously inept MP martinets and Holmsby's "boys" as he called them, who, to hear him tell it, clung to him like chicks to a mother hen. Not that I blamed them. Stationed at the sink, shredding lettuce, trying not to laugh as he stood over the grill poking the steaks, I remembered perfectly how rotten, scary and, most of all, lonely it had been.

After dinner, we carried our beers back into the parlor, and I settled on the sofa again while he sank comfortably into his armchair. I'd taken him up on his offer of a cigar, and was tugging at it reflectively when he said, "Tell me about them letters."

I puckered and sucked and puckered and sucked, then sent a miniature steam train flume of smoke into the air. I didn't look it him, responding in as nonchalant a manner as I could manage, "The ones I dreamt?"

He pulled his own smoke from between his lips and rolled it slowly between his thumb and first two fingers. He studied it like it was some new pleasant fabric caressing his skin. "Things have been bad for the colonel since..." His voice tapered off.

"The war?"

He clamped the cigar back between his teeth and shot his gaze up toward me. "Whatever you think you know, it ain't true."

"That covers a lot. I think I know plenty, some of it doubtless untrue." I watched him warily, keeping my tone light but ready for him to turn. "I don't mean to implicate you or him in Ramona Wyman's murder. But I need those letters. The journal, too. But I think mainly the letters."

He sat staring at the toes of his slippers. He edged his words around the cigar butt clamped tightly between his teeth. "There ain't no letters."

I breathed in deep through my nose. "You fed me a swell steak and provided this excellent beer and smoke, but—"

"You ain't listening. There ain't no letters. Even if there might have been. There ain't no more."

My breath came out in a sudden disheartened sigh. "Ah, hell."

Holmsby couldn't meet my eye. "Yeah. He was...it...I think he really liked her. Adam did, you see? But the colonel...they...I think...I don't know...But I do think they discussed things, certain individuals, for instance, and he was afraid."

I combed my fingers roughly through my hair. I was staring at the carpet and thinking about how much I had been relying on those letters and how puffed up I had allowed myself to get at the idea that I was going to solve this thing. And how relaxed I had been the last hour or so and how phony that whole hour had been. Then the guilt came. And then the anger.

"So what? Did he burn them? Did you see him do it?" I slid forward on the sofa and rose slowly to my feet. "Or did you do it for him?"

Holmsby had no trouble looking at me then. He watched me the way I had watched him a moment or so before. "You want me to get up so you can knock me down?"

"What I'd like." I stared at him, then abruptly cut toward my hat and jacket. They lay draped carefully over the back of the sofa. "Thank you for the steak. And the beer."

"You're mad," he said like I might not have realized it myself. "Have another."

"I better go." I shoved my arms brutally down the sleeves of my jacket, then decided it wasn't so high class I might not easily rip a seam if I wasn't careful. I took another deep breath. "Jeez."

"I know." Having risen, Holmsby stood beside the armchair watching me.

I turned back and looked him square in the eye. "You don't know. You don't know or you wouldn't have let him do it."

CHAPTER TWENTY-ONE

If you take Dolores south from Market, it swings slowly down into a gully before working gradually up another hill. Toward the top of that rise, you find your path bisected by Twenty-Fourth Street and, on your left, you'll spy some fine old examples of prewar opulence squeezed onto undersized lots, playing peekaboo with you from behind young but majestic poplar and cedar and the ever-present peppers. Dolores itself is a broad majestic stretch of road. Doubtless, perhaps before the earthquake and fire, someone had supposed it would provide an elegant and coveted corridor into the Mission. But it's only been since the war that money has started to reclaim the district, bringing new blood and resurgent property values and, according to Walter Cobb, long-time resident and owner of the Cobb Detective Agency, too much noise and lousy kids.

As mad as I'd exited Holmsby's quaint cottage, it took me hardly any time at all to figure my next move. Probably that had to do with the fact that the idea had been skirting around the back of my cranium since Joe Lovejoy's friendly phone call the previous morning. Only my natural inclination to avoid the underlying unpleasant ramifications had kept me from pursuing the lead earlier. As it was, my wristwatch was closing in on nine o'clock when I snagged a parking spot just two houses down from Casa Cobb's front door.

He answered himself, in shirtsleeves with no vest, his tie in place but relaxed, exposing the undone top button of his collar. His eyes neither squinted nor widened when he found me on his stoop. He was too cagey for such a blatant tell, but he pinched his not unsubstantial tufts of eyebrows together up over his enormous mangled chunk of nose. "Declan?" He was quite clear that it was a question, only the question had nothing to do with my name.

"Mr. Cobb." I tried to make it equally clear that mine was an answer. I nearly even nodded to show him, yes, I really was standing unannounced on his doorstep. It interested me that I found myself half turned, nearly glancing over my left shoulder at him. "Were you expecting me?"

"Expecting you?" His expression struck me as genuinely taken aback. "I've been calling you for days, and you haven't seen fit to answer. Why would I be expecting you?"

That allowed me to face him head on, and I made the move casually, edging my shoes around on the smooth concrete as quietly as possible. "I thought maybe—"

He lowered his eyebrows back to their default positions, then dropped them even lower. "Why are you here? It's late."

"Yes, sir. I believe we have things to discuss."

"Which would explain why I've been telephoning." He managed to keep his tone lighthearted, despite the petulance of his words. There was even the hint of a wry smile at the corner of his wide mouth. He glanced down, not at my shoes or the stoop, but possibly at options, then tossed another quick glance back over his shoulder. "You know I prefer to conduct business at the office."

"Yes, sir."

He gave me another look, and made it an open study. I knew he liked me. It wasn't just that he'd said as much on occasion. Talk is, as they say, cheap. But he'd let me know in other ways, such as laughing in my presence and sharing a drink from the private reserve of Irish he stowed in his bottom desk drawer. And he was letting me know again on the stoop, because his look said quite plainly anyone else would be told to call for an appointment. I was told, "Wait here a moment."

I nodded once, but he was already closing the door. I heard myself exhale again and took a step back, still facing the door. I dipped my right hand into my jacket pocket, and made a mental tally of all my shooters—the three that reside full-time at the office, the Colt currently visiting them, the ugly snub under my mattress—none of which I'd thought to bring along. I really could be stupid.

I'd heard about two dozen of my own breaths before the door opened again, Cobb standing sideways this time, gesturing, and telling me, "Please come in."

He led me through the foyer to a tall narrow hall. From there, double doors on the left led to the front parlor. And though I heard nothing behind the closed doors, I gathered the room beyond was not vacant. Probably the old man's brief departure had been to clear a pathway to his study at the back of the house. We passed the stairs and the open doorway to the dining room, the narrow hall to the kitchen, and finally reached the small cluttered room where he preferred not to work from home. Nowhere along the way did we see or hear another soul. After I entered the study, he told me to take a seat as he closed the door behind us.

"This is about that murdered girl," he said, his hand still on the doorknob.

My sitter had barely touched the cushion, and I paused in the act of settling myself to shoot him a glance. But I stopped the look before it got more than a start. I forced myself to concentrate on sitting in the chair. Comfortable. At ease. "I sincerely hope not."

He didn't say anything as he stepped around to the rolltop desk against the wall and claimed the worn swivel chair. He slid a box from the back of the desk toward the corner nearest me. He opened it, revealing a stash of plain white smokes. He waited patiently for me to lean forward and take one before snagging his own, closing the box, and sliding it back to its original position. He produced a lighter, but I'd already dug out my own matches so he lit only himself. He tasted it, got some tobacco on his tongue, cleared that, then rubbed his thumbnail across his lips. He looked up at me and sat back in his groaning chair. Comfortable. At ease.

"How can I help?"

I hoisted my right ankle and settled it over my left knee, resting my elbows comfortably on the arms of the chair. My back was pressed against the rest perhaps a bit too firmly. I exhaled. "What do you know about Ramona Wyman?"

He betrayed no expression. "She's the dead girl you hope you're not here about."

There was a pause as if he thought I might respond. When I didn't he told me, "Not much. I read the papers. And Andy…" He caught himself, thought better of something, and continued. "Ackerman and I have discussed it briefly." He gave me another of his probing looks. "I let a fellow called Lovejoy poke around that family on a previous, unrelated matter. Have you seen him? Joe's his name. You might remember he helped out on the Folsom Heights Exchange matter. Good-looking kid. Dark hair. Moustache." Cobb shook his head. "It's been days since he's reported in, and he hasn't been staying at his apartment from what I gather."

"So you're saying you haven't been in contact with Lovejoy?"

He smiled. "Sloppy. Look at your hands."

We glanced down together to see that I was gripping the arms of the chair. Not white-knuckling them, I wasn't that far gone, but hardly resting comfortably. I relaxed them because it would have made me look even more foolish to deny that he was right. I exhaled again.

He shifted in his chair, turning to address the top of his desk. "And remember your breathing." He pushed aside some paperwork to access a panel among the drawers at the back. He slid the panel aside, revealing a secret compartment from which he drew a tiny Derringer. He held it by the barrel as he offered it to me. "She's an antique. You'll only get two shots, so make them count."

I made no move to take the gun, just glared at it a moment and then at him. He wasn't smiling with his mouth, but his eyes were gentle enough to make me feel like he'd busted my jaw.

He put the Derringer down on the desktop as he settled back, facing me again. "You didn't bring your own gun, which gratifies me somewhat. But you've been paying lots of attention to your hip pocket, so I know you were wishing you had."

I figured the quicker we moved on, the better for my self-esteem. "Lovejoy's involved."

Again he managed to keep any hint of emotion far from his face, but his voice hardened noticeably. "It will take extraordinary evidence to convince me. Not that I consider him above reproach, but because I'd hate to think after all these years I could commit such an error in judgement."

"You said he hasn't checked in."

"That's extraordinary, I suppose, and possibly evidence. But of what? Are you claiming he killed the girl?"

"No. I believe I know who did that."

"The chauffeur."

"He was a mechanic. Well, he drove some too, I suppose." I shrugged. "Maybe it was him."

"Ackerman seems to think so."

"Which is why I don't." I put both feet back on the floor and leaned forward to rest my elbows atop my knees. Actually relaxed now, but in such a way as to allow myself to start getting keyed up. "Not being contrary. I mean the fact that the evidence points clearly to the Papalia kid doing it. And I think Ramona—Miss Wyman—was killed because someone was scared. Papalia had been scared too long for it to make a difference at this point. No, it was someone who felt secure and then got scared because..."

I stopped and looked up at him. Relating my theories, I had been staring at the space in between us, but just then I needed to see his eyes.

He nodded. "I'm following. You think Papalia was framed, or at least he was a handy stooge."

"Worse. I think I cast him in that role."

He shrugged. "Yes, well, we often overestimate our own importance in such matters. Events like these usually require long periods of gestation. You may have helped tip the scales in one direction or the other, but most of the weight had already been placed." He cleared his throat. "None of which is what you had started to say. You were saying the killer got scared because."

"Yes, sir. Joe Lovejoy."

"Joe scared the killer?"

"No, sir. I want to talk to him."

"As do I." He looked at me as if I might have a suggestion that could satisfy us both. I merely sat looking him in the eye. Finally I was rewarded with just the faintest hint of a squirm. It was perhaps one of the great moments of my career so far. "What is it exactly you suspect Joe of doing?"

I shook my head feeling, admittedly, a bit cocky. But also greatly relived that my worst fear, that the great Walter Cobb might have knowingly sullied his hands in this matter, had been at least somewhat allayed. "No, sir. I'm sorry."

He hoisted one of his massive eyebrows. "By God, you actually suspect me of something."

For a moment, I had to fight to contain my smile. "No sir. I confess I may have allowed myself to get screwy a moment and harbored foolish doubts about certain aspects. In fact, what I suspect is that I've made too many blunders so far. You may be in the same boat. No offense, sir, but you confess you still trust Lovejoy."

"I still have faith in my own abilities to read a man."

"Yes, sir. Either way, we need to talk to him."

It was Cobb's turn to draw a breath, and apparently he didn't care how much I heard about it. He also stroked his broad chin, a definite tell. He continued to study me while chewing over something he didn't seem to like the taste of. "You have a suggestion as to how we might make that happen?"

Another smile tried to worm its way onto my phiz. I killed it even more thoroughly than the previous one. "I do. Maybe. It isn't his only play, but it's his primary one. Lana O'Malley. Lovejoy scored big there. In more ways than one."

"Don't be vulgar."

"I apologize."

"How does that help us?"

"Because she's got an itch. No, it's more like a burr. Deep." I nodded. "You may know about it."

"Her father was murdered."

"That's just a symptom. Her obsession. It isn't her father's death. Only my plan won't work from here. We'll need to go to my office."

Cobb looked at me a moment longer, but only a moment. He wasn't one to hem and haw. "Let me tell Muriel."

CHAPTER TWENTY-TWO

M r. O'Malley."
I was back at my desk, in my office, seated in my own chair, leaning forward on my elbows. Walter Cobb was seated across from me in the client chair to the right. It was his first time there, and he was making a show of not looking around. I was concentrating on the telephone and my client. "I hope I'm not disturbing you."

"No. No, indeed. I'm glad you could return my call."

"Yes. I mean, no, I'm not. Sorry. Did you call?"

"More than once. I left messages."

"Sure. I got them, of course. But I've been busy. And I'm calling to report. Success."

"Success?" You might deduce he'd never heard the word.

"Yes, in the matter you asked—

"But the police said that was settled. Hector killed himself. They said he murdered Ramona."

"Oh, no. Not that matter. I mean the murder of your father."

"The murder of..." I would not be overstating to say he nearly shouted that. But neither would I like to mislead you by putting too much emphasis on it. It simply took him momentarily by surprise . "I don't understand."

"That visit we paid to your family's home, when I searched Miss Wyman's room. I confess that I thought it best to keep it secret at the time, but it paid off. I did find something, only I wasn't quite sure what it meant until now. I mean, sure, she had it hidden in a safe place, which is why the cops missed it, but I needed time to look it over thoroughly. That's why—"

"Wait. Are you claiming Ramona had something to do with father's murder?"

"Oh, no, no, no. Listen, Mr. O'Malley, clearly I'm not explaining this well at all. Perhaps we should meet in person. Can you come to my office first thing in the morning?"

He did not respond at first, but neither did it sound like he stepped away or even fiddled with the receiver. He simply considered the question. "Ten o'clock?"

"Perfect. And, of course, you should invite your sister. I know she'll be very interested in what I have to say."

That required a bit more consideration. "I don't know. Perhaps you and I should—"

"No, sir. I really have to insist. Or no, that's wrong. I really want to request as a favor that you invite her. I promise she won't regret it. Nor will you."

"But you must know how she feels."

"Exactly. But this will completely change her opinion of me."

"I don't know," he said again, though the second time something in his tone prompted me to play an advantage.

"I hope you do trust me, Mr. O'Malley."

"It isn't that at all, Mr. Colette. In fact, part of the reason I've been calling was to tell you—"

I got a sudden gut-wrench of a feeling my advantage had gained me too much. I needed to head him off. "Then you will call and invite your sister? Tonight? It's late I know, but she may need to rearrange her schedule."

"If you think it's that important."

"Great. Then I'll see you both first thing in the morning." I didn't make it a question. He needed to get used to the idea it was settled.

"Yes. But while I have you—"

"You will call her right away?" It was chancy to push so hard, I knew. He hadn't impressed me as a complete imbecile, and I had no idea how astute he might actually be. But he only laughed, probably deciding that I was the fool.

"Yes. I'll call her the minute we hang up."

"Then I'll let you go. I apologize again for disturbing you so late."

"It really isn't—"

"Goodnight." And I immediately severed the connection by pushing down the pin on the telephone set with my free hand.

As I was replacing the receiver in the cradle, Cobb told me, "Two things. First that was clumsy. You should have led him to suggesting he invite his sister. You not only suggested it, but reiterated it another half dozen times."

"Half dozen?"

"I lost count."

"And the second thing?"

"I'm even more confused. How does this help us? Are we going to wait here until ten in the morning?"

"I doubt it will take that long. He'll call her, and if she's home, I doubt we'll wait anytime at all."

"And if she isn't home?"

"Where would they be? Joe hasn't reported in. He must know you'd have eyes out looking."

"I don't have eyes out looking. Not specifically. I haven't accepted your supposition that Joe is involved in this affair."

"But if any of your boys were to spot him, they'd report it right away. Joe knows that."

He shrugged, dismissing our argument without actually acquiescing. "Now, tell me what exactly you suspect Joe of."

"Maybe we should wait."

"Maybe you should remember who you're speaking to." Amazingly, I heard absolutely no threat in his tone at all. He was merely reminding me that he considered me worthy enough of trust to follow from his home in the middle of the night, and I might be decent enough to do the same.

"You know a good-looking guy, probably five-ten or eleven, blond, with a very prominent scar splitting his left eyebrow?"

He let me see that he was considering it, reviewing mugshots in his brain. "Scar?"

"Yeah." I drew my fingertip through my eyebrow in as close an approximation of the highwayman's scar as I could recollect. "About here. Most likely from a knife, but not necessarily."

"Sam Rickey, maybe? He used to work at Zenith. Now I think he might snoop for some lawyer."

"He wouldn't be working for Marty Velasco?"

"Not if it is Sam Rickey. He's bent enough, but I never heard he went over."

"And this Sam, he might know Lovejoy?"

"I suppose. It's a big city on a small parcel of land."

I sat back, lighting up another cigarette. "Well, someone matching Rickey's description waylaid me and a friend on a quiet road in Marin yesterday. He and two others. The idea was that they'd been sent by Velasco to collect a debt and possibly warn me off. I suspect they were there for the latter purpose only. Well, maybe not to scare me off. I doubt even Lovejoy is that thick. But to lead me astray."

"Waylaid you?"

I provided him a brief summation of my adventure with the widow O'Malley, concluding with, "I doubt she came up with that on her own."

"But you say Joe has hooked the daughter. Lana?"

"Hooked, yeah. Been hooked by? I'd say the widow. You've probably seen pictures, but let me tell you, they don't tell the story by half."

Cobb stroked his chin again. "Well, if he did fall, it would be over a woman. But only if she could convince him that he held the reins."

"She could convince him he had her saddled and shoed. Even while clamping the bit between his teeth."

"So it's her you suspect?"

"No."

"No." He stared at me some more but I was saved by the telephone.

"Hello?"

"Colette," came Lovejoy's voice over the wire.

"Joe."

He then offered to do me a favor, or at least what he probably considered a favor, though, honestly, he isn't my type. "I called to say that Miss O'Malley is disrespectfully going to decline your invitation."

"Well, she's relaying the message through you, so I'd say she got the disrespectful part right."

"I'm not wasting any more breath on warning you."

"That's something, I guess."

"You've made your bed. Now you'll just have to deal with Cobb."

"Listen. You tell—" And I admit the clever center in my brain thought it might be a hoot to bad-mouth the old man with him sitting there in front of me, but I came to my senses in time. Or lost my nerve. "Never mind. I'm not worried about that. This time tomorrow, the whole affair will be wrapped up, and I'll be sitting pretty on a nice bundle of cash. If not from Miss O'Malley than from some other interested party."

Personally, I hadn't expected things to go so smoothly. And his long pause, during which I could practically hear him chewing over my words, managed to somehow lower him two more rungs on my respect ladder. Finally he asked me in a manner he might use to address some annoying kid, "What is it you found exactly?"

"Sorry, buddy. This is *my* lucky break. My golden goose. Did it even occur to you to check out the girl's room?"

"But you didn't find anything."

"Says who?"

But, of course, he couldn't say who said without offering up even more of a confession than he already had. Still, I wasn't completely confident he'd take the bait. He might rabbit. Or sit down and think things over. Neither of which fit my plan.

"And, besides, there's plenty of implication in this letter—er, I mean, this thing I found—to go around. Maybe I won't be the one facing the wrath of Mr. Cobb."

That got me a shorter pause with less chewing. When his voice came again, the words were clipped, like his lips were stretched thin and he was biting off bits of air as they came out of his mouth. "Listen, Colette. I don't know what you think you found, but whatever it is, you're confused. The police are sure that the grease monkey killed the girl. It's settled."

I let him hear how disappointed and disgusted I was. "Oh, hell. Are you that far behind? I thought I made it clear in my message to Miss O'Malley that this wasn't about the Wyman girl. This is about the matter she came to consult me on Tuesday morning." I savored a long, loud breath through my nose. "Or are you just playing stupid, boy? Because you should know, at this point you seem to be laying it on thick."

He covered his mouthpiece. He didn't even try to be subtle about it. He and whomever he had with him were still arguing when he came back. He hissed, "Yes, yes. Will you trust me?" and then aimed his words toward the transmitter. "We need to meet."

"Who? Me and you?" I sounded confused.

"Yes!" He practically screamed it. The brief disagreement at his end had apparently stoked some passion in him. "I'm telling you as a friend. There's more to this than..." Unable to come up with a suitable comparison, he let it hang. "If you really do have your mitts on a golden goose, there will be more than enough gold to go around. I can make you rich, boy. Both of us rich."

It was my turn to act stupid, but I didn't want to risk laying it on as thick as he had. "I ain't your friend."

And the weasel actually managed a quick laugh. "Ain't, he says." I admit it was a cunning maneuver. And it made it even easier to pretend to fall for it.

"Fine. You know where I am. I have things to prepare. If you can get here quick, I might hear you out."

Relief colored his voice in pinks and green. "You won't regret it."

"Huh," I said, moving the receiver back over toward its cradle. But he was right. I almost certainly wouldn't regret it.

CHAPTER TWENTY-THREE

So, how was that?" I leaned back in my chair, lacing my fingers behind my head and hoisting my heels up onto the corner of my desk. I admit I was feeling pretty swell.

Walter Cobb was too busy lighting a cigar to pay proper attention to my exhibition. He didn't make a production out of it the way Holmsby had, but it held his focus. It occurred to me, watching him, that this case had come down to me relying on two mostly square old geezers and one probably dirty young gigolo. Of course, at that point, I didn't know a third, even older geezer waited in the wings. Like most everyone else, I had written him off. How wrong we all were.

Cobb waved out his match and leaned forward to drop it into the ashtray I'd placed at the far corner of my desk for him. "I only heard your half, but at least you didn't invite him here yourself." He settled back and squinted his left eye at me. It's quite a trick and I never failed to swallow it hook, line and sinker. "You know I think highly of you, Declan."

I fought to keep a stupid grin at bay. It's silly how much I admire that man. And then I started to feel uncomfortable because I thought he might decide to remind me that I had possibly suspected him of malfeasance. Placing my shoes back onto the floor, I asked him, "Would you like a drink, sir?"

He responded favorably, and I poured us two whiskeys. Meanwhile he rose and took a brief tour of my digs, meaning he glanced at my license and tossed a gander out my window at the alley. While he stood appraising the yellow sofa, I delivered his beverage.

"I'd heard reports…"

The bend of his lips couldn't quite be labeled a frown, but it certainly wasn't a smile. I wanted to tell him that just the other day a client had complimented me on that sofa. I opted instead for a bald-faced lie. "It's not as comfortable as it looks."

"How could it be?" He sampled some whiskey and turned back toward his chair. "Kenny Dolman worked for me two years. And when he left, he took seven good clients with him. Allowed him to set up a nice shop over in Oakland."

"Yes, sir." I pointed to the far corner, behind my desk. "I'm thinking of getting a plant to put there."

That put a pin in the topic, and we moved on to his wife and kids. He was telling me about his daughter Moira and some fresh-faced young gunnery sergeant when we heard the ping of the elevator. The outer door opened. Firm, measured footsteps came through the reception area, then Joe Lovejoy waltzed in, looking handsome and self-assured. Neither of which lasted long.

He darted his dark eyes back and forth between Cobb and me before settling on the old man. "Boss!"

"Joe." Cobb's face was stern but not smoldering. He pinned Lovejoy without assaulting him. I confess to having a dopey grin on my own mug. It was some pleasure to watch Lovejoy squirm.

"But, what are you doing here?"

Cobb indicated the client chair next to his own. "Have a seat, Joe."

That Lovejoy immediately complied was perhaps more a testament to the old man's nature than his own. I would have done the same thing. The back of his lap hadn't quite made it to the cushion, however, before he stopped, shot a glance at me, then made a show of looking quite serious for Cobb. "I hope this clown hasn't been telling you stories, sir."

He must have liked the way that sounded because, as he settled into the chair, casually flipping back the corners of his trench coat and confidently crossing his legs ankle to knee, a bit of the self-assurance reasserted itself on his comely kisser.

Cobb sighed. "No, Joe. No one tells me anything. For instance, you. Last I heard, you were following up a lead. That was two days ago. How often are my operatives expected to report?"

And Lovejoy's self-assurance went right down his throat with a mighty gulp. "The nature of the lead, sir. I was waiting for a chance to report. The Wyman girl. Ramona Wyman as we discussed Wednesday morning."

"Wednesday morning. It's Friday night. Nearly Saturday morning. I had a top man assigned to that case and yet my most thorough report came through Andy Ackerman at Homicide."

I thought, *top man!* But I held my tongue. Lovejoy, on the other hand, was sputtering something that sounded suspiciously like deep cover. Cobb dismissed him by clamping his teeth tightly around the butt of his cigar and growling, "Report."

Joe's features clenched and then relaxed. He cast a glance at me indicating I might offer them some privacy. When I ignored his look and sat there merely being interested in hearing his report, he began.

"I spent most of Wednesday a.m. attempting to reconstruct the girl's movements of the previous day. It's summertime, so she doesn't attend school. My investigation mainly involved questioning the house staff. As you can imagine, the household was not only bereft, but had endured police interrogation most of the night."

"You sure do talk purdy," I crooned in my best Western drawl.

Lovejoy's head snapped up on his neck so that he could glare at me with narrowed eyes. Cobb cleared his throat, which I translated as a firm cease-and-desist order. But I leaned back again, feeling more than comfortable and offering Joe the sort of grin usually reserved for cats feasting on canaries.

"As you know," Lovejoy continued, turning back toward Cobb and winning the valiant struggle to meet the old man's eye, "my *in* allowed me access to the entire family. Not merely access, but I had been able to nurture a certain amount of trust. I think—"

I couldn't resist interjecting, "Your *in* being Lana O'Malley."

"Shut up!" That was from Joe, looking like he meant it. And, moreover, looking quite prepared to follow up his command with hands-on persuasion if I wasn't willing to comply. His attitude did away with my smug grin, but I confess it left me feeling tingly all over.

Cobb offered me a slow, disapproving frown. Sitting there, he did not look anything but bored by Joe's report, but I figured he was boiling. I saw tell-tale signs: the way his fingers worked the arms of his chair, and the fact that his legs were neither crossed nor stretched out, but rather folded so that his feet were under him like he was ready to pounce. Of course, he was a few years past the days of deadly pouncing, but I figured like Wayne Holmsby, he could still manage a sting or two. And at that point, I also figured most of his rage was directed at someone other than me, but his frown warned me I was edging dangerously close to shifting the distribution.

As if he'd read my mind, he sighed and moved his hands off the arms of the chair, using them to rub his knees. "It's late, Joe. Get to the point."

"Yeah, boss. I'm sorry. Everything I learned leads me to agree with the police. For whatever reason, either lured or of her own volition, Ramona Wyman left the mansion to meet with Declan Colette."

"You weasel," I said.

"Sit down," Cobb told me, and I realized I was on my feet. As mentioned before, given the old man's nature, I complied without considering any other option.

Lovejoy's dark eyes glinted at me under the overhead light. "It appears she accepted an offer of a lift from Hector Papalia, the man responsible for the automobiles and also George Kelly's driver on occasion."

"The suicide."

"Yes, sir. What exactly transpired between them can only be surmised at this juncture, but I imagine it was sexual in nature. He made advances, etcetera, which the girl spurned. Resulting in a crime of passion."

Lovejoy sat back in his chair, signaling completion. He was attempting to appear alert and professional, but again, the signs were contradictory. He was clutching his right ankle, which was lodged atop his left knee, too tightly with both hands. His heavy, manicured eyebrows were cocked too high. And he was swallowing about twice as much as any honest man would need to. Not surprisingly, I suspected him of chicanery. And if I suspected it, Cobb not only knew it but could probably explain exactly which parts of the report had been subterfuge, which had been exaggeration, and which had been outright lies.

But the old man took a different tack. "So, basically, you're telling me you've got nothing."

Startled, Lovejoy shifted in his chair. "Well, no. I—"

"You're saying the police solved the case ahead of you, even though you were right there on the scene, having already established contacts and trust."

"Actually, boss," Lovejoy said, foolishly letting a hint of frustration sharpen his tone, "Papalia solved it by offing himself. The police just found the body."

The old man fiddled with his cigar. "But everything you've just told me I heard from Andy Ackerman twelve hours ago. Am I paying Ackerman's salary? Should I be?"

"That's not fair, boss."

I had to wonder if he always addressed Cobb as boss, or if that wasn't something he was doing for my benefit. Perhaps he did it to remind both Cobb and myself of where the old man's loyalties should lie. It wasn't a poor strategy, if that was indeed the case. Though, like Ackerman at the crime scene referring to Cobb as Walter, it felt to me Lovejoy was laying it on a bit thick.

"So tell me about Marty Velasco," Cobb said.

"Marty Velasco?" Lovejoy was completely befuddled. And also astounded. And he let us both see that he didn't care who knew it. "What about Marty Velasco?"

I noted Cobb's visible relief. Lovejoy, too busy force-feeding us his own reaction, probably missed it. "Thank God," the old man said. He settled back in his chair, stretched out his legs and crossed them at the ankles. "So you aren't working for Marty Velasco."

Lovejoy sputtered. "Working for..." Then he slid forward, clutching the arms of his chair, putting both feet on the floor under himself, preparing to pounce. It was as if he and Cobb had decided to swap poses. But Lovejoy was staring at me. "This is you!" He jabbed a finger toward me, probably to ensure both Cobb and I knew exactly to whom the pronoun referred. He appealed to the old man, "I don't know what lies he's been spreading."

"Calm down," Cobb told him, and it partly worked. But even if Lovejoy had wanted to comply, he was too excited.

"But, boss!"

"Tell me about Sam Rickey."

"Sam Ric—" It undoubtedly occurred to Lovejoy that he'd just sung that tune, and a reprise so soon might not fly. He swiveled his head back and forth, gaping at Cobb then me then back.

"What have you gotten yourself into?" Cobb asked him, every inch the concerned patriarch.

Lovejoy recovered with a visible jerk. He instantly relaxed, sliding back and flattening his tie. He went to brush his fingers through his hair and knocked the magenta fedora, which he'd forgotten to remove upon entering and discovering the trap he'd walked into, to the floor. He made no move to retrieve it. He just showed me a wicked smirk. "You cheap bastard. This is you trying to weasel your way in." He shifted his attention with a distinct snap onto Cobb. "Listen, boss, this character is a snake. He used that poor girl's murder to get into the O'Malley's mansion and then threatened Mrs. Lawrence O'Malley. Tried to blackmail her. Thanks to me, that didn't work, and now he's trying to get my job."

I wasn't even tempted to rise to that bait. It was too pathetic. I merely shook my head to show how sad it was to see him squirming through the wreckage. Whether or not he bought my insincere sympathy, who can say?

Cobb said, "Right now I'm trying to help you save your job. Maybe salvage your entire career. Now, tell me—"

"God damn it!" Lovejoy leapt to his feet. As abruptly as he'd calmed himself, he was furious again. The olive skin of his cheeks had deepened nearly to the same magenta as his hat. He spun, put a foot against the front edge of the chair he'd been sitting on and sent it tumbling across the floor. Turning back to face Cobb, he hoisted his arms in a large, histrionic gesture of futility. "So, what, you're just gonna take this faggot's word over mine?" He tore off his trench coat and flung it to the floor. "Get up!" he told me.

I was already rising, shrugging out of my jacket.

"You aren't going to fight," Cobb told us both.

"Sure we are," I said.

Lovejoy was tearing off his own jacket, still staring at me. Still livid.

"Damn it," Cobb said. "It's late, and I'm tired."

"This won't take long," I told him.

"Fuck you," Lovejoy told me. He was rolling up his shirtsleeves as I started around the corner of my desk, and he sidestepped away from me over toward the yellow sofa. The area behind the client chairs and in front of the sofa provided perhaps fifty square feet of open floor space. Perfect for some fisticuffs.

Cobb didn't bother to turn his chair to watch us. "No knives or saps. No brass."

"No, sir," I said.

"Joe?"

"I won't need them," Lovejoy assured him.

"Then you won't mind putting them here on the desk."

Lovejoy made some sort of tsking sound, nothing like my own standby, and looked up and over at me. I had positioned myself in front of my desk, in approximately the same spot the second client chair had occupied before being kicked across the room. Rolling up my own sleeves, I returned his look, figuring my expression conveyed exactly what I was feeling: pleased and eager.

Undoubtedly that was the bully in me rearing his ugly head again. I outweighed Lovejoy by nearly twenty pounds, and just a glance at his effete hands with their long, graceful fingers and manicured nails told you he wasn't one for lowering himself to hit things, at least not very often.

He came over, walking boldly right up beside me while simultaneously not even deigning to acknowledge my proximity, and hoisted his left foot up onto the edge of my desk. He tugged his pant leg higher still, exposing a short stiletto strapped to his shin. Yanking it from its sheath, he tossed it onto the desk. Lowering his foot back to the floor, he withdrew from his right hip pocket a shiny set of brass knuckles.

"What about the Betty?" Cobb said. "And the noose?"

"All that stuff's in my coat."

Cobb beckoned to him. "Give it here."

Lovejoy stepped around me to retrieve his hat and coat. He tossed the former onto my desk next to his knife and knucks and handed the latter over to Cobb. The old man performed a slow and methodic search of the garment, tossing up items as he discovered them.

Despite my previous crack about Lovejoy being the sort to carry tools, I was surprised by the extent and variety of objects that clattered atop my desk in the following minute or so. A sap, another set of knuckles, two more blades, and a nasty length of cord with handles attached at each end. It was a wonder the man didn't rattle when he walked.

By the time Cobb had finished and folded the coat on my desk, the flaring tempers and raging testosterone had subsided somewhat. Which is why the old man runs a twenty-man operation while Lovejoy and I do grunt work. Not that either of us was ready to back down. I had been looking forward to this for days, and Joe's anger, though more recent and intransigent, had hardened into an icy determination.

The fight itself proved something of a letdown. Not that Lovejoy couldn't dance. He knew the steps, and he had the reach on me, but I was smart enough not to let us spend too much time upright. Once he'd tagged my left cheek, I tackled him to the sofa, and we bounced onto the floor. From there we grappled and poked and twisted and grunted and strained and cursed until I managed to bend him into a sort of reverse double chicken wing. We were pretty much seated, facing one another, in the middle of the floor, but with him bent painfully forward, his head tucked securely under my right armpit. His arms were stretched straight back, reaching toward the ceiling. I had them locked in a noose formed by my own arms, my hands gripped tightly to one another. His legs were stretched out to the sides, and I sat between them, my own legs scissoring his waist. He was pretty much ready to be branded.

"Give it up, Joe," Cobb told him. "For Christ's sake."

Lovejoy actually grunted and strained his arms to try and break my hold. I reciprocated by tightening my legs around his waist. "You bastard," he told me again, his muffled voice coming up from somewhere in the vicinity of my right hip pocket. "You goddamned fairy bastard."

I flexed my arms that time, threatening to wrench his shoulders from their sockets. Right up until he'd said that, I'd actually been feeling a bit sorry for him, proof that I wasn't all bully. But I wrenched him good then, and he rewarded me by crying out and then yelling, "All right! All right! Let me go!"

A moment later when I continued flexing my arms, Cobb said, "Declan." Neither shouting nor pleading, just reminding me he was there.

I opened my fingers slowly, until just the tips of one set were tugging at just the tips of the other, and then the pressure of Joe trying to straighten his shoulders pushed my arms apart in an explosive rush. I unhooked my ankles and slid my butt back across the floor. He gave up some sound between a groan and a sigh, tipping over onto his left side. Figuring he wasn't above kicking me even after the bell had sounded, I kept sliding until I felt the sofa against my back. I leaned into it, breathing heavily and watching him try to get his joints back into alignment.

Cobb rose, offered up a good-sized and heartfelt sigh of his own, then stepped slowly over to offer Lovejoy a hand. Scowling, Lovejoy turned away and rolled over onto his knees without assistance. Cobb put his hands on his hips. "You have to see you're finished, Joe. Not just with me. Maybe truly finished."

I thought for a moment Lovejoy was going to curse Cobb the way he had me, but his good sense prevailed. "Fine." He worked himself to his feet, staggering over toward my desk and his hat and coat and toys.

"But not until you explain. You owe me that, I think."

Lovejoy spun on his heel and nearly went down. He gaped at Cobb. "I owe you?"

"An explanation, at least. No? Why you betrayed me."

"I didn't betray you, boss." Lovejoy turned back toward the desk, propping himself up on it with both hands. His head hung heavily down between his aching shoulders. "Or maybe I did. I made a mistake. I thought I was...I thought I was doing right."

"No," Cobb told him, as simple as that. "I want the truth now. No more evasions."

Lovejoy turned again, this time wedging his keister against the edge of my desk. "But it is the truth!"

"It's not and you know it. If you'd truly thought that you were doing right, you would have reported in. You would have returned my calls. And you wouldn't have come here tonight."

CHAPTER TWENTY-FOUR

B abe, it's me."
I've suffered my fair share of indignities in life. Actually, depending on my mood, I might claim I've suffered more than my fair share. For instance, some things that transpired in a certain dank cell in Waterford, England, during the middle of March, 1945, while I was waiting to get shipped off to an army hospital. But watching Joe Lovejoy sit in my chair, behind my desk and make that call on my telephone damned near topped anything that came before it.

He had, of course, relented and bared his soul, such as it was, to Walter Cobb. He explained that he and Lana O'Malley had developed a mutual admiration during his initial investigation into her father's murder. He admitted with carefully chosen words that he had perhaps needlessly prolonged the investigation, insinuating that Miss O'Malley certainly knew what he was doing, and therefore tacitly, if not expressly, condoned it. He did not state categorically that he had shared her bed. He knew, as did I, that Cobb would see such a verbalization as disparaging the lady's reputation. For all his talent and insight as an investigator, the old man was nevertheless a product of his generation. Of course, Lovejoy had obviously enjoyed many breakfasts at the O'Malley apartment.

He was sketchier as to how exactly he had entered into relations with Mrs. Lawrence O'Malley. But I don't think his reticence had much to do with caution. I think while he had perhaps attained the summit of that particular peak, he simply had yet to manage planting his flag, so to speak. And since his behavior seemed that of a man in thrall of the mountain, he was embarrassed to reveal how thoroughly he had been played.

He claimed they had consulted several times prior to late Wednesday night when she had told him, in some distress, that I had attempted to blackmail her. He was again vague on the details of my exact scheme, which, again, I was willing to attribute to Mrs. O'Malley. She knew damned well I hadn't done any such thing. Unfortunately for Joe, hearing his recitation of the tale, Cobb and I weren't nearly as receptive an audience as he had been hearing hers.

He laid the phony banditry all on her. And while perhaps less than gallant, I figured it had to be true. Lovejoy believed wholeheartedly the skit was performed to convince me Mrs. O'Malley was already on the hook with Marty Velasco, and that I, upon learning of the gangster's previous claim, would look elsewhere to stake my own. Lovejoy clearly didn't know, and I didn't enlighten him, that the holdup wasn't staged for my benefit at all. I was just a happy witness who had ultimately flubbed his part.

Joe did admit to gathering the cast and writing the script and even setting the stage. In addition to Sam Rickey, Lovejoy had recruited Lyle Stout and Max Darrow. That final name had elicited a growl from Cobb. Darrow was another of his own men. Lovejoy claimed that no one had ever been in any real danger. The guns hadn't even been loaded. I thought he ought to tell that to the bruise on my shoulder, but kept quiet because the truth is, the main thing wounded were my feelings.

Cobb didn't sit completely idle. He offered an assortment of questions—fewer early on, more toward the end—feinting and poking in a seemingly random exploration of what appeared to be the soft spots, checking to see if any might be widened into actual holes. But Lovejoy had stayed near enough to square that his confession held up. He'd been a louse to Lana O'Malley, not simply latching onto her as a meal ticket and plaything, but parlaying their friendship into an entrée to her stepmother, probably in hopes of trading up.

As much as I had disliked him before, that last part had me despising Joe Lovejoy all over again. While Lana and I would never be bosom pals, mainly because she was an obsessed paranoid bitch, she wasn't an idiot. And considering the object of her paranoid obsession, if she were ever to find out the whole truth about her paramour, she'd probably go off the rails completely.

"Well," Cobb sighed. "What now?"

He had addressed me. I sat on the sofa, where I'd been since stretching Lovejoy's arms. Remaining out of the way and keeping silent had struck me as the savviest play. Confessing was laying Joe low enough without his being reminded of the fact that I was watching. But I looked up and over at him then.

"Now I finish him off, and we go home to bed."

Cobb breathed in, calming himself. "Do I need to remind you that I was already at home ready for bed?"

I frowned. "Well, what comes next depends on him. What's his status?"

Cobb turned to Lovejoy, who stood looking like the proverbial deer, in this case confronted by two sets of headlights coming from two directions at once. He swung his head back and forth as he tried to decide which of us to gape at. Cobb kept looking at him, but said, apparently to me, "I think he's ready to help you."

I swallowed a handful of remarks I wanted to make and told Lovejoy, "Then call your girlfriend, Miss O'Malley, and tell her it's true. Only it's even bigger than I let on. It blows the lid off everything."

Lovejoy stared at me, then switched to Cobb. "What does? What's he talking about?"

"My evidence," I said. "What I found in Ramona Wyman's room. Only tell her—"

"What *did* you find?"

"Don't interrupt. Tell her that it's deep, and you're going to stay here and look it over. Tell her to call the family and see if she can't stage another pow-wow like the one they had on Wednesday. Reiterate how big it is. How explosive."

"But what is it? I don't understand."

I frowned at Cobb. "Clearly he's not ready to help."

"But, boss!"

"This is your chance," Cobb explained in a calm, fatherly tone. "Do as he says."

"I don't understand."

"You understand enough, I think, to do as he says."

Lovejoy rubbed his face, which was already splotchy and somewhat green. Rubbing didn't help; it merely raised crimson patches on his cheeks. He gaped at me some more, gradually narrowing his eyes into squints, though whether because he glommed to my angle or merely resented taking orders from me, I can't say.

He took a few shallow breaths, then told the space half way between Cobb and me, "She won't buy that you and I are working together. And she certainly won't buy that you handed over the info willingly."

I could see what he was hinting at and shook my head, arching a brow in admiration. "Then sell it, my lad. She's a *chica* and that's your specialty. It's why the old man keeps you around."

Cobb pivoted his head so he could look at me, all affronted dignity. "What did you call me?" He doubtless was well-aware that nearly all his men and business acquaintances referred to him in those terms. They simply didn't do it within earshot.

"Yes, sir," I said. "Slip of the tongue."

And that was how Joe Lovejoy, the louse, the cut-rate Tyrone Power, the ladies' man detective, ended up in my chair, behind my desk, on my telephone, lying about how he whooped me in a fair fight. "Yeah, babe," he said, "Well, I guess some guys only look tough. I think you might have been right about him. He sure folded up like a queer when I got started on him."

I nearly pulled off my shoe and threw it at his head, but Cobb saved me the trouble by issuing a warning sound from deep in his throat that actually made Lovejoy jump. Apparently, though, Lana had her own objections. Joe's voice grew even more obsequious. "I know, honey. I'm sorry. He's a good kid."

He cleared his throat. "Listen, I want you to start calling as soon as we hang up. I'll be here another hour at least. I got to look this thing over. It's deep. But I tell you, everyone's gonna want to know about it. Tell them we'll meet first thing in the morning. First thing!" He listened some, then shot glances at Cobb and me before lowering his voice. "Me too. See you soon. Only don't wait up."

He replaced the receiver in the cradle and sat back, looking so smug I thought about yanking off my shoe again.

Cobb told him, "You shouldn't have laid on that queer stuff so thick. You know I can't abide that manner of talk."

Joe looked down at his hand, at his fingers drumming on the top of my desk. He didn't dare look at me because he knew I had weapons far more deadly than a shoe around that office. "Sure, boss. Only, *her brother* really is a queer."

The old man set his hands firmly on the arms of his chair and climbed laboriously to his feet. He always did look ancient to me, in a wizened, elder statesman sort of way, but he possessed a measure of vitality in his office between the hours of, say, eight to six. There in my office, nearing midnight, he looked haggard and pale. "You think that should do it?" he asked me.

I shrugged. "I think that should do something."

"I want Joe to remain here with you."

"No, sir," Lovejoy and I said nearly in unison.

"Yes. No argument. You're grown men and professional, licensed detectives. I expect you can act like it for a hour or so." He paused for a breath. "Or rather like gentlemen, which would probably be better." He pivoted his head to Joe. "Call me a cab."

Lovejoy picked up the phone again as I stepped over to shake Cobb's hand and thank him for his help. He reminded me with a look and a certain edge to his voice, that I'd left him little choice. I'd suspected him of malfeasance. But I was quite willing to abase myself with a woeful smile and plenteous thanks.

Cobb asked Joe to accompany him to the sidewalk, robbing me of the pleasure of dragging the louse from my chair but allowing me a few moments of quiet peace, back in my perch with a tumbler of whiskey and a cigarette. When Lovejoy returned, he stood just through the door from the reception room, looking over at me cautiously.

I let him remain that way for several moments, then pointed out, "It may take a while. Have a seat."

He sat on the sofa, which is as far away from my desk chair as he could get in that room. Then we each pretended we were alone, me sipping my whiskey and him no doubt wishing he'd brought some of his own. After about a quarter of an hour, he said, "I expected you to fight cleaner than that."

"I expected you to fight dirtier."

Another five minutes passed before I appended, "You boxed some. In school?"

He shrugged. "A little. And in the service."

I sat forward. "That thing you did with your right, after the left feint, that could have done some damage if it'd landed."

"Hell. Hitting you was harder on my hands."

I fought down a smile but pulled out a second tumbler. Splashing some whiskey into the bottom, I said, "I think this bruise I'm gonna have on the side of my neck tomorrow is proof to the contrary."

He got up and moved slowly over to the left client chair, which I'd picked up and put back into position while he'd gone down with Cobb. He took the tumbler I slid across to him. "What are we waiting for exactly?"

"A murderer."

"And you know who that is?"

"I think so. I expect so. I'd be surprised if I was wrong."

We said those things back and forth, lapping up our booze, looking at the floor or our tumblers, the desk, telephone, window, or coat rack. Anything but each other. It was easier that way. Another quarter of an hour passed, and by then we were exchanging barbs and discussing Fagan and O'Doul's thus far unsuccessful attempts to turn the Seals into an honest-to-God baseball team. It was all very masculine and reserved, but we had to pass the time somehow. And even though I got the feeling Lovejoy didn't know much about sports, he made an effort to keep up.

When we heard the ping of the elevator, I had a sudden brainstorm and whispered at Joe to take my seat again. I put my back to the front wall, placing me opposite the window that overlooked the alley. To anyone coming into the main office from the reception area, I'd be invisible until they were through the door.

Our visitor didn't wait that long, however. I estimated he was still at the door to the hall when he called, "Hello?"

I saw Lovejoy's face light up, just as mine fell into a hundred befuddled pieces. I came off the wall, stepping toward the door. Morgan O'Malley and I nearly collided at the doorway to the office.

"I knew it!" Lovejoy said. "I goddamned knew it!"

I ignored him, placing a hand to Morgan O'Malley's chest and pushing him back a step. His eyes widened

"What are you doing here?" I said.

"Lana telephoned me with some wild jazz about Joe Lovejoy tossing you out a window." He made it sound as ridiculous as he no doubt knew it to be. Certainly Joe hadn't mentioned anything about a window, and I doubted Lana would have invented such an embellishment on her own. None of which distressed me nearly as much as the dopey look of pleasure and relief that I saw in O'Malley's eyes. He must have felt how uncomfortable I was, because he turned his head a few degrees to the left to glance over my shoulder toward the desk. "Hello, Joe."

"Were you followed?" I asked.

"Followed?"

"The police."

"No." He shook his head. "I don't think so. George said the police had stopped all that."

I enjoyed a very deep breath, realized my hand was still on O'Malley's chest and used it instead to grab his arm. I pulled him into the office and along the wall I'd been hiding against. He followed me without resistance, his legs jerking like those of a drunken marionette. "You shouldn't have come," I told him. "Damn it. But you can't leave now. We're expecting someone."

"Wait," Lovejoy said, "you mean he's not it?"

"It?" O'Malley was looking even more confused. "What's *it?*"

But the brainstorms continued. I jerked my head up suddenly, and I pinned O'Malley with my gaze. "Did you talk to anyone else besides Lana? Your stepmother or Mr. Kelly or Jasper Reed?"

Something in my expression must have alerted him to the fact that this was important, because he didn't even bother to remind me not to refer to Miranda O'Malley that way. He simply shook his head.

"Wait here!"

I made the hall in what felt like three bounding steps. I paused there holding my breath, listening, as I glanced up and down the empty corridor. The elevators were to my left, but a murderer intent upon stealing a piece of damning evidence in the middle of the night wouldn't take the elevator.

I turned right and crept down to the stairwell door. I carefully placed my ear softly against the smooth wood. I'm not sure what I expected to hear. Maniacal laughter? A whispered confession? But, for the love of Mike, I swear I sensed someone standing just on the other side. I reached down with excruciating caution for the door handle, then grabbed the handle, twisted and threw my shoulder against the wood.

The collision was not monumental, but succeeded in throwing the other person back even as the door rebounded into my shoulder. I flung it wide, hearing an exclamation of pain and surprise as the other figure teetered at the top of the stairs. He grabbed hold of the rail to keep from falling.

I straightened up, pushing my tie flat. "Mr. Kelly. Don't you want to join the party?"

CHAPTER TWENTY-FIVE

George Kelly straightened up as well, continuing to steady himself with the railing. The stairwell was dim; a single low wattage bulb positioned just to the side of the doorway offered the only illumination. But the bulb was behind me, and it cast a sickly yellow pall over his haggard face. His eyes were wide and wet and frightened, but also sagging around the edges, perhaps the most truly exhausted eyes I'd seen in several years. He had to swallow several times to clear his throat enough to speak.

"Is my cousin here?"

"Morgan? He just arrived. We've been waiting for you."

"For me? But I—" He abandoned whatever course he'd been set on and switched to an expression of petulant concern. "I want to know the meaning of this. I just received a strange telephone call from Lana, claiming that Joe Lovejoy—"

I showed him my palm, along with a commiserating smile and shake of my head. "Don't bother. I've read the letter, remember? Why don't you come in and we can discuss it."

His collision with the door had knocked his hat off, and it had fallen on a step one up from the landing below. Kelly watched me a second, then turned to retrieve it. He descended with slow, measured steps, then crouched. When he stood up again, the hat wasn't the only thing in his hands.

"I brought my own this time."

I nodded appreciatively. "And she's a beaut."

I wasn't merely talking. The revolver looked to be an old-style Remington six-shooter, polished and clearly treasured. I learned later that before the war, Kelly had spent most of his adult summers on a dude ranch in Colorado. I was told he could ride too.

"I don't suppose three more will make much of a difference at this point."

The look of determination given to him by the gun in his hand faltered a bit. "Three more?"

"Me, Morgan, and Joe Lovejoy. That's two shots each." And then, when I could see the bewilderment in his eyes, I added, "She isn't just for show?"

He wiped his mouth with the back of his free hand. Like everything else about him, his lips were puffy and sagging. Wiping them that way stretched his mouth sideways into a gruesome parody of a scream. His wide eyes seemed to spasm in his head, jittering from side to side, as if he was struggling to focus on some hazy mirage right in front of his face. "No," he said. "I'm not going in. You go get the letter and bring it out here to me."

I shook my head again. "That's no good. I'd just get one of my own guns and we'd end up in a shoot out." I was watching his gun hand, which, rather like his eyes, was none too steady. "You're used up, Mr. Kelly. You were used up last night. If I was half the detective I think I am, I would have seen it. I mean, I met you, what? An hour after you shot Papalia through the head? And I didn't even realize it. That must have disappointed you. I know you wanted me to figure that out.Well, I sussed it this morning, only I also managed to figure out why it was Miranda married O'Malley. See, I was at the beach and—"

"Shut up." Unlike Joe Lovejoy an hour or so before, Kelly didn't shout that at me. He said it quietly, pathetically. His hand drooped an inch or so, not enough to inspire me to heroics. He looked down.

"Yeah, that must have hurt. That she preferred even that old man."

"She's evil, Mr. Colette. Wicked."

He sounded sick to me, which I guess he was. But he also sounded less deserving of my pity, and I felt my lips twisting up. I shook my head one last time. "She's really not. She's just never loved you."

His head came back up, his mouth and his eyes widening even more. "But why?"

And then he lurched toward me, or rather toward the wall to my left, and only after he was falling did I register the three shots. I still flinched, even as I watched the Remington sag and drop from his hand. I stood frozen a moment, wondering where the bullets had hit me. Even seeing the life drain from Kelly's eyes, I couldn't convince myself he hadn't fired. Then I heard the commotion in the hall behind me, and Morgan O'Malley's big frame filled the doorway.

"George!" He tried to push past me, but that spurred me into action. I wrapped my arms around his chest, holding him back. Lovejoy was behind him, looking startled but carrying a sweet little Suicide Special in his hand. I wondered where he'd had that stashed.

"Let me go!" Morgan commanded me, but I said, "Wait, goddamn it! Wait!" I pushed him back through the doorway and into the hall. I didn't release him, however, I simply called back over my shoulder. "Are you through?"

From the darkness below the landing came a frail, ragged voice. "Is he—?"

You have to wonder about the type of man who can pump three slugs into another guy's back, then balk at the word *dead*. Or maybe he'd meant to say *still alive*.

The sound of that other voice tempered Morgan's struggling. We exchanged looks—his asking for an explanation, and mine requesting time to formulate one. I released him cautiously, letting him know with a timid nod of my head that I was trusting him not to make any rash moves. I turned my back to him, blocking the doorway as best I could as I tried to examine George Kelly.

Kelly lay sprawled halfway down the steps. He had hit the wall, then slid facedown. He wasn't completely still. His left leg was bent, the knee lodged on about the middle step, but his right leg was stretched out, his foot nearly touching the landing below. It was twitching spasmodically, which told me one of the bullets had probably landed close to his spine. His chest was jerking too, expanding and contracting irregularly while he made faint choking sounds. He wasn't dead, but I doubted there was much hope. The other two bullets had probably punctured his lungs, and he was drowning in his own blood.

Still, I called, "I'll check," my voice about what you'd expect from a man in the midst of getting his neck wrung. O'Malley took hold of my left arm from behind. I shrugged him off, croaking, "Don't shoot me."

I went down to Kelly and rolled him onto his back. His eyes were still wide, and his blood-coated lips were working, but I doubted he was seeing anything. I figured speech was out of the question. He tensed up a moment, looking even more startled, then faded out completely with a ragged sigh. His leg kept twitching a moment longer.

I watched him until everything grew still, then I touched the side of his neck. His skin was surprisingly hot and sticky, but I felt no throbbing pulse below it. I lifted my head, peering into the darkness. "Yeah. He's dead. Why don't you come up, Colonel?"

I heard O'Malley's gasp and the old geezer's footsteps simultaneously. Jasper Reed ascended the stairs with all the *joie de vivre* of Sisyphus attacking that mountain for the thousandth time. Only in the Colonel's case, his boulder was a dull, silver Luger lodged tightly to his chest and aimed straight ahead. As he made the landing, he bent his form sideways, keeping the body and me—though mostly, I imagine, the body—directly in his line of sight. I've never seen the expression of an old duck in cardiac arrest, but I figure it looks something like Reed's face did as he turned toward me.

O'Malley actually said, "Uncle Jay." I wanted to tell him to keep it zipped, but I also didn't want to turn my back on the man with the gun. Reed, for his part, didn't seem to hear O'Malley at all. His tired eyes were wide and rheumy as he stared at George Kelly's immobile form.

I cautiously lowered my right foot down another step. Reed had crossed the landing, standing poised at the bottom of the set of stairs leading up from the landing to the third floor. I stretched out my right hand, almost like I was offering to help him, even though the last time he'd tried to bash my brain with his walking stick. What I really wanted was for him to hand over the Luger. If he really was done, he wouldn't need it any more.

I flexed my fingers. "How about you let me take that for you, sir?"

He didn't appear to hear me, but he extended his right arm, raising it slightly and aiming the barrel of the Luger at my chest. Then his hand went limp, and the gun sagged. I tugged my handkerchief from my breast pocket and transferred it to my right hand, then moved down another step to where I could just, leaning forward and stretching, take the Luger by the barrel. It was hot even through the cloth, and I dropped it quickly into my hip pocket.

I climbed back up a step. "Can you help him, Mr. O'Malley?"

When that didn't seem to elicit any sort of response, I looked back. O'Malley stood there ashen and nauseous, and not unlike I'd asked him to lick a toad. But when I stepped down to offer Reed an arm, O'Malley came back to life and hurried forward to join us.

When we got the old man around the body and to the top of the stairs, I told Lovejoy that I'd telephone and he should stay with the body. I threw a glance at O'Malley, who still looked in need of some air, and suggested he get some. I asked him to go down to the lobby and wait for the police. He frowned, studying the old man he called Uncle Jay with disgust, then said, "No. I'll stay with George. Joe, you go down and wait for the police."

I didn't argue. I just told him for God's sake, don't touch anything. And then, as I was escorting Reed into the hall toward my office, I glanced back once and saw him standing resolutely at the top of the stairs, his arms folded tightly across his chest.

I got Reed all the way into the small reception area, where I piloted him into one of the chairs in the corner near the old magazines. The Luger was tugging heavily on my pants, so I placed it on the corner of the desk. I wedged myself onto the edge of the desk in front of the gun, blocking it from sight. Then I watched the old man a moment, wondering what the chances were his face would ever really regain its color.

"Can I get you anything, sir? Water? A whiskey?"

He shook his head ever so slightly, keeping his glassy eyes fixed on a point in the air between us. I let him study that a while, then told him, "So, you didn't burn the letters after all."

That appeared to penetrate the fog. He focused his eyes, and his Adam's apple slid all the way down and back up. He blinked. "The letters are gone."

I took a slow deep breath. "Sure. You don't have to talk. Especially not to me. You're a lawyer. You know that."

As I watched, a long series of expressions played across his face. It was like the muscles were rebelling. His lips twitched. "Besides, there was really nothing to them. A brief mention of having met George for a weekend at Malta. Another of George having arranged for Adam to get a new driver." He swallowed again, so thoroughly I could practically hear it. "It was the journal, of course, that brought me here. The arrogant, silly child writes of having managed to convince Papalia to teach her to drive by insinuating something about the letters." He looked at me. "She didn't even know what she had done."

I nodded. "It was all a big misunderstanding." I said that not because it was the truth, but because it was what he wanted to hear. He knew as well as I did that Ramona Wyman died because she knew Jasper Reed had written the letter to Lana. She had called my office and arranged to meet me because she didn't want the old man exposed and embarrassed. By then, she had probably elicited a promise from him that he wouldn't do anything of the sort again. Only she had asked George for my name—probably because one of the kids, Morgan or Lana, had discussed their consultation with him—and George, having already been alerted by Papalia that Ramona was on to something, had listened in to our telephone conversation and jumped to the wrong conclusion.

So, maybe in some ways, it was a big misunderstanding. But she was still just as dead.

The elevator pinged again, and I slid off the desk and stuck my head out the door. It wasn't the cops. Wayne Holmsby stood in the hall before the open elevator doors, looking both ways with his mouth hanging open.

"In here," I called.

I resumed my perch on the someday-receptionist's desk and offered the chauffeur a commiserating smile when he stopped in the doorway. He looked from me to the colonel and then back to me before spying the Luger lying on the desk behind me. He moved toward it with a purpose, and I jumped up and pivoted around the desk, opening the top drawer and pulling the gun across the desktop with my knuckle. It dropped over the edge and into the waiting drawer, which I snapped closed with my hip.

I stood pressing my weight against the drawer and offered him another commiserating look, this time without the smile. He stopped, staring me straight in the eyes, but let it stand at that.

EPILOGUE

Monday morning, I was back in my office behind my desk, with my ankles crossed and my heels resting on the open bottom drawer. I hadn't quite recovered enough from the long weekend to get my feet up onto the edge of the desk itself.

Across from me in the right client chair sat, not a client, but Gig Barton, my reporter friend from the *Bay Clipper*. He had, by then, been over the story a dozen times with a dozen different sources and even published two articles, one of which had been picked up by the AP. But newspapermen always seem to want more. And, in this case, I felt obliged to humor him.

"So somehow the girl figured out that George Kelly had arranged for Adam's death?"

I frowned at him. He knew that wasn't right and posed the question merely to show he'd been paying attention. "No. She managed to make Papalia think she'd figured that out. I don't honestly think she suspected him at all."

"But when she showed an interest in you, Kelly thought she was moving to expose him."

"That's probably right. One of the many things we'll never know is what exactly George Kelly thought." My telephone began to ring, and as I lowered my feet and picked up the receiver, I explained to Gig, "We don't really even know if he or Papalia murdered the girl." I put the telephone receiver to my ear. "Hello?"

"Mr. Colette?" Morgan O'Malley's voice sounded two entire registers below its usual tone.

"Sir." I can't quite claim I was expecting the call, but neither was I wholly surprised by it.

"Sir?" He tried to laugh and bring his voice back up where it belonged. "That's a bit formal."

"Unfortunately, I'm with a client. Perhaps I could telephone you back?"

"Oh, I see. Yes. Well." He coughed. "Do you think you could manage it today? I mean, it's nothing urgent, only…well, you did receive the check I sent you?"

"Yes, sir." I had received both a two hundred dollar check and an accompanying gift. I looked at the far left corner of my desk where the crystal cigarette holder stood. It was a sparkling, expensive piece of work and had no business being in that office. Which, naturally, made it the perfect metaphor. "You should receive a full accounting of charges by the end of the week."

"Wonderful. Only, I mean, I could pick it up. Or you could drop it by." He took a deep, preparatory breath. "I did invite you to dine once, and you were busy. I'd very much like—"

I cut him off. "As I said, sir, I'm with a client. You're at the home number?"

"Yes. I'm sorry. Yes, I am at home and should be all afternoon." He paused then, and though I did not hear him draw a breath, I calculated that he was working himself up to something again. "Listen, Colette, just so we're clear. I talked to Hobie Wainwright about you. I mean, he referred me to you in the first place, I suppose you know, and, well, I…I figured if anyone could…I'm referring to that business…I mean, what that policeman said at the house. Well, Hobie told me…he told me about your friend."

"My friend?"

"The sailor. The one who—"

I found myself sitting forward again, frightened by the sound of my voice. "Sir! I'll telephone the moment I'm free. Now, really, I must hang up."

"Yes! Yes, of course." He sounded apologetic and maybe slightly frightened himself. "I just wanted you to know that I knew. That I *understood.*"

And as soon as he said that, I realized that of course he didn't understand at all. One thing you learn talking to shrinks is that when they say they understand, you can bet it means they're measuring you for a straightjacket. I told him goodbye and barely waited for his goodbye back at me before returning the receiver to the cradle. I sat back but didn't put my feet up again.

"Who was that?" Gig wanted to know.

"You ever heard of Hobie Wainwright?"

His eyes widened. "That was Hobie Wainwright?"

"So you know him?"

"Sure. He owns *Bayside Sunset Magazine* and about a dozen papers up and down the coast. How do *you* know him?"

"I don't," I admitted. "Never heard the name before."

"That's cause he's super rich. Doesn't deign to mix with those of us down at street level. Why was he calling you?"

"He wasn't. That was an ex-client. Something about a billing problem." I tried to clear my head by jerking it up suddenly. "What were we talking about?"

Gig thought he might like to pursue the Hobie Wainwright angle, but I wouldn't indulge him, mainly because I really had never heard of the man before. Still his name kept tugging at the back of mind as we rehashed the details of Ramona Wyman's murder. Just like the crystal cigarette holder kept drawing my eyes. And Morgan O'Malley's telephone number kept repeating over and over in my head.

I finally got rid of Gig, dialed O'Malley's number, and managed to arrange to meet him without too much discussion. In fact, his eagerness confirmed for me just how imperative our meeting was.

He joined me at nine-thirty outside The Rusty Spike, down near the bayside wharfs, where the quiet streets and well-spaced lamps made it easy to slip unnoticed into the nearby alley.

He was suitably receptive to my placing both hands on his shoulders and guiding his back to the wall. Even though he tried to sneer and tell me, "You know, I don't normally patronize dives like this one."

I pushed up against him, nudging his chest with my own. I lowered my head, and he was just enough taller than me that I could butt my forehead against that heroic chin of his. "You like me, don't you?"

"You certainly have your allure, Mr. Colette." I couldn't see it, but there was the sound of a grin in his voice. "Declan."

"Yeah." My eyes were clamped shut, and I had to force the words up my throat. "I like when you say my name like that. Say it again."

"Declan."

I slid my hands down off his shoulders and onto his arms, kneading his biceps beneath the layers of his shirt and jacket. I pushed his right arm back, guiding it gently around behind his waist until I could snake my own right hand down and around and take hold of him by the wrist.

Apparently finding his arm pinned behind him wasn't quite cause for alarm. He made a purring sound, like a tiger rather than a kitten, deep and sexy. "What's this?"

I didn't answer, but I shoved him more roughly up against the wall. I put my left hand on his chest, pressing there before rubbing down his belly then back up, slowly, teasingly. He felt hard as granite to me under the rich fabric of his shirt. Michelangelo's *David* indeed. He tried to kiss me. His lips brushed my forehead as I nuzzled the side of his neck. His big powerful body was moving slowly against mine.

"Declan."

He continued to squirm slowly, sensuously giving himself over. But I had his right wrist securely locked in my right hand, pinned at the middle of his back. His broad shoulders were pressed firmly up against the stone wall.

"Jesus," he said at last, his voice hoarse and gasping. "Kiss me."

I did, angling my face up suddenly just as I slid my left hand around his throat. It was tight, but not enough to keep him from turning his head, breaking the kiss he'd demanded a moment before.

"No." It wasn't the sort of no that means, I know I shouldn't but more please. Just to be crystal clear, he told me, "Stop that."

My lips moved up close to his ear. "Make me, big guy. You're tough, ain't you? Make me stop if you think you can." I pushed up against him, crushing him between my form and the wall. My grip constricted his throat, then I could hear it in his voice.

"I said stop."

I ignored him, waiting for the full panic to set in, wondering just how foolishly brave he might be.

He made a choking sound, a gurgle, an abortive attempt to draw breath. "I don't like this!"

I chuckled in his ear. "I know what you like. You spoiled rich kids are all the same." I caught his earlobe between my teeth and clenched my fist tighter. I dug into the flesh at the back of his neck with my fingertips. His larynx trembled beneath the pad of my thumb. He pushed at me with his left hand. His legs jerked as his shoes scuffed the dirty alleyway. He began to buck, but my feet were planted. I had all the leverage and his good arm rendered useless. He tried to make a fist in my hair. When that didn't work, he pushed against the side of my head. Failing that, he punched me.

It was his left arm, and I was too close for him to get a proper swing, but he managed to make the most of it. I suppose he had been aiming for my jaw, but his knuckles landed just above the hinge of it, square between my temple and my right ear. He probably didn't know it, but that was more effective. And painful.

The first one only served to make me tighten my grip, but he fed me two more, each rougher than the one preceding it. After the third one landed, I released him, staggering back. I wobbled over to the opposite side of the alley lodging a hand against the bricks to steady myself. Those were good punches. He might be sensitive and artistic like Gig had claimed, but he had an arm.

"You maniac!" He was bent at the waist, his left hand braced against his thigh as he massaged his throat with his other hand. He didn't look up even when he told me, "Get the hell away from me!"

That was what I was waiting for.

I complied, taking the first few steps carefully, then hitting my stride and pulling back my shoulders and straightening my tie. He continued to gasp and sputter, but I figured he'd be fine once he calmed down. I didn't look back.

I picked up another bottle of Old Crow on the way home and had polished off half of it before crossing my threshold. I got my jacket off, dropping to my knees in front of my dresser. I pulled out the bottom drawer again, this time all the way so that its contents spilled across the carpet.

Among the many pieces of junk was a tin box that once had held an assortment of toy soldiers. But the soldiers were gone, replaced by old letters, some postcards, and a few snapshots. Also some dog tags, including mine, though those weren't the ones I picked up. Catching the chain tightly in my fist, I saw one snapshot had slid clear of the others and lay face up, reflecting the dull light from overhead. The picture showed two young men in uniform—one army, one navy— side by side, with the Golden Gate Bridge in the background. The soldier, who looked a lot like me, only happy, had his arm draped across the sailor's shoulders. They were both grinning at the camera, full of life and the false promises of that sunlit afternoon.

I crawled over onto the bed, carrying the dog tags and the whiskey and rolled over to face the wall. My head was on the pillow, but when I brought the bottle to my lips, I spilled half of what I'd saved down the side of my face. Well, he never did approve of my drinking anyway. I tossed the Old Crow on the floor and then pushed the soaked pillow after it. Then I brought the dog tags to my lips, not so much kissing them as just reminding myself of how cold and lifeless they were.

My life is cluttered with perfect metaphors.

It still hits me like a punch to the middle of my chest to think of him down there, wrapped in all those thousand tons of steel, buried forever with the rest of the cheap beasts, forgotten by everyone but me. Of course, they're all forgotten except by those who loved them, no matter what folks claim about Armistice Day or Memorial Day. And my greatest fear is that I'll somehow forget too. Get distracted. Fall in love.

My only hope is that my plan works, and I succeed enough or fail enough at this stinking profession I've chosen for myself that somehow, sometime, someone ends me too and dumps my corpse into the Pacific.

The ocean is wide and deep. But the same waves crash on Sonoma and Monterey as do on Okinawa and Omaha Beach. The same water weighs heavily on the wreckage of the USS Bismarck Sea, and the shattered remains of the kamikaze plane that put her there. And with a little luck and a sympathetic current, I'll find my way to the bottom. To the dark and cold and forgotten.

Then we can be down there together, forever.

About the Author

Growing up, Jon Wilson wanted to be a stunt man, a professional wrestler, or a rodeo clown. After breaking his neck in 2001, he decided writing might be safer.

He was wrong.

Currently living in California, he is occasionally hard at work on his next novel.

Declan Colette will return in *Every Unworthy Thing*.

Coming Fall 2015

Books Available from Bold Strokes Books

Buddha's Bad Boys by Alan Chin. Six stories, six gay men trudging down the road to enlightenment. What they each find is the last thing in the world they expected. (978-1-62639-244-1)

Dark Rites by Jeremy Jordan King. When friends start experimenting with dark magic to gain power, Margarite must embrace her natural gifts to save them. (978-1-62639-245-8)

Play It Forward by Frederick Smith. When the worlds of a community activist and a pro basketball player collide, little do they know that their dirty little secrets can lead to a public scandal...and an unexpected love affair. (978-1-62639-235-9)

GingerDead Man by Logan Zachary. Paavo Wolfe sells horror but isn't prepared for what he finds in the oven or the bathhouse; he's in hot water again, and the killer is turning up the heat. (978-1-62639-236-6)

Myth and Magic: Queer Fairy Tales, edited by Radclyffe and Stacia Seaman. Myth, magic, and monsters—the stuff of childhood dreams (or nightmares) and adult fantasies. (978-1-62639-225-0)

Blackthorn by Simon Hawk. Rian Blackthorn, Master of the Hall of Swords, vowed he would not give in to the advances of Prince Corin, but he finds himself dueling with more than swords as Corin pursues him with determined passion. (978-1-62639-226-7)

Café Eisenhower by Richard Natale. A grieving young man who travels to Eastern Europe to claim an inheritance finds friendship, romance, and betrayal, as well as a moving document relating a secret lifelong love affair. (978-1-62639-217-5)

Balls & Chain by Eric Andrews-Katz. In protest of the marriage equality bill, the son of Florida's governor has been kidnapped. Agent Buck 98 is back, and the alligators aren't the only things biting. (978-1-62639-218-2)

Murder in the Arts District by Greg Herren. An investigation into a new and possibly shady art gallery in New Orleans' fabled Arts District soon leads Chanse into a dangerous world of forgery, theft... and murder. A Chanse MacLeod mystery. (978-1-62639-206-9)

Rise of the Thing Down Below by Daniel W. Kelly. Nothing kills sex on the beach like a fishman out of water...Third in the Comfort Cove Series. (978-1-62639-207-6)

Calvin's Head by David Swatling. Jason Dekker and his dog, Calvin, are homeless in Amsterdam when they stumble on the victim of a grisly murder—and become targets for the calculating killer, Gadget. (978-1-62639-193-2)

The Return of Jake Slater by Zavo. Jake Slater mistakenly believes his lover, Ben Masters, is dead. Now a wanted man in Abilene, Jake rides to Mexico to begin a new life and heal his broken heart. (978-1-62639-194-9)

Backstrokes by Dylan Madrid. When pianist Crawford Paul meets lifeguard Armando Leon, he accepts Armando's offer to help him overcome his fear of water by way of private lessons. As friendship turns into a summer affair, their lust for one another turns to love. (978-1-62639-069-0)

The Raptures of Time by David Holly. Mack Frost and his friends journey across an alien realm, through homoerotic adventures, suffering humiliation and rapture, making friends and enemies, always seeking a gateway back home to Oregon. (978-1-62639-068-3)

The Thief Taker by William Holden. Unreliable lovers, twisted family secrets, and too many dead bodies wait for Thomas Newton in London—where he soon discovers that all the plotting is aimed directly at him. (978-1-62639-054-6)

Waiting for the Violins by Justine Saracen. After surviving Dunkirk, a scarred and embittered British nurse returns to Nazi-occupied Brussels to join the Resistance, and finds that nothing is fair in love and war. (978-1-62639-046-1)

Turnbull House by Jess Faraday. London 1891: Reformed criminal Ira Adler has a new, respectable life—but will an old flame and the promise of riches tempt him back to London's dark side...and his own? (978-1-60282-987-9)

Stronger Than This by David-Matthew Barnes. A gay man and a lesbian form a beautiful friendship out of grief when their soul mates are tragically killed. (978-1-60282-988-6)

Death Came Calling by Donald Webb. When private investigator Katsuro Tanaka is hired to look into the death of a high profile lawyer, he becomes embroiled in a case of murder and mayhem. (978-1-60282-979-4)

Love in the Shadows by Dylan Madrid. While teaming up to bring a killer to justice, a lustful spark is ignited between an American man living in London and an Italian spy named Luca. (978-1-60282-981-7)

Cutie Pie Must Die by R.W. Clinger. Sexy detectives, a muscled quarterback, and the queerest murders...when murder is most cute. (978-1-60282-961-9)